Praise for

Falcon's Mistress

"An intriguing and tender tale of love, passion, and mystery."

—*Fresh Fiction*

"Full of twists and unexpected surprises. I thoroughly enjoyed it for the engaging characters and its unpredictability . . . Hard to put down . . . A book readers won't want to miss."

—*Romance Reviews Today*

"Birdsell's novel entwines elements of a spy thriller, a gothic suspense, and a love story to more than satisfy readers."

—*Romantic Times*

"If you want to read a novel with amazing depth and beautiful writing, be sure to pick up *Falcon's Mistress*." —*Rakehell*

The Painted Rose

"A betrayed beauty and a devastated artist find hope and healing in *The Painted Rose*, the lyrical and richly emotional debut by talented newcomer Donna Birdsell."

—*New York Times* bestselling author Mary Jo Putney

"In *The Painted Rose*, a passion for art and flowers weaves a web of healing between past pain and present love. A delightful debut romance." —*New York Times* bestselling author Jo Beverley

"Donna Birdsell's terrific debut novel, *The Painted Rose*, is a deeply moving story that truly celebrates the healing power of love. With an emotional story that is both dark and tender as well as intelligent, and with sympathetic characters, this is a must-read for lovers of romance." —Jacqueline Navin, author of *The Beauty of Bond Street*

conti

"Moving, utterly romantic . . . Beautifully written with compassion and sensitivity, the book's poetic prose flows from the page into your heart, even as the suspense builds and you're drawn into the mystery. Birdsell has a marvelous future awaiting her as her career blossoms into full bloom."

—*Romantic Times* (Top Pick)

"Ms. Birdsell's debut historical romance is touching, emotional, and beautifully rendered. She has the talent to get the reader so involved in the story that, once started, you can't put it down. I anxiously await her next book." —*The Best Reviews*

"A deeply emotional debut . . . a gripping historical romance; there's no way to read it and remain unmoved."

—*Romance Reviews Today*

"A terrific tale . . . Fans will enjoy Donna Birdsell's delightful debut and look forward to more historical romances from this talented newcomer." —*BookBrowser*

Berkley Sensation titles by Donna Birdsell

WOLF'S TEMPTATION
FALCON'S MISTRESS
THE PAINTED ROSE

WOLF'S TEMPTATION

Donna Birdsell

BERKLEY SENSATION, NEW YORK

THE BERKLEY PUBLISHING GROUP
Published by the Penguin Group
Penguin Group (USA) Inc.
375 Hudson Street, New York, New York 10014, USA
Penguin Group (Canada), 90 Eglinton Avenue East, Suite 700, Toronto, Ontario M4P 2Y3, Canada
(a division of Pearson Penguin Canada Inc.)
Penguin Books Ltd., 80 Strand, London WC2R 0RL, England
Penguin Group Ireland, 25 St. Stephen's Green, Dublin 2, Ireland (a division of Penguin Books Ltd.)
Penguin Group (Australia), 250 Camberwell Road, Camberwell, Victoria 3124, Australia
(a division of Pearson Australia Group Pty. Ltd.)
Penguin Books India Pvt. Ltd., 11 Community Centre, Panchsheel Park, New Delhi—110 017, India
Penguin Group (NZ), Cnr. Airborne and Rosedale Roads, Albany, Auckland 1310, New Zealand
(a division of Pearson New Zealand Ltd.)
Penguin Books (South Africa) (Pty.) Ltd., 24 Sturdee Avenue, Rosebank, Johannesburg 2196,
South Africa

Penguin Books Ltd., Registered Offices: 80 Strand, London WC2R 0RL, England

This is a work of fiction. Names, characters, places, and incidents either are the product of the author's imagination or are used fictitiously, and any resemblance to actual persons, living or dead, business establishments, events, or locales is entirely coincidental. The publisher does not have any control over and does not assume any responsibility for author or third-party websites or their content.

WOLF'S TEMPTATION

A Berkley Sensation Book / published by arrangement with the author

PRINTING HISTORY
Berkley Sensation mass-market edition / October 2006

Copyright © 2006 by Donna Birdsell.
Cover art by Robert Papp.
Cover design by George Long.
Interior text design by Stacy Irwin.

All rights reserved.
No part of this book may be reproduced, scanned, or distributed in any printed or electronic from without permission. Please do not participate in or encourage piracy of copyrighted materials in violation of the author's rights. Purchase only authorized editions.
For information, address: The Berkley Publishing Group,
a division of Penguin Group (USA) Inc.,
375 Hudson Street, New York, New York 10014.

ISBN: 0-425-21261-0

BERKLEY SENSATION®
Berkley Sensation Books are published by The Berkley Publishing Group,
a division of Penguin Group (USA) Inc.,
375 Hudson Street, New York, New York 10014.
BERKLEY SENSATION is a registered trademark of Penguin Group (USA) Inc.
The "B" design in a trademark belonging to Penguin Group (USA) Inc.

PRINTED IN THE UNITED STATES OF AMERICA

10 9 8 7 6 5 4 3 2 1

If you purchased this book without a cover, you should be aware that this book is stolen property. It was reported as "unsold and destroyed" to the publisher, and neither the author nor the publisher has received any payment for this "stripped book."

For R.M.B and C.E.B.,
my two beautiful little heroines.

Acknowledgments

Many thanks to James Wagner, whose knowledge of historical detail is invaluable. And thanks to Joy Nash, Anita Nolan, and Sally Stotter, for their advice and support.

CHAPTER 1

London
November 1776

Tobacco.

The rich, pungent scent of it tickled the edges of Ethan Gray's senses. He breathed deep, his pulse racing.

Could she be the one?

The one who'd held a pistol to his temple in the dark warehouse? The one who'd threatened his life if he continued to search for the hidden cache of arms? He'd been looking for her for months. If this were the same woman, what was she doing here, at Lady Jersey's masque?

It wouldn't be the first time he'd happened upon her at a party. She'd stolen letters from Lord Shelbourne's desk the night of a soiree there, while Ethan hid behind a settee. He hadn't actually seen her, for he hadn't wanted to reveal his own presence in Shelbourne's private study. But he'd smelled tobacco that night, too.

Tonight, though, he'd come across her quite by accident,

plucking her from the crowd for a dance. She stumbled against him, grabbing his hand for balance as he pulled her toward the dance floor. If this was the woman he sought—and every instinct affirmed that—well, it was almost too easy.

Surely, the heavens smiled on him tonight.

There was one small problem. He couldn't exactly arrest her for treason in a saloon full of Society's finest—none of whom knew he was the Wolf, spymaster for Lord North's Anti-British Activity Committee. To them he was merely Ethan Gray, the rogue who seduced their wives and ruined their daughters' reputations.

He had to devise a way to get the peacock alone. He struggled to keep his voice even as he spoke to her. "Lovely mask."

Colorful plumage framed kohl-lined eyes and splayed across rouged cheeks, leaving a pair of delectable pink lips exposed. And beneath them, a delectably creamy décolletage.

"Thank you," she replied. "Yours is most fierce."

Ethan had come as a tiger, the ultimate predator. The Wolf, dressed as a cat. Unfortunately though, tonight he felt more like prey. The harbormaster's wife, with whom he'd had a fruitful affair but who had since lost both her usefulness and her novelty, had been stalking him through the ballroom since he'd arrived.

He now regretted telling her what kind of mask he planned to wear.

Ethan led the peacock to the middle of the dance floor, where they fell easily into step with the other couples. He had her in his arms only moments before she was whisked away by another partner in the cotillion.

She moved gracefully around the circle, dipping and turning, bewitching each partner with her secretive smile before they were finally reunited for a promenade in the middle of the floor. He gave her an appreciative nod. She might be his enemy, but a finer-looking opponent he'd never laid eyes on. He almost wished she wasn't the woman he sought, for he would have enjoyed seducing her.

"I wonder, would you care to take a bit of air with me?"

The question, from her lips, took him aback. *She* wished to be alone with *him*? This night really was too good to be true.

He hesitated for a moment, so as not to seem overeager. "A breath of night air with such a beauty would rescue my week from mediocrity."

She laughed—a sound that resonated like the low octaves of a harp—and said, "You needn't flatter me, Sir Tiger. I've been assured you'll give me exactly what I want."

She'd been assured—? Could it be that some well-meaning friend had set this all up?

"Who, dear lady, has assured you of that?"

She only smiled as if it were all a merry prank.

He danced her to the outer limits of the ballroom floor and behind a towering topiary. He reached for her mask, but she stopped his hand. Her touch was light on his wrist, her fingers long and delicate. "Do you have something for me?"

The brazen invitation sent an instant rush of heat over him. She looked startled, as if she'd felt the attraction, too. Without thinking, he bent and kissed her. Her lips were like sun-warmed silk beneath his. He cupped her cheek in the palm of his hand, stroking her chin with his thumb.

A small noise of surprise caught in her throat, as if a kiss wasn't the "something" she'd been expecting. She released his wrist from her grasp, and he took her by the shoulders, deepening the kiss. When he pulled away, she seemed stunned, like a rabbit in the sights of a fox.

Or a wolf.

She held a trembling hand to her lips.

"I am sorry," he said. "I thought you wanted . . ."

"The key. I want the key."

"What—?"

A commotion on the dance floor caught his attention. People moved aside as Lady Jersey marched amongst the guests, as if looking for someone. She stopped to speak to the harbormaster's wife, who pointed in Ethan's direction.

Lady Jersey waved him over.

He attempted to ignore her, but when she sent a footman in his direction, he knew he would have to answer her call or risk creating a scene. He swore under his breath.

"It would seem I am being summoned by our hostess," he said. "I won't be but a moment."

"Meet me out on the terrace," she murmured.

He nodded, once again thanking the gods for his good fortune.

Lady Jersey met him halfway, her expression of concern comical beneath her heavy Egyptian makeup. "Ethan Gray, is that you beneath that mask?"

"Yes."

"Good! There are two tigers prowling about tonight, and I was afraid I might have the wrong one." Lady Jersey grabbed his elbow and steered him into the relative quiet of the salon next door. He made a concentrated effort to hide his annoyance as she bowed her head close to his. "Lady Frederica needs you."

"What's wrong?" he asked.

"She's crying her eyes out, the poor dear."

His annoyance gave over to concern. It wasn't like his sister Freddie to shed unnecessary tears. He could remember only two other occasions when she'd cried. The first was when she was seven, and Father refused to allow her to take fencing lessons with her brothers. The second occurred was when she was twelve, and Mother forbade her to wear breeches ever again.

But Freddie could wait. He had to get back to the peacock,

before his good fortune ran out. "I am sure my sister will be fine, Lady Jersey. Where is her friend Jane? Would she not be a more able hand in this situation?"

Lady Jersey frowned. "How ignoble of you, Mr. Gray, to leave your sister in such a state."

He sighed. "Where is she?"

Lady Jersey signaled to a servant, who hurried to her side. "Show Mr. Gray to the library, please."

Freddie huddled beneath a lap blanket on an oversized velvet chaise, a handkerchief pressed to her nose, her butterfly wings and mask flung carelessly on the floor beside her.

She regarded him with red-rimmed eyes. "Oh, Ethan. I've made such a mess of things."

Ethan mentally braced himself. Such a confession could not be good, coming from one so adept at making messes. He sat on the edge of the chaise, taking Freddie's hand in his. It was ice cold.

"I'm certain things cannot be that bad."

She shook her head. Her copper curls bounced wildly. "But it is. I confessed . . ." She swiped her eyes with the handkerchief. "I told Josiah Blackwood I love him." She gave Ethan a defiant look—the same one he'd seen hundreds of times as they were growing up.

He bit back the urge to scold her. "Do you think that was wise?"

"I couldn't help myself. He told me he was leaving. His ship . . . it's been fitted for war. He's returning to the colonies to fight the privateers."

"'Tis a noble cause."

"'Tis foolishness, as is all war. What if he's killed!"

Ethan sighed. "Freddie, it is the price we must pay for our country."

"I shall never be happy again."

"Nonsense. This so-called war with the colonists will be over quickly, I assure you. A small group of treasonous rebels is no match against Britain's forces. It won't be long before your Captain Blackwood returns to you."

Freddie's eyes brimmed with tears. "He won't be coming back. At least, not to me."

"What makes you think so?"

"He called me a . . ." She sucked in a breath. "A spoiled child!"

Ethan bit his lip and said nothing.

Freddie glared at him. "I'm sure you are happy things have ended between us."

"Of course not." In truth, though, he was. Captain Blackwood was ill-suited for his sister. Too rough, too colonial, and too scandalous by far. And although he was but twenty-three, he seemed much older.

On the other hand, Freddie was, in fact, little more than a child. She'd had her debut only last season, and had just reached her eighteenth year. She'd led a relatively sheltered life, and was no match for the likes of Captain Blackwood.

Ethan patted her hand.

"You never approved of our match," she said, with a hint of girlish petulance.

" 'Twas more a flirtation than a match, no?"

"But I love him!"

Ethan sighed. "There have been many beautiful women enamored with Captain Blackwood, but none so beautiful as you. If you have not captured his heart, dear sister, perhaps it is because he does not wish it to be captured at all."

Freddie sniffed. "Perhaps."

"Now, dry your eyes, and take heart. If I ever lay eyes on Captain Blackwood again, I promise to thrash him within an inch of his life."

"You will?"

"Absolutely. Besides, there are dozens of gentlemen here

tonight willing to do battle for your affections. Not that I approve of any one of them," he added quickly. "But at least they might serve as a distraction."

"I don't want to be distracted," she groused, but rose anyway, and picked up her wings and mask.

"Let me give you a bit of advice. The best way to attract a gentleman is to play your hand close to the vest," Ethan said. "A bit of intrigue goes a long way."

"Is that what tickles your fancy?" Freddie asked, as he hustled her back toward the ballroom.

"What?"

"Intrigue."

Ethan thought of the pretty peacock awaiting him on the terrace. He had more than a few questions for her, and suspected that he wouldn't mind interrogating her one bit. Yes, intrigue was a powerful thing.

He deposited Freddie with her friend Jane, and made for the terrace doors, only to be intercepted by the harbormaster's wife.

"What is the hurry, Ethan? Your pretty peacock has flown away."

Ethan's stomach tightened. "What do you mean?"

"She's gone, darling."

"Gone?"

The harbormaster's wife smiled. "I gave her a friendly warning. One woman to another."

He grabbed her elbow. "What did you say?"

Her eyes blazed, and her smile hardened. "I told her Ethan Gray wasn't a man to trifle with. I told her you'd tear her heart out and eat it for breakfast." She laughed. "She couldn't get away from here fast enough."

Ethan raced from the terrace toward the stables, the pounding in his ears growing louder as he ran. He soon realized it wasn't his heart, but the beat of hooves on the drive as the peacock thundered past on a mount, her feathered costume billowing behind her.

He ran to the carriage house, past a cluster of drivers and footmen, and into the stables, saddling the first horse he came upon. Amid shouts from the drivers and stable hands, he flew from the stables, hoping to catch his quarry before she reached the cover of the trees along the north road.

He caught her in his line of sight. He pushed his mount, closing the space between them to a quarter league until the moon disappeared behind a cloud, throwing them into utter darkness. He was forced to slow, and when the moon reappeared, the peacock was gone.

He rode for a while before reaching a fork. At the crux of it, in a ditch, lay something pale and motionless.

The peacock!

Ethan leaped from his mount and kneeled beside her, sifting frantically through the mass of feathers.

"Damn me." He swore to the moon.

It would seem his luck had given out. He'd found the peacock's feathers, but the bird herself had flown.

Chapter 2

Birmingham Gun Quarter
March 1777

The little room was dark save the light from a street lamp outside.

Ethan held the gunsmith's ledger up to the window to read it, fearing to light a candle in an office so close to the street. He flipped through the pages.

March. July. November. Each of these pages marred by an ink stain, a watermark, or a missing corner. Each of them incomplete, lacking the one vital piece of information he sought. Who had placed the orders for large weapons shipments bound for Africa?

He could not question the gunsmith directly, for fear of tipping his hand. This was delicate business. He had no idea who was involved in this intrigue, and the last thing he wanted to do was alert anyone to his investigation.

Although, it would seem as if at least one person knew.

Everywhere Ethan had gone, it was the same story. Logs

obliterated. Papers destroyed. The bank, the warehouse, the docks. Anywhere there should have been a record of transactions related to these shipments, they were gone. He needed one man's name, but he could not get it. And Ethan knew exactly who was responsible.

The peacock.

Damnation. He would have had her at the masque if he hadn't been snared by Lady Jersey.

He'd since learned that on the night of the ball, one Miss Mortimer-Smythe had been on her way to the masque when her coach was waylaid by a marauder. She was stripped to her underclothes and bound to a tree along with her aging driver and two stunned footmen, none of whom had been able to protect her.

Before her wig and costume were so rudely purloined, she'd been dressed as a peacock.

Much to his frustration, Ethan had spent the past four months searching for the woman at the ball, with not one clue as to whom, or where, she might be. It was as if she'd turned to vapor on the road, leaving Miss Mortimer-Smythe's costume with nothing to hold it aloft.

Who—or what—had drawn her to the ball? And what key had she sought?

Ethan snapped the ledger closed and returned it to the gunsmith's desk, considering his next move.

The man who ordered these guns had skimmed hundreds of weapons from the Africa shipments. The guns were then secreted in cargo sent to the American colonies, meant for the hands of colonial traitors. British soldiers would die because of those weapons, and Ethan couldn't stop it.

He'd never felt so bloody ineffective. Perhaps what one of his men had said, however jokingly, was true.

He'd lost his edge.

* * *

The ride back to London was endless. Ethan thought of nothing but the soldiers whose lives were in danger because *he* couldn't find one man.

If he'd been a drinker, he'd have gone straight on to his club and drowned himself in a bottle of whiskey. But other than an occasional mug of ale to quench his thirst, he'd given up spirits years ago.

Instead he headed for home and the comfort of his well-appointed library. Books were his liquor. His escape.

He loved every kind of book, from philosophy to popular novels, and each one held a special place on his bookshelves. He routinely ordered large shipments from Millar's of London, spending hours cataloging and shelving and rearranging the titles.

As soon as he entered the haven, his breathing came easier. The giant oxblood leather chair beside the fireplace beckoned. But when he got to it, it was already occupied.

Freddie lay curled up in the deep cushions, sound asleep. A waterfall of copper-streaked curls spilled over the arm of the chair. She snored softly, like a kitten who'd spent the day chasing mice.

"Freddie." He nudged her shoulder gently, and she opened her eyes. In an instant, the kitten bared her claws.

"There you are! I've been waiting for you all night."

"What's the matter?"

"I have a bone to pick with you."

"A bone to pick . . . ? Good lord, Freddie. Can't this wait until morning?"

"No, it cannot." She uncurled and stretched, and climbed out of the chair. "Will you please explain why you had to break Winifred Sandler's heart?" She gestured to the chair, and he sank into it with a weary sigh.

"Freddie, I hardly know the girl. How could I have broken her heart?"

"Did you not escort her to the theater? To several parties? To the Royal Exchange?"

"I did. However, that hardly passes for courtship."

She planted her fists on her hips. "If a gentleman treated me so, would you consider it a courtship?"

He dragged a hand over his face. "Freddie, this isn't any of your concern."

"Winnie is one of my dearest friends. Or, I suppose to be more accurate now, she *was* one of my dearest friends. You all but begged me to make an introduction. You spent a week acting as if she'd won your undying love, and now you act as if you hardly know the poor girl."

He felt a momentary twinge of guilt. The truth was, he didn't really know her at all. She seemed a nice-enough girl, but unfortunately one who wasn't the type to talk about her brothers' comings and goings. Therefore, she was absolutely useless to Ethan.

So he'd moved on to her ladies' maid, who was equally familiar with the Sandler brothers' activities, and more than willing to discuss them. In bed, of course.

The two brothers' names had come up as possible links to a merchant who smuggled goods from the colonies—mostly cotton and tobacco—and Ethan had been trying to discern whether they might in any way be involved with the weapons case.

"Ethan, I cannot help but feel as if something isn't right. Tell me, why are you doing this?"

"I'm sorry, Freddie. I truly am. But wouldn't you rather I ended things with Miss Sandler as soon as I realized we had no future? 'Tis better than leading the lady to believe we might . . . well, that it might continue on."

Freddie's frown softened. "Listen to you. You cannot even utter the word *marriage*. I daresay it is time, dear brother, for you to conquer that impediment. Find a wife. A woman to bear your children. A woman with whom to share your life."

The Devil's teeth. There wasn't such a woman alive.

His profession was steeped in secrecy. What woman would understand his comings and goings in the middle of the night? What woman would accept that danger played a prominent role in his life? In any case, taking a wife would severely limit his ability to romance information from willing wives and daughters and sisters.

His mother and grandmother put up with it, each being married to agents themselves, but they were rare women. Strong and self-assured, patient, and confident enough to know they owned their husbands' hearts. In all his life, Ethan had never met such a woman.

In fact, there was only one woman he'd ever entertained the thought of marriage with, and trusting her had cost the lives of two good men.

Ethan had shown mercy to Winifred Sandler by not bedding her, out of respect for Freddie. But in the world of espionage, he had no time to coddle the weepy female temperament.

He herded Freddie to the library door. "May we discuss my need for a wife in the morning?"

Freddie chewed her lower lip. "Perhaps I shall make it my season's endeavor."

Lord save him, for Freddie was relentless in her "endeavors."

"Perhaps your season's endeavor should be to find a husband for yourself," he countered.

Her expression darkened. "I've decided I shan't marry. Ever."

Ethan bit back a grin. "Does this have anything to do with Captain Blackwood?"

"Of course not. I've simply realized that I would much rather be an independent woman."

"A spinster?"

"No, an intellectual."

"A *bluestocking*!"

"I've already begun reading Rousseau."

"Don't let Father and Mother hear that."

Freddie shrugged. "They'll find out soon enough. In the meantime, I shall begin a list of eligible women for you. How about the Countess Van Helsenberg? You've always gone in for tall Dutch ladies. Or Miss Emily Pickwick? Oh, wait. I believe she was married off last year, to that awful young man with the bad skin. How about Viscount Entwhistle's daughter? No, she's much too thick in the legs. . . ." Freddie wandered from the library, muttering beneath her breath.

Ethan rubbed a knot at the back of his neck, trying hard not to think about what names might appear on that list.

Feeling much older than his thirty-five years, he selected a book, newly arrived from Millar's, and trudged back to the leather chair. He cracked open the tome, relishing the feel of the stiff leather binding in his palm, and the smell of ink and vellum. The knots of tension in his shoulders eased.

The volume was new, but the book he'd read once before—Fielding's *Amelia.* He preferred it to the author's *Tom Jones*, which he always thought a bit tedious.

He read: ". . . To speak a bold Truth, I am, after much mature Deliberation, inclined to suspect that the Public Voice . . ."

Ethan shot upright in his chair. He read the sentence again. "To speak a bold Truth . . ."

With his finger marking the place in the volume, he hurried to his desk, unlocking one of the drawers and twisting the pull down to the left. A false bottom sprung open in the drawer, revealing a thin stack of papers. He sifted through them, withdrawing a letter.

The one he'd stolen months ago from the desk of Lord Shelbourne, one of two men arrested in connection to the weapons investigation. The other was Lord Chadwick. A third man, Sir Ambrose Hollister, had eluded capture, and the fourth man was the one he couldn't seem to find out anything about.

Authorities, including Lord North himself, had questioned Shelbourne and Chadwick numerous times, with no success. Both men denied knowing the whereabouts of Hollister. And both refused to admit they'd had a fourth partner, most likely fearing the repercussions.

Ethan was certain the missive he'd stolen contained important information about the arms shipments, but thus far he hadn't been able to discover anything of note amongst what seemed like idle gossip written in neat, unremarkable script that did not match any one of the other men's.

The information was there, though. He was sure of it. The woman who smelled of tobacco—the woman he'd come to think of as Peacock since Lady Jersey's masque—had taken two other letters from Shelbourne's desk—letters Ethan had intended to take for himself before she so rudely interrupted his thievery. They both were written in the same hand as this one. If the letters were harmless, why would she have risked stealing them?

He unfolded the letter with some excitement, skimming it quickly although he knew it by rote.

He found what he was looking for at the beginning of the third paragraph. "To speak a bold Truth . . ."

It was a cipher. In this sentence, the letter's composer informed Lord Shelbourne of the book to use to solve the clues embedded in his words.

Ethan pored over the letter, searching for clues. Paragraph five read: "She'll be three years on the sixteenth of April."

What did the numbers mean? Page and paragraph? Chapter, paragraph, line? He'd used a similar cipher with his men several times. After a few false starts, he cracked the code.

He opened *Amelia* to chapter Three for "three years," went to paragraph sixteen for "sixteenth," and then to the fourth line for "April," because it was the fourth month of the year.

He read: "When this was ended, they set forward to survey the *gaol* . . ."

The jail. What about a jail? Perhaps they'd met near a jail to exchange information. If so, which one? There were hundreds in England alone.

Ethan skimmed the letter again. "For the use of the land, he paid ten Bantam hens, two calves, and three geese."

Ethan turned to the book. Chapter Ten, paragraph two, third line. "He did not stop at his Quarters, but made directly to London . . ."

Back to the letter. "The two of them bought five horses. Five! They'll keep them at St. Martin's."

The book, chapter Two, paragraph five, fifth line: "She then put a bank bill of 100*l* into Mr. Booth's hands . . ."

St. Martin's. There was a St. Martin's Dock not far from the warehouse where the peacock had threatened him. And a jail just a block or two from there.

Adrenaline coursed through Ethan's veins. He hunched over the letter, working every possible bit of the code until he'd uncovered a wealth of information.

None of it meant anything now. The letter was old and the intelligence it yielded no longer valid. But it was his first—nay, his *only* piece of solid evidence that a fourth man existed in this conspiracy to supply arms to the colonists.

And what might this man's motive be?

The motives of the other three varied. Lord Shelbourne was a banker, Chadwick a lumber merchant, and Sir Ambrose Hollister a shipping company operator. The three stood to lose a great many profits due to the embargo against the colonies. The more quickly the disagreement between England and the colonies was settled, the more quickly their profits would return to normal.

He took up the letter again. It was, naturally, unsigned. No address. No mark. No readily decipherable code to identify the composer. He'd been over it a thousand times.

He folded the letter carefully and replaced it in the desk, latching the false bottom and taking care to lock the drawer. He kissed the volume of *Amelia* before placing it back on the bookshelf.

Whistling to himself, he made his way to his chambers, the frustrating turn at the gun maker's office all but forgotten.

Chapter 3

10 Downing Street
London
April 1777

The clack of ivory balls, the familiar masculine comfort of the room, put Ethan at ease—a state foreign to him as of late.

Lord North enjoyed a good game of billiards, but much preferred to play in the comfort of his own home rather than in the clubs. Ethan was one of the privileged few invited into his sanctuary.

"One of General Gage's regiments in the colonies uncovered a large cache of weapons in Concord, just before the battle in Lexington," Lord North said as he lined up a shot at the billiards table.

"Yes, I'd heard."

"I'd wager some of those guns were sent from London's docks."

"Undoubtedly."

Lord North withdrew a handkerchief from his sleeve and mopped his brow. "There are still many good, loyal English citizens in the colonies, but there are many enemies as well. We cannot allow weapons of unknown quantity to find their way into the hands of traitors. Every rifle, every speck of powder, endangers our men."

Lord North did not attempt to hide his frustration. It was an emotion Ethan understood well. "I fully realize that, sir."

The older man's tone softened a bit. "I know you do. But you see why I am beginning to doubt the wisdom of leaving this mission solely in your hands."

"I will find the person responsible for the shipments, sir. I give you my word."

"It has been nearly five months since your last lead," Lord North said. "Haven't you come up with anything else?"

Ethan thought of the peacock. Surely she'd been the cause of most of his ill fortune as of late, obliterating any useful information. If only he'd been able to catch up with her on the road the night of the ball.

"I have informants in every quarter," Ethan said. "It's only a matter of time."

"Yet time is something we lack. Perhaps we should assign someone to help you. You haven't had assistance on this case since the Falcon."

The Falcon was Ethan's cousin John Markley, the Duke of Canby, who'd helped him build evidence against Shelbourne and the others, before his identity as a spy was revealed and it became necessary for him to leave England. Now, everyone but Lord North and Ethan believed him dead.

Ethan slid a cue stick through his fingers, completing his shot with little effort. "I would prefer to handle this myself, sir. There is much at stake."

"Indeed there is." Lord North took another shot, making a noise of disgust when his ball missed the pocket. "There is no shame in asking for assistance. It has been a while since you've taken on a mission with such a scope, and your father is concerned that you cannot handle it alone. Shall I assign you a partner?"

"No." The word echoed off the paneled walls, coming out more forcefully than he intended. He took a breath, and lowered his voice. "No, sir. I really would prefer to finish this myself. One of my sources has confirmed that another large order for guns has been placed with the same gun maker on Price Street recently. If my estimations are correct, that shipment will arrive at the quays next month. I will find that shipment, sir, and keep each and every gun from reaching the colonies. I swear it."

Lord North took his shot and leaned on his cue, his face unreadable. "Very well, Gray. If you won't accept help with the weapons investigation, perhaps I should assign someone to take over your other duties until this case is resolved."

Ethan faltered, his shot missing the leather basket by a good hand's width. "You mean to head the committee?"

"Yes."

Ethan placed his cue against the edge of the table. "I won't resign."

"I am not asking for your resignation. But perhaps you aren't capable of handling all of your responsibilities. If that is the case, you must choose between remaining spymaster or returning to the field."

Ethan's stomach knotted. He would not relinquish his hard-won position as head of the committee his own grandfather created. The position his father had held before him. It would be an affront to his family. It would be a mark of shame on him.

But neither could he give up on this investigation. Not now. How could he maintain the respect of his men if he were no longer able to match their skills in the field? If he couldn't show them he was willing to put his life on the line, just as they did?

They'd jokingly accused him of going soft. Of trading adventure for the warm beds of society mavens. But Ethan knew that within every jest lay a kernel of truth.

Lord North set his cue on the table. The time for games was over.

"I know this relatively tame life in London isn't nearly as exciting as working as an operative," Lord North said. "Tactical affairs can never match the thrill of getting your hands dirty, as they say, but your post is an important one, Gray. Essential. Make no mistake. If you cannot put every ounce of thought into it, then you must let me find someone who can."

The walls of the billiards room seemed suddenly closer. Ethan wiped the sheen of perspiration from his forehead with his sleeve. "Give me one more month, sir. If I haven't found the bastard who is shipping those guns by then, I will resign from the committee completely."

Lord North sighed. "I do not care to lose you, Ethan. Disregarding the debacle with the Sparrow when you were first named as your father's replacement, I think you've done a fine job as spymaster. I fought for you then, and I believe in you now. But I wish you would reconsider finding a partner. In fact, I have the perfect person in mind."

"Oh? Who might that be?"

"The Raven."

The Raven had been an operative with the committee for only three years, but had proven quite useful by forming an association with a group of French expatriates who still enjoyed frequent contact from their homeland. The result was a steady stream of information about the personal habits and business dealings of several members of King Louis's inner cabinet.

Information that would become extremely valuable,

should France prove to have an alliance with the American colonists.

Ethan shook his head. "I must respectfully decline, sir. I am not accustomed to working with strangers, especially on such a dangerous and sensitive mission. Besides, the Raven is firmly entrenched in the south. How do you know such an assignment would be welcome?"

"I don't. But I shall leave it up to you to ask, if you so desire. The Raven awaits us upstairs." The prime minister moved to a bell pull in the corner.

"He is here?" Ethan said, surprised.

"You've never met the Raven." It wasn't a question, but a statement.

"No. I've tried to arrange several meetings, but they've fallen through."

"Then there is something I should tell you before—" Lord North's gaze drifted toward the door. "Ah, but I am too late."

Lord North's butler entered the billiards room, followed not by the Raven, but by a rather plain-looking young woman dressed in a high-necked black gown.

Lord North dismissed the servant and closed the doors, escorting the woman to where Ethan stood.

Upon closer inspection, she wasn't as young—nor as plain—as Ethan had first thought. Each of her features individually was nothing to comment upon. Her nose was a bit large, her lips too full, her sharp blue eyes too angled for his taste. But together, they formed an interesting landscape that wasn't entirely displeasing. Her hair was hidden beneath a rather large bonnet, which she had yet to remove.

Her gaze took him in, as well. And though he was thoroughly accustomed to the blatant admiration of ladies, her scrutiny seemed less designed to strip him of his clothing than to bare his inner thoughts.

He shook off that disturbing sensation when she extended a hand. He bent, kissing the air above her fingers.

"Wolf," said Lord North, "may I present to you the Raven."

Ethan froze, releasing the fingers that suddenly seemed to burn hot in his. He straightened, his eyes meeting hers. She did not blink.

"The Raven?"

She nodded.

"Forgive me, but—"

"You assumed I was a man."

Ethan said nothing.

"Precisely why I've put off our meeting, Mr. Gray. I wished to prove my worth to you without carrying the burden of my sex."

"Why would you imagine your sex a burden?" Ethan said. "Lord North and I would not consider it so."

The Raven smiled. "Come now, Mr. Gray. We both know that whenever a woman endeavors to perform what is considered a man's work, her head is assumed to be empty unless there is rigorous proof to the contrary."

"Proof that you have provided most authoritatively, Miss Winter," Lord North interjected.

"Miss Winter?" Ethan repeated.

She removed her hat. "Yes. Maris Winter."

"Gavin Winter's daughter?" He needn't have asked. He knew from the white-blond hair she'd just revealed that she could be no other.

He went cold.

"It is a pleasure to see you again, Mr. Gray. It has been a while."

"Nine years."

He studied her anew. She'd certainly changed. When he'd last seen Gavin Winter's daughter, she'd been an awkward girl of seventeen years, distraught over the death of her father. He'd hated to bring the news to her. But she'd looked at him with grateful admiration when she learned that he'd been there, trying to save her father's life. He couldn't tell her that her father's death had been his fault. . . .

Her youthful admiration had apparently disappeared over the years, as had some of the sadness. Now, her eyes were guarded. Wary. He wondered if her experiences as a spy had made them so.

"So you have decided to follow in your father's footsteps?" he said.

"As you did. I imagine it wasn't easy to step into your father's shoes as head of the committee."

In fact, Ethan had worked doubly hard to prove to his father and Lord North that he deserved it. And although Bernard Gray, Earl of Maldwyn, would never let Ethan forget his mistakes, in the end, even *he* had to allow that Ethan had now earned his post.

"The intelligence you've sent us has been of great benefit, Miss Winter," said Lord North.

"I am honored to serve the Crown in any way I can, sir."

"I am glad to hear it, for I have a new assignment for you."

Ethan shot the prime minister a questioning look.

"Of course I shall accept any charge you bestow upon me," Miss Winter said. Lord North escorted her to a bank of chairs lined up at the far end of the billiards room. She settled onto one of them, alert, waiting.

Lord North waved Ethan over. "This concerns you as well, Gray."

He strode to the chairs, but did not sit. "Yes, sir."

"Miss Winter has discovered that an American merchant ship, a privateer, has captured one of His Majesty's naval vessels. An armed transport bearing supplies for our troops in the colonies. All officers aboard have been taken prisoner. All sailors were set a drift in a whale boat. Two of them are dead," Lord North said in a grave voice. "The Americans have had the audacity to sail our ship into a French port and intend to sell it, and all of its contents, there."

"To what end?" Ethan asked.

"The money from the sales will undoubtedly fuel the colonists' war efforts," Miss Winter answered.

"Exactly," Lord North said.

"What is it you wish from me?" Ethan asked Lord North.

"Not just from you, Gray, but from Miss Winter as well." The prime minister studied them both for a moment before continuing. "I wish for the two of you to work together on this matter."

"Together?" The Raven's shock mirrored Ethan's own.

What could Lord North possibly have to gain by sending him on this mission? Time away from England was time away from investigating the weapons shipments.

"With all due respect, sir, do you think that is wise?" Ethan said.

Miss Winter moved closer to the edge of her chair. "I am certain I could manage this on my own. I—"

"I think not," Lord North interrupted. "You could not possibly inquire about such dealings as a woman. However, your knowledge of the situation and your contacts in France could be invaluable, and would aid immensely in the investigation of this matter. And Gray, your negotiation talents and overall experience are essential to this delicate work. The combination of your skills will allow you to make quick work of this together, don't you agree?"

Said agreement was not forthcoming from either Ethan or Miss Winter, a fact that Lord North chose to ignore.

"Miss Winter, did you not report to me that this auction will be an international affair?"

"Yes. Word of it has gone out to parties in several other countries."

"That presents an interesting opportunity for anonymity, does it not?" Lord North leaped up from his chair, rubbing his chin. "Ah. I have it. Ethan, you will pose as a foreign merchant. Dutch perhaps. How is your Dutch? Better than your French I hope."

"Somewhat."

Lord North continued. "You are interested in making France your home. Miss Winter, you are his French-born wife, who has learned of this sale through relatives closely connected to the court."

Maris nodded. Although Ethan couldn't be certain, it appeared as if she'd turned a few shades paler.

"A Dutch merchant and his wife?" Ethan said.

"Precisely," said Lord North. "Of course, you are free to work out the finer points amongst yourselves, but I think it is an excellent start, don't you?"

Ethan frowned. "I don't—"

Lord North skewered him with a look.

Ethan sighed. "If that is what you wish, sir."

"It is." He turned to Maris. "How about you?"

She nodded, but did not look at all pleased by the turn of events.

Lord North gave a contented nod. "Now, Miss Winter, will you please excuse us? Gray and I have some additional business to settle. I shall send word when you and he are to leave for France. Be warned, though, it shan't be more than two or three days. Can you be ready?"

"Of course." Maris nodded at Ethan. "Until then . . ."

Ethan bowed. "Until then."

Lord North followed her to the doors and murmured something before he closed them behind her.

"I will not work with a woman," Ethan said, as soon as she was gone.

Lord North's eyebrows shot up, disappearing beneath his wig. "Why not?"

"Because—" Ethan stopped himself. He took a deep breath. "Because they are too easily swayed."

"Swayed? By what?"

Ethan shrugged. "Flattery, seduction, avarice." *Love.*

"Pah." Lord North waved a hand. "You are still rattled by what happened between you and the Sparrow."

Ethan said nothing.

Lord North gave him a fatherly look. "That was a long time ago. It was a mistake, Ethan. But it wasn't your fault. None of us knew that Madeline was . . ."

"A treacherous whore?"

"A traitor."

"I should have known. But I was blinded by her—"

"You were human, Gray. You are smarter, now. You learned a valuable lesson."

"Unfortunately, men had to die because of it. They walked into an ambush because of me. Because of my involvement with Madeline."

"They were as much to blame as you," North said. "They should have been more careful. They knew the danger of the mission."

Ethan rubbed the back of his neck. "Still, I cannot work with the Raven."

"We've relied on her information for three years, Gray. She is a fine operative. You've said so yourself, on many occasions."

"That was before I found out she is a woman. And Gavin Winter's daughter, on top of it."

Lord North shook his head. "This point is not negotiable, Gray. You *will* work with her."

Unable to keep his frustration in check, Ethan kicked a chair from his path. "Just what is your intent? Do you mean to undercut the weapons investigation? Do you wish me to fail?"

Lord North looked surprised. "Of course not. But you

said yourself that delivery of the gun order would, in all likelihood, not reach the quays for another month. This trip to France shouldn't take more than a few days' time, provided the weather and tides cooperate."

"But to take me away from England . . . it assures I will make no headway in that quarter. Besides, you've just told me I need to concentrate more on my other duties."

"And you just told me you are capable of handling both. Besides, there could well be a tie between this auction and the weapons smuggling. Perhaps you will find it."

"Or perhaps it will waste valuable time."

Lord North shook his head. "It will only be for a few days. And it will allow you to judge for yourself whether or not you believe the Raven a capable partner for you in the weapons matter. You asked for that chance, did you not? A chance to judge her abilities before bringing her in?"

Ethan gave him a flat smile. "I suppose I did."

The truth was, he didn't need this mission to tell him whether or not she was capable. He already knew the answer to that.

This would not do. Would not do at all. To be in such close proximity to Ethan Gray—

Maris closed her eyes and breathed deep, clearing her mind of negative thoughts. It was a skill her dearest friend, Ajala, had taught her when she was but a child. A skill that continued to serve her well.

She would accomplish nothing if she allowed herself to feel fear.

She'd been close to Gray before—in the warehouse, and more recently at Lady Jersey's masque, where she'd mistaken him for the owner of a shipping interest whom she was supposed to meet.

She'd managed to keep hold of herself in those instances. She could do it again.

In some ways it would be an honor to work with him. His dedication to the Crown was legendary, and his bravery unsurpassed. There were many stories to illustrate his courage, but one in particular had inspired her to work for the committee.

Around the same time he'd become the newly appointed spymaster, Gray had walked into an ambush with the full knowledge he could be killed, in order to try to warn two other operatives they were in danger.

One of those operatives had been her father.

Though Gavin Winter hadn't lived through the attack, Gray had risked his life to try to save him, and for that she would be eternally grateful. Her admiration for the Wolf was one of the reasons she'd decided to become a spy herself.

He was smart, and resourceful, and unafraid. And because of that, he was also a formidable enemy. She'd learned not to underestimate him.

She eased back into the once-plush seat of the carriage, covering her legs with a soft wool blanket. The April air snaking beneath the carriage door to bite at her ankles still held the residue of winter.

Though Gray's companionship the entire way to France and back would undoubtedly unnerve her, she could also look upon Lord North's edict as a blessing in disguise. If she knew where Ethan Gray was, then she would also know where he was not.

And that would serve her purposes far better than anything she could have arranged on her own.

Chapter 4

The ship's bow slapped white-crested waves, spraying Ethan and Maris with the waters of the English Channel as they sailed toward France. It would be a trying journey in more ways than one.

The two had exchanged few words on the carriage ride to the docks, aware that they would have much time together with little to say. The tension stretched taut between them like the hide on a drum.

Behind them, Ethan knew the white cliffs of Dover would soon disappear, shrouded in the fog that lay over the water, obscuring the English shoreline. Then it would be the two of them, alone, with only each other to rely upon.

Not a comforting thought.

The wind whipped against Maris's back, wrapping the skirts of her gown about her legs, and spiriting away the ribbon that held her long braid at her back. Her hair uncoiled and flew about her like a cloud, giving her the aspect of an angel dressed in black.

Ethan bustled her belowdecks, to the cabin they would

share for the few hours' journey to France. There hadn't been enough cabins available on the small ship for him to procure one for each of them, and it might have seemed strange in any event, considering that they were traveling under the guise of a newlywed couple.

The boat pitched as he held open the cabin door. Maris stumbled into the tiny space, striking her shins against the frame of a small bed anchored to the floor.

"Ow!"

Good breeding dictated he go to her, assist her, but her expression kept him at bay. It was clear he was the last person from whom she would accept help.

She dropped less than gracefully onto the cot, rubbing her shins. "These shoes are a horror on slippery wooden decks. Would you mind terribly if I removed them?"

"By all means."

She pulled one shoe off and wiggled her toes. When he continued to look on, she frowned at him until he turned his back to her.

Ethan laughed. "My dear lady, when we depart this ship in Calais, we shall be sharing a carriage, a room at the inn, all of our meals, and most likely an affectionate glance or two, just for appearance's sake. Getting a glimpse of your stocking feet will be the least intimate of our ventures, I am afraid. Are you certain your priggish nature will survive this mission?"

"I am hardly priggish, Mr. Gray—"

He turned back to face her. "Ethan, please."

She gave him a disapproving look. "As I said, I am hardly priggish. But I don't believe in hasty intimacies. We'll do best together if we respect each others' privacy, no matter the circumstances."

"Well then, I shall make an effort to abandon my practice of breakfasting in the nude."

Her mouth drew into a tight line. She busied herself

tucking her shoes neatly under the cot and smoothing her skirts, no doubt awaiting an apology for mentioning the unmentionable in a lady's presence.

Ethan suppressed a grin. No sense stirring the hornet's nest when he had to live with the hornet for the next week.

"I am sorry if I offended you. Let us begin anew. Shall we pretend we are meeting for the first time?"

"Good heavens, let's not relive that moment," she said, collecting her wild hair and taming it back into a braid. "I was painfully shy, and embarrassingly enamored of you and your incredible act of bravery on my father's behalf."

His smile faded. "Yes, well. Happily, that is no longer the case."

If possible, her expression grew even more benign. "Perhaps we should prepare for our upcoming roles." She motioned to a small chair in the corner. "Sit, please."

Ethan quelled the urge to take offense at her superior tone, and sat.

"First of all, let us practice our names. We don't want to give ourselves away over a simple slip. Do you speak French?"

He spoke a few sentences.

Her brow puckered. "Let me hear your Dutch."

He recited a poem he'd memorized.

"Much better. Perhaps you should keep with Dutch whenever possible. I will, of course, speak Dutch when I address you in France."

"You speak Dutch, as well?"

"Yes. And Bavarian, Hindi, and a bit of Spanish, but not enough to get by. I am practicing, though."

"Naturally."

She raised her eyebrows at his sarcastic tone. "Shall we begin?" She cleared her throat. "Hello, I am Mrs. Angelique Ganesvoort." Her French was flawless. She repeated the phrase in Dutch, which was equally perfect.

"I am Bartel Ganesvoort." To the untrained ear, his Dutch was more than passable, but it lacked the subtle perfection of Maris's. He remembered that her father had had a knack for languages as well. He'd spent a number of years spying in India, under the guise of working for the East India Company.

"What are we doing in France?" Maris asked, in Dutch.

"We recently married in Amsterdam and came to France to reside in your ancestral home in Normandy."

"How did we hear of this auction?" she asked.

"I am a shipbuilder. I plan to commission work from the French navy. I have many connections in Versailles."

"Do we?" she asked, in English.

"Do we what?"

"Do we have connections in Versailles?"

Ethan leaned back and draped an arm over the back of his chair, studying her. The whereabouts of the Crown's operatives were a matter of great secrecy. Only Ethan and Lord North knew every one of their locations at any given time.

And while it was apparent the prime minister trusted Maris, Ethan did not. In his estimation, she was hardly a spy. More like a glorified drawing-room gossip.

Ethan knew Lord North would seek his opinion of the Raven as soon as they returned from France. And he would have the great pleasure of reporting her lacking. It was the perfect excuse not to work with her.

"Well, do we?" she said again. "Do we have contacts in Versailles? Perhaps it would be good for me to know, in the event that anything should go wrong."

He rose suddenly. "Come, Mrs. Ganesvoort. Let us go up on deck and take some fresh air."

So, he didn't trust her.

Maris slipped her shoes on and followed Gray from the tiny cabin.

His condescending attitude pricked her usual self-assuredness. She'd spied for the Crown for more than three years now, with exemplary results. There wasn't a man who'd worked harder for the committee than she had. How dare he treat her like some senseless ninny?

"We'll accomplish nothing unless you trust me," she said, just loud enough for him to hear over the wind. "If you don't, we could get ourselves killed."

"I promise you, we won't be killed." He gripped the ship's rail, his knees bending, his hips moving easily to offset the pitch and yaw of the boat.

"You obviously don't believe you need my help," she said. "And to be truthful, I don't believe I need yours, either. But our mutual friend deemed it necessary that we embark upon this journey together. He obviously had his reasons. And since we are stuck together, I suggest we make the best of it."

He turned and looked out over the water.

There were no other passengers on deck, just crew members scraping brightwork, setting sails, and heaving lines. A few men gathered at the scuttlebutt for a dipperful of water, but most were engaged in activities that left them no time to wonder about her and Gray.

Maris's stomach churned. She withdrew a crumpled handkerchief from her sleeve and unwrapped the contents, slipping a small piece of gingerroot into her mouth. Another trick she'd learned from Ajala.

She choked back the feeling of loneliness that always threatened when she thought of her friend, and turned her attention instead to Ethan Gray's profile.

The wind swept russet hair back from his face, laying bare every sinfully seductive angle. A razor-thin scar cutting into his upper lip did not mar his good looks, but rather served to give him an air of danger that made him infinitely appealing.

His eyes, as stormy and gray as the waters around them, stared off into the horizon as if already searching for answers on the shores of France. The man was too handsome for his own good. Or the good of any woman who happened to fall prey to his charm.

His method of seduction, and his subsequent unburdening of female companionship, was beyond legendary. It bordered on scandalous.

The Wolf had proven himself a rake of the first order, earning his moniker in spades. To women, he was the ultimate unattainable gentleman. Therefore, they wanted nothing but to attain him.

Some ladies forbade their daughters to so much as dance with Ethan Gray. But the marriage-mart mamas didn't know what Maris knew. Maris understood him. Just as hers had, his trysts served a purpose. The Wolf used women for information.

What she didn't know was whether or not the Wolf and Ethan Gray were two separate men. Did Gray ever want a woman for anything more than information? Did he ever seduce a woman for the pure pleasure of it?

Had he ever been in love?

After he'd tried to rescue her father, the dashing Mr. Gray had been at the center of all Maris's girlhood daydreams. She'd thought about him almost incessantly in her fantasies of love and marriage and family.

But she wasn't a girl anymore. She had no more illusions about the Wolf. Or about any man, for that matter.

A sail came about and the boat lurched suddenly to port, pitching her from the rail. Gray caught her before she ended up sprawled facedown on the deck. He pulled her upright, bracing her against his body as the ship righted itself. "Are you hurt?"

Her heart drummed against her chest. *So this is what it feels like in the arms of the Devil.*

He smiled, almost as though he could hear her thoughts. It was not a warm, companionable smile, nor even a friendly one. It was as duplicitous a smile as she'd ever seen.

And still it managed to twist her stomach into excited little knots.

She chewed the piece of ginger in her mouth until the knots in her stomach loosened, suspecting she'd need quite a bit more of it to get her through these next few days.

The sun had just begun to set as they disembarked in Calais. The tides and wind had been merciful, and they'd only had to wait a few hours to dock.

Maris had never been to Calais, and she looked about her with curiosity. Evidence of the medieval English occupation was everywhere in the port city. From the architecture to the English spoken all around them, Calais seemed almost a part of England itself. Indeed, it was the closest point in France to her own country, and on a clear day, her homeland was visible from Calais's shores.

At the bottom of the gangplank, Gray stopped her. "Wait here a moment. Let me find out where we might stay tonight."

As he conferred with the captain, Maris ignored his order and wandered a ways up the shoreline. As far out into the channel as the eye could see, ships bobbed on the waves, which abated only slightly in the harbor.

Mooring ropes groaned against the currents, holding their charges fast despite the whitecaps that knocked against the hulls. Amidst the rocking, the crew of the *Oiseleur* struggled to unload a carriage they'd transported from Dover. A nervous young man, perhaps at the start of his Grand Tour, looked on apprehensively.

Maris tented her hands over her eyes to shield them from the sun's reflection on the water, her gaze scanning the ships docked there. Most were ferries or aging merchant ships, their hulls green with algae. But in a slip a quarter-mile away floated a handsome frigate with bright blue gun whales, its brass fixtures gleaming in the sunset. It bore no flag. She squinted, trying to read the name on the side of the boat.

"Dear God, no," she whispered. What in the hell was Samuel doing in Calais?

She glanced over her shoulder. Gray was still speaking to their captain, his back toward the rest of the harbor.

She hurried back to the middle of the dock, and stood beside him while the men concluded their conversation. Maris clutched his arm. "Are we ready, my love? Let us hurry."

The captain winked at Gray. "An eager piece, isn't she?"

The two men laughed, and the captain went off, belting orders to the crew unloading the carriage.

"Which way is the inn?" she asked.

He pointed past her. "A short way up that street."

The opposite direction from Samuel's frigate. Her heartbeat slowed just a little. She released his elbow. "Shall we be off, then? It is growing dark."

"Cover your hair, please," Ethan said quietly.

She looked as if she might argue with him, but tied her bonnet over her haphazard braid.

Ethan took Maris's arm so as not to lose her amongst the fevered activity of the waterfront. "Your hair is unusual enough to draw comment. Let us not attract undue attention to ourselves until we are able to assess the situation here."

She nodded her assent. Her cheeks bore a greenish hue, no doubt due to the rough waters on their journey. The delicacy of a woman's constitution could not be concealed,

Ethan thought with satisfaction. With any luck, the waters on the way home would prove equally inhospitable to her.

But for the time being they were land-bound, tired, and hungry. He and Maris walked to a nearby inn with the unfortunate moniker of The Pig's Foot, where they would sup and take a room for the night.

"I daresay your color is much improved," he said, in Dutch, when they arrived at the door to the inn.

"The fresh air did me good."

"Ah, of course. After all, there was precious little fresh air aboard the ship."

She ignored his barb, raising the lace hem of her gown to step over the threshold of the inn.

Ethan looked about them, dismayed. It was a filthy place, with grease stains generously coating warped wooden floors, and the smell of sour ale steeped into the walls. The cellar below was sure to be teeming with rats and other vile creatures.

It was the sort of place Ethan avoided at all cost, but almost worth entering just to see the look on Maris's face. A woman would never tolerate such a hole.

Only, the place did not seem to disturb her.

Unfazed by the filth, she headed straight for an empty table in the common room, removing her gloves on the way. She waved to him from the table, and he reluctantly took one last breath of unpolluted air at the doorway.

"Will we stay here tonight?" she asked, apparently not at all disturbed by the thought of it.

He nodded. "The captain said it is the only place in town not filled to the rafters with lodgers. I can see why."

She looked about, as if noticing for the first time the inn's obvious deficiencies. "Not the finest accommodations, are they?"

"To say the least."

To his annoyance, she looked amused. "My dear Bartel. You've become too accustomed to luxury."

"I hardly think cleanliness is a luxury, *Angelique*."

A man in a leather apron approached. "May I help you, Madam? Monsieur?"

"Are you the innkeeper?" Ethan asked in Dutch.

The little man frowned. "I don't speak Bavarian."

"It is Dutch," Maris said with a smile. "I am afraid my husband's French is not so good, so I will make the arrangements. Do you have a room available?"

"But of course."

As Maris spoke with the innkeeper, Ethan took note of their surroundings in case they needed to make a quick exit for any reason. He hoped she would think to request a room with a window.

"Our trunks are aboard the *Oiseleur*," she told the innkeeper. "Will you have someone fetch them?"

"But of course, Madame." He motioned to a serving girl who looked as if she hadn't seen a bathtub or basin since Michaelmas. "Would you care to sup before I show you to your room?"

Although Ethan's appetite had been quelled by the thought of rats in the cellar, Maris ordered them a hearty meal.

After the innkeeper and the serving girl left them, she leaned in. "What do you think?"

"I think you are insane if you eat anything that is cooked in this rat-infested hovel."

She shook her head impatiently. "How will we find out about the auction? We cannot simply show up in Bolougne tomorrow and expect to be included in it, no matter what our supposed 'connections.' "

"True. But there are ways to garner an invitation."

"How, when you don't even know who is running it?"

He shrugged. "Leave that to me."

* * *

The thought of Gray following her so closely up the creaking staircase made the greasy meal they'd eaten churn in Maris's belly. She concentrated her gaze on the innkeeper's apron strings as he led them to the top of the stairs, and then to the end of a narrow hallway.

"Our best quarters for you, Madame. Monsieur." The innkeeper stepped aside.

Maris's heart stopped beating momentarily.

There was but one bed, of course. One very small, lumpy bed in one very small, cold room. She would be alone with the Wolf tonight. It was inevitable.

She'd known this, of course. But the reality of it was something else, again.

"Thank you," she said to the innkeeper, her voice unsteady in her own ears.

It was late, and she was bone tired, but she didn't imagine she'd get much sleep this night. She placed the sputtering tallow candle she carried on the bedside table beside the lamp that was already there, doubling the amount of light in the room.

Gray pressed a coin in the innkeeper's palm and closed the door behind him.

"Well. What do you think?"

She turned her back to him, pressing her fist to her stomach, breathing deep until her nerves settled. "I've seen worse."

"Really?" He sounded genuinely incredulous. "Under what possible circumstance?"

She turned to face him. "While *you* might spend the majority of your time between the silken sheets of well-born ladies' beds, your operatives often must suffer a few discomforts to acquire the information we seek."

Even in the dim light, she could see his expression turn

stony. He took two steps toward her, until his face was inches from hers. "Don't presume to know anything about me," he said in a low voice.

A chill swept the hairs on her arms to attention, but she did not back away. "I would expect the same courtesy."

His eyes blazed. He leaned in, his lips a breath away. She steeled herself against a kiss, furious that he would take such a tack with her. Such a common strategy might work on his simple-minded society ladies, but Maris liked to believe she had a bit more spine.

She worked herself into a moral outrage over that kiss.

A kiss that never came.

Instead, Gray reached around her and snatched the faded quilt from the mattress. "You may have the bed. I will sleep on the floor."

Ethan lay in the dark on the hard, cold floorboards, staring up at the ceiling, which he could not see.

It would seem the Raven was of similar opinion to the rest of his operatives. She believed him soft. Weakened by too many years in London. Spoiled by too many comfortable beds.

He'd like to know when last *she'd* slept on a floor.

On the other side of the tiny room—hardly more than five steps away—he heard the ticking rustle beneath her. She was restless; perhaps wondering if he would attack her during the night. That thought gave him some satisfaction.

Not the thought of attacking her, but the fact that she might be worrying over it.

He found he enjoyed antagonizing her, which was so very unlike him. Seduction was more his fashion with women. Extreme courtesy and a gentle manner caught the fairer sex off guard when they were expecting wickedness.

However, he doubted the Raven had faced too many men who wished to seduce her. She was far too serious, and much too plain. There was absolutely nothing tempting about her.

Except, perhaps, her toes.

And her hair. Oh, yes. Definitely her hair. The way it had floated about her shoulders on the ship, like strands of white silk on water—

He blocked the image from his mind. Even if she weren't an operative, working for him—and with him—she was far from the kind of woman about whom he would entertain such thoughts. There was simply no intrigue there.

His thoughts strayed unwillingly to the peacock at Lady Jersey's masquerade. Her lips, so lush and pink, so soft against his. Her startled blue eyes glittering behind the mask. Her breasts spilling like lush fruit from the bodice of her gown . . .

He pushed that image from his thoughts as well. She might be intriguing, but the woman was a traitor. The enemy.

Forbidden.

He rolled onto his side and closed his eyes. Of the two birds that plagued his every thought of late, all things considered he much preferred the peacock to the Raven.

The ride to Boulogne-sur-Mer could only be categorized as wretched.

Aside from an occasional surly look, Gray barely acknowledged her as the coach bumped and wheezed over the seaside road. The day was raw and misty. Wind buffeted the vehicle constantly, adding to the already nauseating movement. The only good thing about it was that it was taking them farther away from Samuel's ship.

Maris had run out of gingerroot, and prayed she could find some more before the journey back to England. Assuming, of course, she'd make it back to England in one piece. She figured that if the French didn't catch on to her ruse and kill her, Gray might do it himself.

Clearly, he hated her. For what, she had no idea, but she wasn't sure she even wanted to find out. She'd thought this might be the perfect situation to learn more about him. Maybe to find out exactly what he knew about Samuel. But she was too close for comfort now. Especially with Samuel traipsing about Calais. All she wanted now was to collect the information they'd come for, and go home.

The coach jerked to a stop on a windswept cliff. Below them, a river opened into the channel, where half a dozen boats sat bobbing on the waves.

The driver poked his head in the window. "The view is beautiful, no? Just the place for lovers, no? We stop to look."

Gray shook his head. "Thank you, but we just want to—"

The driver winked, and scrambled back up to the box.

"Wonderful," Gray muttered. He pushed open the door. "I suppose we must take a look."

They disembarked from the coach and stood on the edge of the cliff. Wind tugged her hat, and caused the ruffles of Gray's neck stock to flap like flags against his green velvet coat. The cold mist penetrated her woolen traveling attire, chilling her to the bone. She hardly noticed.

"It is spectacular," she breathed. Blue mist curled through a riverbed populated by stark white rocks.

"The River Liane," he said in Dutch, pointing to the estuary below. "There is a legend that claims that early in the seventh century, a boat appeared there quite mysteriously, pulled by a swan and carrying a statue of the Virgin Mary. There were no oars. No sails, or sailors. The villagers declared it a miracle, and carried the Blessed Mother to the church on their shoulders. The statue was credited with many miracles."

"Perhaps we should pray for a miracle ourselves," she said.

"We won't need one." He absently fastened an open button on the collar of her cape. "Just stay close to me. Follow my lead, and by all means, do not try to involve yourself in business best left to gentlemen. It would not be well-received."

"Oh, but of course! I am happy just to have a strong man to tell me what to do." Her voice dripped with annoyance she couldn't even pretend to try to hide.

If Gray thought she'd spend this entire mission contentedly basking in his shadow, he was mistaken. She was no longer the awestruck girl who would have kissed his feet. She'd worked hard to dig up every shred of intelligence for this operation, and she would not be pushed to the background now.

Gray shook his head and opened the carriage door, ushering her inside just as it began to rain. He instructed the driver to take them to a decent inn in Boulogne.

As the coach lurched into motion, Gray said, "I've begun to think you're not particularly grateful for my protection, or the skills I bring to this endeavor."

"Perhaps because I do not need your skills, nor your protection."

He raised his eyebrows. "You think you could manage this mission on your own?"

"I know I could."

He snorted. "Might I remind you that we aren't in some drawing room at your uncle's country house, gossiping with misplaced French dandies."

"Of all the arrogant—" She bit her lip in frustration. Heat climbed her neck and ignited her cheeks. "I don't have an uncle, and I don't gossip. But I might remind you that in this pursuit of the vermin who have killed our countrymen and intend to sell our navy's assets from beneath us, there will be precious few women to seduce to get the information you need. This time, you just may have to rely on your instincts. Or have they, as rumor holds, escaped you, Mr. Gray?"

His eyes narrowed. The air between them was as thick as the mist outside. He extended a gloved hand across the short distance between them. Maris thought he might strike her. But he surprised her once again, brushing a fingertip over her cheek.

"Do not underestimate the power of seduction. What if I were to turn that power to you? Do you think I could seduce you, Miss Winter?"

Alarm wrung the air from her lungs. She sat as still as she could amidst the bumping of the coach, and said nothing. At last, he withdrew his hand.

"Do not mistake me for one of your women, Mr. Gray," she said quietly.

In a voice dripping with amusement, he said, "That would be quite impossible, Miss Winter."

Chapter 5

Ethan could scarce remember when he'd ever been in a fouler mood.

Seduce her?

Seduce *her*?

What had led him to even joke about such a thing? After what had happened with the Sparrow, he'd rather cut off his own hand than pursue such a dalliance. But he hadn't been able to stop himself from taunting her.

He shook his head in disgust. It hadn't been a joke. He'd meant to intimidate her, but it hadn't worked. He'd only succeeded in disgusting himself.

The coach stopped before an inn in Boulogne-sur-Mer. The Flying Gull was a palace compared to The Pig's Foot. Heaps of trash were noticeably absent from the gutters, and there wasn't one stray dog skulking about in front of the door. At least, not in the downpour that currently assailed them.

He and Maris dashed through the driving rain, into a pleasant common room where a fire blazed in the hearth.

Maris stood dripping upon a braided rug as Ethan made arrangements for them in halting French. He did not think Maris any more capable than he to do it, with the way her teeth chattered.

Their bedroom matched the simple comfort of the rest of the inn. Two large windows overlooked the water with a view which, at the moment, was blurred by sheets of rain. Beneath the windows, a large red roof jutted out over a porch, blocking their view of the street and giving them some measure of privacy. A large fireplace dominated one wall, emitting a welcome wave of heat.

"Oh, lovely." Maris went to the fire directly, standing as close as she dared without singeing the lace from her gown. But it appeared the heat could not penetrate the chill that had settled over her. She shivered violently beneath the wet wool of her traveling attire.

He stripped the embroidered coverlet from the bed and took it to her. "If you hope to get warm, you will have to remove your clothing."

She narrowed her eyes.

"I did not mean to imply—" He rubbed the back of his neck. "Dammit. What I meant to say is that I will take my leave while you—"

"Fine."

"You'd best turn your back for a moment," he warned.

He shed his wet jacket and shirt, retrieving fresh clothing from his trunk. He decided his breeches and stockings, although damp, would have to stay put. "I'll go downstairs, pass the word that I am interested in the auction."

Maris wrapped the coverlet he'd given her around her shoulders, and sat on the edge of a chaise before the fireplace. She bent, attempting to unlace one of her boots with shaking fingers.

He kneeled down before her. "Let me help you."

She watched him as if he were some sort of dangerous animal that might devour her from the feet up.

He unlaced one of her boots. Taking the heel in his hand, he tugged gently until the boot slid from her foot. Without thinking, he took her toes between his hands. They were ice cold.

He rubbed gently, using the friction of his palms against her silk stocking to warm her.

She really did have lovely toes.

He placed her foot gently on the floor, and reached for the other boot.

"No!" Her voice wavered. "I-I will do it myself. Thank you."

Reluctantly, he stood. "Keep the door locked. I will be back in an hour."

As soon as he'd gone, Maris let out a long breath.

With trembling fingers, she unlaced her other boot. Sweet Mary, she didn't think she could bear to have him touch her again.

The way he affected her was . . . well, it was simply contrary to all common sense.

She worked the buttons of her wet gown, which she hadn't removed in two days—also contrary to all common sense. She'd slept in it the night before, as much for warmth as for the protection it afforded should Ethan Gray attempt to debauch her.

She'd been peculiarly disappointed when he did not.

Of course, he was accustomed to the company of women far more handsome than she. No one would ever mistake her for a great beauty, although she'd had her share of gentlemen admirers, and more than one clandestine note confessing undying love.

But that would never be Ethan Gray's method, would it?

A full-on assault? He was much more likely to impart slow torture—like warming toes.

And she was nothing better than a fool to obsess over his methods of seduction.

She peeled away the layers of her traveling clothes and stood before the fire in a damp chemise, feeling the warmth seep into her bones. On a small table nearby sat a carafe of port and two small glasses. She poured a bit of the ruby liquid into a glass and sipped it, letting it warm her insides even as the fire warmed her skin.

When the heat grew too intense, she wrapped herself in the coverlet and sat on the edge of the chaise. Her eyelids flagged. She'd been on edge since she'd seen Samuel's boat in Calais, but now that there was a comfortable distance between them, she could finally breathe.

She stretched out on the chaise, watching the fire dance in the grate, feeling truly warm for the first time since she'd left England.

The common room of The Flying Gull was all but deserted. It was between mealtimes, and the place didn't have the inviting air of a workaday pub. If Ethan were to find out anything about the auction, it wouldn't be here.

He wandered out onto the street. The rain had finally stopped, but not before it had turned the road into a patchwork of ruts and puddles. He weaved around them, making his way toward the docks, instinctively seeking the lower places. Places where whispered conversation drew no attention. Where information could be bought along with whisky, women, or deceit.

He found it at The Coxswain.

Lightermen, sailors, and dockers of all persuasion milled about outside. The door swung open, emitting three members of *Le Regiment Des Gardes Suisse*, King Louis's elite guard. One of them held it open for Ethan as he entered, and Ethan noticed the man was missing the tip of his middle finger.

Ethan wondered what the guards were doing in Boulogne. And more specifically, what they were doing at The Coxswain.

Inside, the place was steeped in shadows, but was not uninviting. A fire burned in the hearth beneath a giant cooking pot. The smell of soup mingled with ale, and the brine of the harbor wafted in through the doorway, clinging to the clothes of the patrons.

Though the tables were filled, the bar was nearly vacant. Ethan sidled up to it, resting an elbow on the pitted surface. "*Aal*," Ethan said. Ale.

The barkeep raised his eyebrows. Ethan repeated his request, this time in French.

The barkeep set a pewter mug before him.

"Merci." He took a long pull, and set the mug back on the bar. "Might I make an inquiry? I am seeking a special *veiling*."

The barkeep shook his head.

"An auction. Of a ship."

"Why would I know anything about it?"

Ethan shrugged. "You look like the kind of man who knows things."

"If I did, why would I tell you?" The barkeep's voice took on an edge of hostility.

"Because you know the value of useful information."

"And what is that?"

Ethan drained his mug before removing a leather purse from the inside pocket of his waistcoat. He withdrew several gold livres, dropped them into the mug, and pushed it toward the barkeep.

The man removed the coins and pocketed them. Then

he refilled the mug and handed it to Ethan. "Wait over there, at the table."

The barkeep disappeared through a door behind the bar.

Ethan took a seat in a corner, nursing his ale as he listened surreptitiously to the conversations around him. French. Dutch. Spanish. English. Italian. Greek. Intrigues hatching across nationalities. He'd always enjoyed working in seafaring cities for just that reason.

A dark-eyed serving girl stopped at the table, displaying her wares as she leaned over to pick up his mug. "More?"

"No, thank you."

"Something else?" She winked.

"No, thank you."

She gave him a disappointed look before moving on to the next table, her hips undulating beneath her skirts.

Ethan smiled. Not because of the serving girl, but because it felt so damned good to be out of London and in the field again. He tried not to let the fact that he was partnered with a woman ruin his mood.

An hour later the barkeep reappeared, followed by a short, oily-looking man with thick eyebrows. The man slid onto the chair across the table, his dirty lace sleeves smearing the layer of grease from its surface. His eyes never left Ethan's face. "*Wie zijn u?*" Who are you?

"Bartel Ganesvoort."

"Should that mean something to me?"

"That depends. Who are *you*?"

The man leaned back in the chair, eyeing him across the table. "Our friend"—he indicated the barkeep—"he told me you are interested in attending an auction?"

"Yes."

"Where did you hear of this auction."

"My wife's uncle. He is a close friend of Jacques Necker."

"Necker? The king's minister of finance?"

Maris had learned Necker would be visiting his sister in Marseilles for the next fortnight, and therefore could not be contacted in time to deny any knowledge of a Bartel Ganesvoort.

Ethan nodded. "Necker knows I am interested in acquiring ships for the Dutch navy."

"I trust you have letters of recommendation?"

"But of course."

"Where are you staying?"

"At The Flying Gull."

The man removed a vellum card from his pocket and laid it on the table. On it was written an address, nothing more. "Come tomorrow at noon. Bring your credentials."

Ethan celebrated his success with one more mug of ale, and a brief flirtation with the serving girl. Then he walked the streets of Boulogne for an hour, looking for the king's guard, without success.

Eventually he was forced to face the inevitable. He would have to return to The Flying Gull—and Maris Winter. He took his time getting himself there. Perhaps if he waited long enough, she would be sleeping.

When he returned to the inn, the door to their room was locked, as he'd ordered. He entered quietly.

The Raven lay stretched out on her side on the chaise before the fire, the coverlet wrapped about her like a toga. Her white-blond hair tumbled over her shoulders, covering her breasts as if she were a Roman goddess posing for a portrait.

Sleep softened her. Gone were the pinched lips, the guarded expression, the prim posture. He studied her as if seeing her for the first time. She couldn't make him turn away now with her disapproving looks.

In sleep she showed a vulnerability that unsettled him.

Her chest rose and fell in gentle rhythm, a testament to the fact that she was a living, breathing person who just might have fears and flaws. So opposite the figure she cast upon the world.

Her face was serene, her lips a deep, delicious red. Her slender white neck lay exposed to him, stirring within him a battle between the primal urges to attack and to protect, as if she were his possession.

He could make her his.

The thought—sudden and urgent—startled him, and he took a step back. A floorboard creaked beneath his feet.

She stirred, and one leg emerged from the coverlet, bared to the thigh. The intriguing expanse of ivory skin beckoned.

Come. Touch.

His mouth went dry. He kneeled before her and reached out . . .

A sudden crash from the direction of the window startled him from his trance.

Maris bolted up on the chaise, and gasped.

Ethan charged toward the noise. In the dim light, he saw one black-booted foot disappearing through the open window. He made a grab for it, but the person attached to the foot twisted from his grasp.

Ethan dove through the window. A knife flew past his ear, lodging in the window frame with a *chunk*.

The intruder rolled across the porch roof and dropped off the side. Ethan scrabbled to the edge of the roof.

"Dammit!"

The street below was already deserted.

Maris's heart ricocheted off the walls of her chest, coming to rest somewhere between its proper place and her throat. She wasn't certain what had happened, but she knew that standing there wrapped in bedding could not possibly benefit her situation.

The aftereffects of wine and sleep impairing her only momentarily, she hurried to her trunk and pulled out a dressing gown, shedding the coverlet and securing the quilted wrapper tight about her waist.

Moments later, Gray reappeared, climbing through the window with a knife in one hand, his face red and his breathing labored. He yanked the window shut, securing the latch.

"What did you see?"

She shook her head. "Not much. There might have been a man kneeling beside me, but I cannot be sure."

If possible, his face grew even redder. "Did you hear any sounds in the room?"

"No. What happened?"

"When I returned, there was someone in the room. I saw him climbing out through the window." He checked the latch again. "Did you keep the door locked, as I asked?"

She put her hands on her hips. "Of course."

"And the window?"

"Closed. I was nearly frozen to death. Why would I open the window?"

As they spoke, Ethan searched the room. "I don't think anything is missing. You will have to check your things, of course. But if it wasn't a robbery, who in the hell was it?"

A knot tightened in Maris's gut. It couldn't have been Samuel. Could it?

It would be just like him, to hunt them down this way. This was all a game to him. If he'd somehow found out she was in Calais, he could have followed them to Boulogne-sur-Mer . . .

"You didn't see anything? You cannot describe him at all?" she asked.

"No. Just a black boot. Whoever it was rolled off the edge of the roof and disappeared before I could catch up with him."

Her belly uncoiled a bit. "It must have been a robber."

Port towns were notorious for them. She tried to sound convincing, for both Gray's sake, and her own.

He went to the basin, splashed water on his face, and ran his fingers through his hair to straighten it. "Dress yourself," he said. "I'm going to summon the innkeeper."

"You plan to tell him of this? Won't it draw an undue amount of attention on us?"

"It will draw more if we don't report it. Any other traveler in this situation would. We must maintain our guise of ordinary travelers, in every sense."

Maris nodded. She could not fault his logic.

She went to her trunk, hoping against hope she'd find something amiss. In fact, there was nothing missing. But there was something new.

A note, written in Samuel's hand.

Go home.

What were Maris and the Wolf doing in Calais?

If they were there, it could only mean trouble. Had they somehow learned of the auction? They must have. There was no other explanation.

Samuel rested his elbows on top of the small desk in his quarters, rubbing his eyes with the heels of his hands.

There was no possible way he could alert anyone here of their presence. He couldn't care less about the Wolf, but it would put Maris in danger, as well. And for as much as she interfered in his business, he did not wish to see her dead.

He would simply have to let things go as planned, and try to fix whatever difficulties arose.

He stared out the small porthole at the churning waters of the channel, longing for this all to be over.

CHAPTER 6

The address on the vellum card turned out to be a haberdashery a half-mile from the waterfront. The building was old but well-kept, with green shutters and a wide window in the front, displaying an array of jackets, waistcoats, and stockings for the well-dressed gentleman.

Ethan tried the door, which was locked. Through the window, they could see that the place was deserted.

"Perhaps we should go around to the back," Maris said. Her gaze swept uneasily along the crowded streets.

He shook his head. "There could be a trap."

"But we're easy targets here. We should—"

He silenced her with a look, and knocked again.

The door swung open. A small man in a handsome suit of clothes in the English style stood in the doorway.

"I am Eugene Gasquet, proprietor of this establishment. May I help you?"

Ethan presented the vellum card.

"Ah. Come in, please." He stepped aside, allowing them to pass.

The little tailor came just to Maris's shoulder, a perfectly proportioned man of miniature stature. He directed them toward the back of the shop, past a painted screen that hid a backroom.

If Gasquet was small, the man just inside the doorway was, conversely, immense—a great leviathan with a flat nose and thick forearms. He stopped Ethan and Maris with a massive hand. "Your papers?"

Ethan presented two letters. One had been forged by the former secretary of King Louis's finance minister Necker, who now worked for the Crown. The other was from a fictional Dutch dignitary, made credible by an official-looking seal. He also presented a counterfeit bank draft, drawn on Necker's real bank account and forged with his signature by the former secretary, in the amount of a hundred thousand livre.

The leviathan passed them on to a man at a small desk behind him, who pored over the letters with ink-stained fingertips, holding them up to a candle and examining the seals.

Ethan held his breath. Would they pass this test, or would they be exposed as frauds? He wondered if Maris felt the same rush of apprehension. The same thrill. He cast a sideways glance at her.

She seemed unperturbed, as usual. The cool exterior she typically presented was apparently no casual act. Or if it was, at least she was able to continue it in the face of extreme duress.

His estimation of her increased a notch.

On impulse, he reached out and touched her hand, curling his fingers around hers and giving them a small squeeze. She blinked.

The man at the desk handed the papers back to the leviathan, who gave Maris a disdainful glance as he passed the packet over to Ethan. "Be seated. The auction will begin shortly."

Ethan swallowed the bile that had risen in his throat. He put his hand on the small of Maris's back, guiding her to an empty row of chairs.

There were, perhaps, two dozen other people in the room. Near them, an elderly, gray-haired gentleman in blue; two bewigged dandies in high heels and tight velvet breeches; a balding, bespectacled man whispering in Bavarian to a man who appeared to be his secretary, who took copious notes on a lap desk; and a young man in the colorless clothing favored by American colonials.

Ethan committed his face to memory, suspecting that he might have something to do with the theft of the ship.

Everyone in the room, with the exception of the guards at the doors, looked well-heeled and breathlessly expectant.

Miss Winter was the only woman present, for which Ethan drew several hostile glances. Apparently, bringing one's wife to an illegal auction went against custom.

Not for the first time, Ethan wondered if he should have demanded, rather than requested, that she stay at the inn. And then he thought that it was unlikely anyone demanded anything of Maris Winter and got it.

"Why weren't we allowed to view the goods before the auction?" she whispered.

"Most likely because they want to check everyone's credentials first. Or perhaps they want only those who are serious buyers to know where the ship and its contents are being held."

Gasquet stepped up on a sturdy block behind a lectern. He resembled a near life-sized puppet, worked by some invisible hand.

"Good afternoon," he said in French. "Welcome. Today we have a very special offering. Several lots of cargo, fine weapons, and of course, a swift and excellent twenty-four-gun frigate."

The Bavarian's secretary whispered to his employer, perhaps translating Gasquet's words.

The little tailor continued. "We will auction the goods in lots. The auctioneer will give the details for each lot, and if you wish, you may bid upon the contents. The winner of each lot will have two days to examine the goods and approve the transaction. If he decides he does not wish to purchase the item after all, it will be awarded to the second-highest bidder. Therefore, whether or not you win a bid, we ask that you remain in Boulogne until all transactions are finalized."

Murmuring. Nodding. Coughing.

Gasquet introduced the auctioneer, who stepped up to the lectern with a sheaf of papers and a mug of ale. He sipped from the mug to prime his throat.

"The first lot to be auctioned," he read, "will be an assemblage of spirits. Forty cases of whiskey, nineteen barrels of ale, and eleven barrels of wine. May I take the first bid?"

For several long moments, all was silent. Ethan wondered if this would happen, after all, or if they might all simply get up and leave. Then, one of the dandies shouted a number. The room exploded with activity.

Lot two. Ninety-one red wool overcoats, eighty-eight pairs of breeches, and two hundred pairs of wool stockings.

Lot three. Two-hundred seventy-five muskets with bayonets. Four field cannons. Thirty kegs of black powder.

Lot four. Forty-six crates of china. Ten crates of crystal wine goblets. Sixty sets of fine silver flatware.

The bidding grew fierce. Ethan stood and removed his jacket.

The Bavarian's face turned a worrisome shade of crimson as he shouted numbers at his secretary, who in turn shouted them at the auctioneer.

The Bavarian did not win this last lot, and shook his fist as he railed at his secretary. Ethan felt pity for the man, who would undoubtedly bear the brunt of his employer's disappointment when the auction was over.

When bidding for the last lot had ended, the room suddenly grew quiet. Quills scratched on parchment. The auctioneer took a sip of ale and shuffled his papers.

"And now, our final offering. A frigate, outfitted with twenty-four guns. English construction, built in the Isle of Wight. Minor damage to the starboard hull and mizzenmast."

The auctioneer said nothing about the ship being an English naval vessel, but Ethan suspected that everyone in the room knew it was exactly that. His stomach clenched at the thought of the lives that had been taken during that "minor damage."

"Who will begin the bidding?"

A turbaned rajah started it off with a ridiculously low sum, but it wasn't long before the bidding grew to staggering amounts, and all but three men had dropped out—the Bavarian, the rajah, and Ethan.

Ethan would win the bid. He could name any sum in the world, for he would never have to pay it, and Necker's line of credit at the bank was nearly limitless.

Ethan would never claim the ship, of course. There was no way for him to get the vessel back to England. But he did need to know where it was docked. He had to be certain it was the same ship that had been overtaken on the Atlantic by the colonial privateer. He had to have proof.

The Bavarian raised the bid by seven hundred livres. The rajah dropped out.

The auctioneer looked at Ethan, and he nodded.

In the midst of the frenetic bidding, while everyone's attention was riveted on the auctioneer, Maris took inventory of the men in the tailor's back room.

Not exactly the criminal sort, unless you counted the men guarding the doors. Most of the bidders looked like well-to-do merchants. Perhaps even noblemen. The fabrics of their clothing, their stature, their shoes, attested to the wealth they clearly possessed. She wondered how each of them had learned of the auction, and filed her observations away in her mind, on the chance that they'd be useful in the future.

Maris had taken great pains to make herself as forgettable as possible—covering her hair beneath a hat, wearing a nondescript gray gown—but the fact that she was the only woman in the room had naturally brought her under great scrutiny.

Gray had asked her to stay at the inn, but she'd refused his request. She still considered this *her* mission, and she'd be damned if Gray would run away with it. In retrospect, her decision may not have been the best choice.

She drew up the fan that dangled on her wrist and opened it, gazing into a small round mirror attached to the tip of one of the fan's ribs. In it, she could see the open door that led to the alleyway behind the shop. A guard stood on either side of the door, but it wasn't the guards who drew her attention. It was the man standing just outside the door.

Samuel.

She went numb. He stared into the shop, as if waiting for someone to emerge.

Maris fought to breathe, cursing the corset that battled against her ribs. *Damn.*

Damn. Damn. Damn.

She glanced sideways at Gray, who was completely caught up in the bidding for the ship. What if he turned? What if he saw?

It would be over.

Maris swallowed the lump at the back of her throat. She'd tried. She'd risked everything, and for what? Samuel was a fool.

The bidding reached a frenzy. Ethan stood, knocking his chair to the ground in his haste. He and the Bavarian shouted at one another, and at the auctioneer. And then, the Bavarian was silent.

Ethan had won the bid.

Samuel disappeared from the mirror. Maris took a deep breath, and turned around. He was gone!

She prayed he hadn't recognized them, and wasn't waiting for them somewhere outside. He'd seen only their backs through the doorway. If she could get Gray out of there as soon as possible . . .

The auctioneer collected his papers and left the lectern. Gasquet stepped up onto his block. "Thank you all for attending. Those who have taken the lots, please stop at the desk on your way out, to make arrangements to inspect the goods."

Gray guided her to the desk, where they stood in line behind the other fortunate bidders who'd won lots. When they stepped up to the desk, the man with the ink-stained fingers had Gray sign a promissory note before handing him a vellum card with another address. "You'll find the ship here."

Gray tried to take the card, but the man held fast until Gray met his gaze. "Perhaps your wife would be more comfortable at the inn."

It wasn't a suggestion, but a mandate even Maris understood.

Gray nodded, and the man released the card.

"I am going with you."

"No, you are not." Ethan slipped a knife into a leather scabbard inside the waistband of his breeches. "It was made clear to both of us that you are not welcome."

"They won't know I am there. I will follow behind."

Ethan buttoned his jacket. "No. We cannot risk it. We don't know the situation."

"Exactly. You need me. What if something goes wrong?"

"Nothing will go wrong, unless they see you trailing behind me like a mother hen."

Ethan was, in reality, quite happy that Maris had been ordered to stay away from the ship. He was much more comfortable handling things himself. Although he did feel the slightest twinge of guilt, knowing that it was the intelligence she had collected that put them onto this operation.

He went to the basin and splashed water onto his face, washing away his misgivings. After all, things could get dangerous at the docks. It was no place for a woman.

Maris handed him a linen to dry his face. "I cannot stay here, trapped in this room. What will I do?"

"I don't know. Sew? Nap? Brush your hair? What is it that women do to pass the time?"

Her expression darkened.

He snapped his fingers. "I've got it! You can plot ways to murder me in my sleep."

"I've already done that." She put her hands on her hips. "I realize you don't take my abilities seriously, Mr. Gray. But—"

"Please, call me Ethan."

"—But since I am the one who first brought this treachery to light, I would like to see the culprits brought to justice by my own hand."

He tossed the linen in a basket and sat on the edge of the bed to change his boots. "As Lord North pointed out, we all work together for the common good. In this instance, your presence will hinder our efforts far more than it will help them. So for the good of the committee, I beg you, desist."

She regarded him in silence for a few minutes before she acquiesced. "Very well. For the good of the committee, I will not accompany you to the docks."

He gave an exaggerated sigh of relief. "Good. Now that that's settled, will you help me off with these boots?"

Help him off with his boots, indeed! Maris threw herself onto the bed and screamed into a pillow.

Gray was gone, on his way to the ship, while she was relegated to nail-biting in this stuffy room. It wasn't fair.

She sat up.

What if Samuel was there at the dock? What if he were somehow involved in the auction?

What if he was the one who captured the ship?

She bolted from the bed and ran to her trunk. Damn. The shirt and breeches she wore for skulking around dark alleys and such were conspicuously absent. She hadn't packed them because she hadn't wanted to draw suspicion should a curious chambermaid happen to go through her things.

Well, she would have to borrow from Gray. She'd move much faster in men's clothing, and be far less noticeable at the docks.

She went to his trunk and rooted through it, withdrawing a pair of soft woolen breeches and a well-worn linen shirt. She held the shirt up to her nose. It smelled of him—that enticing blend of spice and oak. Without thinking, she rubbed the garment against her cheek.

When she caught herself, she threw the offending garment onto the floor and stomped on it.

She stripped out of her gown, laying it neatly on the bed before donning Gray's clothes. The shirt hung from her shoulders like a deflated topsail. The breeches slipped from her hips and pooled on the floor about her ankles.

She pulled the breeches up and stuffed the shirt in the waistband, bunching it in her hand while she searched for something to hold them up. She found a scarf in her trunk, and tied it around her waist like a sash, slipping a small scabbard and knife beneath it, against her belly. Then she covered the whole mess with one of Gray's long jackets.

Knotting her hair atop her head, she hid it beneath one of his hats. As a final touch, she donned the very pair of boots she'd helped Gray remove, stuffing the toes with two of the snowy white cravats he was so fond of wearing.

On her way out the door, she caught a glimpse of herself in the standing mirror. Ridiculous. She couldn't leave the room looking like this.

At least, not through the door.

She went to the window. The roof below stretched out to the street in front and to a narrow alley on the side of the inn. She flung the window open wide and stepped onto the roof, dropping to her knees. She crawled on her hands and knees to the edge. There was no one in sight below, so she swung her legs out over the edge and dropped.

Maris emerged from the alley in time to see Gray and Gasquet in a gray caleche, caught up in the snarl of traffic heading toward the waterfront.

She followed easily on foot as they navigated the rutted thoroughfare running beside the docks. The street was crowded, and the coach moved slowly amongst carts and animals and people. Mules pulling wagons piled high with baled cotton, cloth, tobacco, and other dry goods crossed from the wharfs to warehouses on the other side of the cobbled street.

Maris kept to a path that ran in front of the various businesses lining the thoroughfare—sail-makers, fish houses, coopers, pubs, and inns, pushing her way through throngs of dockworkers, keeping her eyes trained on the back of Gray's head.

But at the end of the street, the crowds thinned. The coach picked up speed. Maris broke into a run, but could no longer keep up with the caleche, losing Gray and Gasquet as a huge fruit wagon crossed in front of her, blocking her view.

She stopped and bent over her knees, breathing hard.

What now?

Gray had taken care not to show her the vellum card with the location of the ship. She had absolutely no idea where it might be.

She caught the last of her breath and straightened, setting off in the direction the coach had gone. If the ship was docked anywhere along the waterfront, she would find it.

Unfortunately for her, the waterfront went on as far at the eye could see.

CHAPTER 7

The ship sat anchored off a quay partway up the Liane River. She was beautiful, despite her cracked mizzenmast and the pockmarked scars from grape-shot marring her hull.

Ethan thought of the men captured in the taking of that ship, and his gut clenched. For the families of those officers, he would find out who was responsible for those deaths.

"You like what you see?" Gasquet stood on the river bank beside him, speaking in halting Dutch. But there was no mistaking his tone. It indicated that he already knew the answer to that question.

"Of course. She is lovely. But what of her gut?"

"I think you will find her pristine, inside and out. The British, they are pigs. But they build fine ships, no?"

Ethan gave him a tight smile. "Yes, they do."

A tender arrived at the quay to take them out to the ship. Ethan and Gasquet climbed aboard, and within minutes the tender skimmed out to the *Majestic*. The rope ladder groaned beneath Ethan's weight as he climbed aboard.

The ship was deserted, save one guard in nondescript uniform who stood on the forecastle. He shot them an intimidating scowl as they boarded.

"Well, Monsieur Ganesvoort, what do you wish to see first?" the tailor asked.

"The gun deck, of course."

As he descended the gangway into the gun bay, Ethan's senses pricked. If this were a trap, he'd be hard-pressed to fight his way out of this hole with only the small dirk tucked in his boot.

He forced himself to move slowly, casually, to examine what he ought to, to look twice at everything, just as he would if he were actually investing the small fortune he'd bid at the auction. He opened the gun ports, examined the powder decks, inspected the futtocks, poked his head into the wardroom.

"How did you happen to get your hands on such a fine vessel?" he asked casually, as they passed through the galley. "Who brought her to you?"

Gasquet gave him a sharp look. "Why do you ask?"

Ethan shrugged. "I just thought to congratulate such an enterprising soul, should we ever happen to cross paths."

Gasquet smiled. "I doubt that will ever happen, monsieur. *Le capitane* rarely travels to Holland."

"But my wife and I plan to reside in France, you see."

The tailor shook his head. "I am afraid he rarely visits France, either."

"Pity. He would be welcome in my home anytime."

"Come." Gasquet motioned to the narrow door. "Shall we take a look at the bridge?"

An hour later, they were seated in the tender, headed for the bank of the Liane. Several men waited for them as they disembarked from the small vessel.

"Monsieur Ganesvoort," Gasquet said, "I would like you

to meet Adolphe. He will finalize our agreement, if you so permit."

Adolphe extended a hand. He was missing the tip of his middle finger on the right hand.

The guard from The Coxswain.

"Did you find the ship to your liking?" Adolphe asked.

"Very much so."

The guard nodded. "You wish to make good on your bid?"

"Of course."

Adolphe produced the bank draft Ethan had given to the accountant at the auction, along with a quill and a small pot of ink. "Necker has authorized this amount? He can cover it?"

"Yes. I will reimburse him when I return to Paris."

Ethan kneeled beside a piling and, using it as a makeshift desk, signed the bank draft. He waited until the ink had dried before handing it over to the guard. "Is that all?"

The guard studied the paper. "*Oui.* Thank you, Monsieur Ganesvoort. Good luck with your new ship."

The guard secreted the bank draft in a courier's pouch, adjusting the straps across his chest. He pulled Gasquet aside, and the two men spoke in low tones. Ethan was unable to hear what they said. When they finished speaking, the guard left the quay by coach.

Gasquet returned to Ethan's side. "I ask that you take care not to . . . shall we say *flaunt* your acquisition."

"Of course. The very picture of discretion. Are we finished?" Ethan asked.

"Not just yet. There is someone Adolphe wanted you to meet. He should arrive soon. In the meantime, would you like to visit your new ship again?"

Ethan declined. He'd hoped to follow the guard, but the prospect became less and less likely the longer he and

Gasquet waited by the river. He watched a chaise carry Adolphe—and the courier's pouch—out of sight. The pouch that contained what might be the only connection between King Louis and the auction.

Ethan made a great show of checking his watch. "My wife, she will be worried . . ."

"Ah!" Gasquet pointed to an approaching carriage. "There he is now."

Several men disembarked from the coach, including a tall, blond man with hooded blue eyes. His dress was foreign.

Dutch, Ethan thought.

He went immediately on the alert. Had he been set up?

The blond came to them at once, and stood before Ethan. "You are from Amsterdam?" he asked, in Dutch.

Ethan said nothing, but looked at Gasquet.

"Adolphe thought you might enjoy meeting a fellow countryman," Gasquet said. "You and he have much in common." His smile seemed genuine. But then again, so did a strumpet's.

"I am Hendrick Osterhoudt," the blond said. "A shipbuilder in Aalsmeer."

Ethan nodded.

"You are from Amsterdam?" Osterhoudt repeated.

Ethan resisted the urge to tug at his neck stock, which suddenly felt as if it were strangling him. His Dutch might be passable when he was speaking with French or Englishmen, but could it pass the scrutiny of a Hollander?

"*Ja*, Amsterdam."

"You know Caspar Ampte?" Osterhoudt asked.

Caspar Ampte's name was forged on one of the letters of recommendation Ethan had given Gasquet.

"Yes, through my uncle."

The blond nodded. "A good man. And how is his wife?"

"Very well."

Osterhoudt's gaze slid to Gasquet, and then back at Ethan.

"I must pay Ampte my respects when I return to the city. But you will save me much embarrassment if you remind me of his wife's name."

Ethan's hand flexed into a fist. He had, indeed, been set up.

He assessed the half-dozen men around him, choosing the one he thought the weakest. That was the man he would attack first, in the hopes that he might clear a path to escape.

He prepared himself for battle. "Ampte's wife? It is Betje."

Osterhoudt's eyes narrowed. "Ampte's wife, *Lotte*, died three years ago."

The men moved closer, like a pack of jackals surrounding fresh kill.

Ethan forced himself to remain impassive for a moment longer. Forced himself to act as if he didn't notice the growing hostility. "I am sorry, sir. But when did you last speak with him?"

The Dutchman gave Ethan a sly look. "Not more than six months ago."

Ethan smiled. "Ah. Then you did not hear! Ampte married his housekeeper, Betje, just three months ago."

Osterhoudt seemed confused. "He married again?"

"Yes. About the same time I did."

The jackals relaxed. Gasquet moved forward, to stand between Ethan and Osterhoudt. "Well, I am glad to have introduced two such influential men. I am surprised your paths have not crossed before this. But perhaps now that you have met . . . ?"

"Of course." Ethan nodded to Osterhoudt. "Until we meet again." Then he turned to Gasquet. "May we go now? I really would like to return to my wife."

"As would any eager new husband," Gasquet said with a laugh. "Are you afraid she will have disappeared?"

"She will be there," Ethan said, as much to convince himself as Gasquet. "She will be there."

Maris walked the waterfront for more than an hour, but found no ship that remotely resembled a British naval ship. Not that she'd truly expected to find it. Even the French would not so openly spit in the face of the most powerful naval force in the world.

The borrowed boots raised blisters on her heels as she made her way to the tailor shop where the auction was held. Perhaps she could find some sort of clue there as to where the ship was docked.

The door was again locked. Maris peered into the window. No movement within. No sign of Gasquet or the guards. She assumed the haberdasher was still with Gray.

She went around to the back of the building, to the door where she'd seen Samuel, but it was locked, too. She debated the merit of breaking into the shop. It would be a risk, and it would take time. Time she could ill afford. But on the other hand, she might find something that revealed the location of the ship.

She circled the building, searching for something to help her. She found it in the form of a broken brick in the gutter, and took it round back. When she was certain there was no one about, she pounded the brick on the doorknob, putting a nice dent in the brass surface.

Another few strikes loosened it. The next few knocked it off completely. She dropped the brick and pushed open the door.

No desk. No lectern. No rows of chairs.

The back room of the shop, which had been transformed into an auction house less than fours hours earlier, now contained bolts of fabric, racks of lace and trim, and boxes of buttons. The colored screen that had separated the rooms was gone, replaced by a plain gray curtain.

She wandered through the stock, searching for signs of the morning's activities. The floor squawked beneath her footsteps, heightening her sense of urgency.

She peeked out through the curtain to the front of the shop. All was quiet. A pedestal for alterations stood on one side of the room, while shelves of lace and linen neck stocks, silk stockings, and gloves filled the other.

A short counter—the perfect size, Maris realized, for Gasquet—stood near the front door. The glass-paned display window looked out onto the street.

Just before she stepped through the curtain, a shadow passed in front of the window outside. A man dressed in the garb of *Le Regiment des Gardes Suisse* moved into view in front of the shop.

The front door opened with a tinny jingle of bells. Maris ducked back behind the curtain, trapped. If she tried to leave through the back, the floor would make too much noise.

She pressed herself against the wall beside the curtained doorway, her hand moving to the knife at her waist.

Two voices. Two men. They spoke in rapid French, although one of them had an English accent. It soon became clear that they had no intention of coming into the back room, and Maris relaxed a bit. She leaned closer to the curtain, attempting to hear their conversation.

"Is it done?" said the one with the English accent.

"Yes. Here is the bank draft from the sale of the ship."

"Do you have the money from the other sales?"

"In gold, as promised. Here." The sound of coins clinking in a purse. "I've taken out the portion we agreed upon. Do you have something for me?"

"Yes."

Maris drew the curtain open by the tiniest sliver. She nearly gasped.

Samuel!

The man with the English accent was Samuel. And at the moment, he was handing a thick packet of papers to King Louis's guard.

Samuel went to Gasquet's counter and retrieved a locked box from beneath. He opened the box and counted out several gold coins from the cache the guard had given him, dropping them into the box.

Maris leaned back against the wall and swallowed the bile that had come up into her throat. What had he gotten himself into now? The only advantage to seeing Samuel standing there, in dealings with the king of France's private guard, was the fact that he wasn't at the ship with Gray.

But what if he had been, earlier? What if Gray had seen him? Or worse, what if Samuel had informed the people selling the ship that Gray wasn't who he claimed to be? Gray could be locked up somewhere right now.

Locked up, or dead.

She took a slow, deep breath, peeking through the curtain again in time to see the guard stow the packet of papers Samuel had given him into a courier pouch, which he strapped across his chest beneath his jacket.

"Please give the king my deepest regards," Samuel said.

"Will you return to Philadelphia?" the guard asked.

"Soon. Very soon." Samuel held open the door. "Godspeed, Adolphe."

With shaking fingers, Maris let the curtain fall back into place.

She needed to warn Samuel of the danger of lingering in Boulogne. Tell him to stop this madness.

But if she did, she would have to let the guard escape her grasp, along with the papers that might provide proof that King Louis was aiding the colonies—and proof that Samuel was entrenched in the whole damned mess.

"Take good care, Samuel," she whispered, as he left through the front door, locking it behind him.

She was gone.

Ethan pounded a fist against his thigh. He should have known better than to leave her alone.

His boots were missing, too. And upon closer inspection of his open trunk, it seemed as if a shirt and breeches and a jacket had disappeared as well.

Good god, she'd paraded through the inn dressed as man!

He would have her head on a pike for this, if Lord North didn't demand it first.

Ethan sat on the edge of the bed and rubbed his temples. Should he go look for her? Or had she already ruined their cover? There could be someone waiting outside to slit his throat that very moment.

He should pack up and get out of there. Let the great Raven pull her own tail feathers out of the fire. If she was as competent a spy as Lord North believed, she'd have no trouble doing it.

He went about the room collecting his things, and threw them into his trunk, slamming it shut. Then he sat on it, cursing under his breath. He couldn't leave an operative. Especially not a woman who lacked defenses. He wasn't heartless.

But he could be a bastard, which Maris Winter would discover when she returned.

If she returned.

The room was steeped in shadows when Ethan heard a rustling outside the door. He stalked over to it and flung it open with a bang, frightening the innkeeper's wife so badly she dropped the tray of food she carried.

"Oh! Oh, my!"

"Madame Derbec, I apologize. I did not mean to scare you," he said in broken French.

"Oh, dear. Oh, dear." She wrung her apron in her hands.

Ethan stepped out into the hallway and kneeled beside the mess, collecting the spilled food with the overturned plates and placing the whole jumble back on the tray.

"Oh, dear. Oh, dear," the innkeeper's wife repeated.

"Do not worry, madame, I will pay for this meal. It is my fault."

This assurance seemed to appease the plump proprietress. She picked up the tray. "Shall I bring another?"

"Yes, please. And will you bring the charwoman, as well? The fire in my room has died, and it is getting cold."

She nodded and bustled off down the hall, muttering to herself. Ethan looked past her, hoping the nosy woman wouldn't run into Maris.

When he went back into the room, it was dark. Ethan bumped about, searching for a candle to light from the lamp on the table outside his door. The creak of a window opening stayed his hand.

The intruder had returned. He could feel a presence, a subtle change in the air. He stood completely still, waiting. The room wasn't large. The man was bound to pass by him eventually.

Footsteps, light and measured, approached. He waited until he felt the air move against his face to strike. His punch landed in the soft spot between the intruder's ribs and pelvis.

"Un-uh."

The intruder dropped to the floor, but not before grabbing the lapel of Ethan's jacket and pulling him down as well.

They grappled on the carpet, rolling toward the bed. Ethan had the intruder pinned against the bedpost by the neck, could feel a pulse beneath his fingers, when something burned the top of his hand. Warm liquid ran down his arm.

Blood. *His* blood.

He'd been cut. The realization hit him just a fraction of a second before the pain.

Instinctually, he brought his injured hand close to his body, holding it against his side and rolling to protect it. The intruder kicked, landing a boot square on his arse.

A knock at the door brought the scuffle to a sudden halt.

"Monsieur Ganesvoort? Are you there?"

"Madame Derbec! Get your hus—"

A hand smacked over his mouth. "Gray? Gray! It's me."

The voice stunned him momentarily. He pushed the hand aside. "Raven?"

"Yes!" Her voice was breathy. Urgent.

"Monsieur Ganesvoort! Is something wrong?" The innkeeper's wife rattled the door handle.

Ethan sat up. "All is fine, madame. I will be there momentarily."

He and Maris struggled to their feet, bumping into each other in the dark.

"Get into the bed," he ordered. "Pull the covers up over your clothes."

He groped along the perimeter of the room, searching for the washstand. He wrapped several wash linens around his bleeding hand before opening the door to Madame Derbec.

She peered over his shoulder into the room. "Is everything well? I heard a bump."

"Yes, yes. My lantern blew out and it is very dark in here without a fire. I bumped into the washstand."

"Well, I have brought a new supper, and Imelda, as you

requested." The charwoman stood beside Madame Derbec, a bucket and a sling of wood in hand. "She will have a fire up in no time at all."

"Thank you." Reluctantly, he stepped aside. Madame Derbec and Imelda pushed past him into the room. The innkeeper's wife deposited her tray on the nearest table. In minutes, the fire burned bright and the lantern was lit, casting its light over the bed where the Raven lay.

Her hair was a cloud of white tangles, her face smudged with dirt. Beneath the bed, the corner of Ethan's tricorn hat poked out.

"Oh, dear, are you unwell?" Madame Derbec clucked, attempting to straighten the covers.

Maris held them tight beneath her chin. "A mild headache, I'm afraid. All this dampness. I am not accustomed to it."

"I suffer from it myself," Madame Derbec said. "Might I fetch some headache powder for you?"

"Oh, that is quite kind of you, but I think a bit of rest is all I need."

Madame Derbec's brow furrowed, as if she couldn't imagine why such a generous offer as hers would be refused. "Suit yourself." She turned to Ethan, and her eyes widened in shock. She pointed to the floor beside him. "Monsieur, you are bleeding!"

Ethan glanced down at his hand. Blood soaked the linens he'd wrapped around it, and dripped onto the floorboards. "I cut myself on the latch of my trunk."

Madame Derbec looked back and forth between them, her expression skeptical.

Ethan took her elbow and steered her toward the door. "Many thanks, madame. You are too kind. We will be generous in both praise and payment when we leave here tomorrow."

Her frown turned to a smile at the mention of compensation. "You are too kind, monsieur. We will be sorry to see you go. Come, Imelda. Let us leave this happy couple to their supper."

Maris threw the covers back and sprung from the bed. She took Gray's fingers in hers. "Let me see your hand."

He pulled away. "I will take care of it." He unwrapped the linens, exposing a shallow cut that ran across the back of his hand, from thumb to pinky.

"You are lucky it didn't go deeper," she said.

"*I* am lucky?" His face turned red. "What did you hope to accomplish by this?" He held up his hand.

"I didn't know I was cutting *you*. I thought you were an intruder."

"You thought *I* was an intruder? *You* climbed in through the window!"

"Into a dark, cold room. I had no reason to believe you were in here. And then I was attacked. Choked. What was I to do, allow you to kill me?"

He glared at her for a few moments before his expression softened just a bit. "No, I suppose not."

She went to him again, and looked at the cut on his hand. It was a nasty affair. The jagged edges would not heal cleanly.

She pulled him over to the washstand and poured water into the basin, submerging his hand. The water darkened.

"It should be sewn," she said.

He merely grunted.

"I can do it for you, if you wish."

He nodded.

She retrieved a needle and thread from her trunk, and heated the needle over a candle flame before threading it.

He allowed her ministrations for a while, flinching only slightly when she first put the needle through his flesh. He watched her work, his face reflecting an emotion she could not name. When she finished he pulled away, and wrapped a fresh cloth around his hand. "I suppose I shall have to ask Madame Derbec for some bandages."

"Here." She pulled the bottom of his linen shirt out of the breeches she wore, and tore off a strip.

He looked at her in disbelief. "That is my shirt."

"Yes, but it's ruined anyway." The part that wasn't tucked into the breeches was covered in dirt and blood.

She took his hand again, and wrapped the strip of linen around it several times, tying it in a knot at his palm. As her fingertips grazed his skin, she felt the oddest sensation, like warm honey filling her belly.

She leaned closer, breathing him in. The warm-honey feeling spread.

He met her gaze—captured it, really—with his. She stopped breathing.

"You look like a foppish pirate in those clothes," he said, his laughter breaking the spell.

She ignored the sudden emptiness as the warm honey disappeared. "It was the best I could do. I have a set of clothes especially for work like this, but did not bring them for fear someone would find them and suspect I am not the French lady I claim to be."

"Clever. But the question remains: Why did you disobey me and leave this room at all? I thought we agreed you would wait here for me."

She put a hand on her hip. "I agreed to no such thing. I merely told you I wouldn't *accompany* you to the docks, which I did not. I made no other promises."

"So, that is how it will be, then?" He shook his head. "I thought you were obedient. I thought you were somewhat intelligent. I thought you realized how important it was for you to remain in the role of dutiful wife."

" 'Tis a role I shall never feel comfortable in, I vow."

"'Tis a role you will never get to play, should you remain the disagreeable woman you are."

Though he spoke in an even tone, his words cut her to the core. Her throat squeezed, and to her horror she realized that she might actually cry.

What did it matter what Ethan Gray thought of her wifely potential? She'd been her own woman, always. She wanted no part of being a wife, and had never considered being agreeable for the sake of any man.

She reached into the breeches she wore, removing a packet of papers, for once not giving a damn about propriety. She threw them on the floor at Gray's feet.

"I might be cold and disagreeable, Mr. Gray, but I am also very good at my work. I believe you will find that these papers provide all the proof we need to confirm your and Lord North's suspicions. France is, indeed, entering the war."

Chapter 8

"Astounding." Ethan finished reading the last of the papers the Raven had given him.

As she'd predicted, the missives provided definitive proof that the French had furnished colonial privateers with both money and arms. Though none of the letters were signed, from the references to cities in the colonies and provoking language it was clear that they'd been written by American colonials.

They all promised shiploads of goods from America in return for funding to outfit merchant ships for war.

The colonial traitors were building their navy.

Ethan folded the papers and secreted them in the lining of the jacket he planned to wear back to England. He would not risk transporting them in his trunk. They would remain on his person the entire way home.

He looked at Maris, who lay on the bed beneath the covers, her back to him, her breathing even. He could not tell if she was awake or asleep.

She'd spoken perhaps a half-dozen words to him since

she'd handed the letters over to him. He tried to find out where—*how*—she'd come upon the papers, but she refused to tell him.

He felt a pang of regret for the way he'd treated her. He had to admit, if only to himself, that she was far more than a drawing-room gossip. He still questioned her abilities against those of a man's, but the Raven had proven herself a resourceful and useful operative of the committee.

More useful than he himself had been on this mission, if he could bring himself to admit it.

His gaze traced the lines of Maris's silhouette, lingering on the curve of her hip. Another thing he had to admit was that his attraction to her had grown as well. That thought made him restless. Unsettled.

He was drawn to her, but as long as their partnership wasn't permanent, he wouldn't worry. And he wasn't about to let it become permanent. As soon as they arrived in England, he'd bid her farewell, tell Lord North he found her lacking and did not wish to work with her, and it would all be done. The Raven could go back to her solitary missions, and he could return to his search for the weapons smuggler.

He removed a folded blanket from the foot of the bed and stretched out on the floor before the fire, his jacket folded beneath his head and one eye on the window.

He couldn't wait to leave France.

The coach that would take them to the docks in Calais arrived at the inn promptly at sunrise. They left The Flying Gull in the same soupy mist that had enveloped the seaside when they'd arrived in Boulogne.

A fitting end for a mission clouded by mistrust and disagreement, Ethan thought.

At least it wasn't raining.

Monsieur Derbec and the coachman loaded their trunks on the boot of the carriage while Madame Derbec waved a tearful goodbye, no doubt sorry to see Monsieur Ganesvoort and his deep purse go.

Ethan and Maris boarded the caleche. Ethan would have been happy to stew in his own thoughts during the ride to the dock, but their coachman had other ideas.

"I suppose you've heard about the murder?" His casual demeanor did not match the excitement in his voice.

"Not at all." Ethan's disinterested tone did nothing to stop the man from continuing his story.

The coachman whistled long and low through his teeth. "A member of *Le Regiment des Gardes Suisse*. The king's guard."

Ethan's head snapped up. "The Swiss guard?"

"Yes! Found with his throat slit on the side of the road, just outside of Boulogne. Imagine!"

Ethan tried to. Maris sat stiffly in the seat, hands folded in her lap, her face expressionless. Her gaze met his briefly before she turned away.

It wasn't possible that *she* killed him?

Was it?

"Why was he killed?" Ethan asked the driver.

"Who knows?" The man spit off the side of the vehicle. "This world is a mad place, is it not?"

Ethan studied Maris's profile. "Indeed, it is."

Ethan was mulling the guard's demise, and Maris Winter's possible role in it, when their ship sailed into English waters.

She'd barely acknowledged his presence the entire way back to England, and with the way he'd treated her throughout the mission, he could hardly blame her for that. He'd been unforgivably skeptical of her abilities, and much too suspicious of her motivations.

She stood on the foredeck, watching Dover grow ever larger on the horizon. She wore the same greenish hue as she had on the journey to France, confirming his suspicions that she suffered from seasickness. Once she'd even released the contents of her stomach over the rail, but she never complained. Never.

He realized that, aside from her wanting to do more, she never complained about anything—their accommodations, the food, the cold, the danger. She was so far removed from the women he typically spent time with, it was almost as if they were of a different species.

And if it really *had* been she who'd killed the Swiss guard? Well then, she'd risen in his regard a thousandfold.

It had been a long time since Ethan had killed a man. He'd killed only three times in his career—not much for a man who'd been a spy for more than a dozen years—but the horror of each deed had stayed with him long afterward. He wondered if Maris would face those same sleepless nights. Those daylight nightmares.

He wouldn't ask her. It was a matter of respect he would extend to any member of this wretched pursuit. Whatever had happened was between her and God, now.

He stood beside her at the rail, their hands perhaps an inch apart. He had a sudden, overwhelming urge to touch her fingers, but she moved them before he got the chance.

"How is your hand?" she asked.

He looked down at the fresh bandages she'd applied that morning. "Stings a bit, but I'll live."

"What a relief."

He couldn't miss the sarcasm in her voice. He smiled. "I'm sure you'll say a prayer for me at chapel on Sunday."

A hint of a smile played on her lips.

They were lovely lips, he noticed. Not quite so lush and pink as the peacock's, perhaps, but pretty just the same.

She caught her bottom lip between her teeth, and a tiny jolt of desire surged through him. He wanted to nibble it, too.

"Maris . . ."

She turned to him, her blue eyes questioning.

He reached out and touched her face, letting his fingertips linger on the silky skin beneath her chin. He leaned in, longing to taste her. Just before his lips touched hers, though, the boat hit a wave, knocking their heads together most painfully.

And knocking the momentary lapse in judgment from his mind.

"Ow!" She rubbed her forehead.

"I'm sorry." He didn't know if the apology was for the knock on the head, or for nearly breaking his cardinal rule.

She looked up at him, her dark blue eyes clear and questioning.

"What I wanted to say is that I am sorry for doubting your capabilities. You've proven an asset on this mission. For a woman, you are quite adept at this business."

Her eyes darkened, like storm clouds reflected in the blue of the sea. "My, what stunning praise. More than I should have expected from you, I suppose." The ever-present stony expression replaced the brief trace of a smile.

In the space of a heartbeat, Ethan wondered why he had ever wanted to kiss those perpetually pinched lips.

The bumpy ride back to Baliforte, Maris's home, did little to improve her disposition.

She'd almost kissed him. She'd actually almost *kissed* him. Again.

The first time, at Lady Jersey's ball, didn't count. She hadn't known who he was. But this time . . .

The pompous, arrogant jackass.

She might tell herself that it was a case of keeping her enemy close, but she knew that wasn't true. Keeping Ethan Gray close was like keeping a snake in her pocket. Far too dangerous.

Or a sweet cake, her mind whispered. *Far too tempting.*

Unfortunately, keeping the Wolf close was the only way to know where he was and what he was doing. It was the only way to protect Samuel.

Maris leaned her head on the back of the seat and sighed. Was there really any way to truly protect Samuel? He seemed hell-bent on getting himself hung. Perhaps it was time to let him go. Let events unfold as they may, without her interference.

But she couldn't. She simply couldn't. She was the only one who could keep him from the gallows. And she would do it, even if she had to die trying. She owed him that much.

Her carriage stopped on the drive in front of Baliforte. The front doors opened, and Riya, their housekeeper, emerged. Maris's mother followed close behind.

Olivia Winter drifted through the doors and emerged onto the portico, suspended there like a wisp of smoke searching for a fire.

Maris imagined a strong breeze might scatter her mother over the countryside. But that was just wishful thinking.

Maris plastered a smile on her face as the footman helped her from the carriage. "Hello, Mother. I'm home."

"I knew it." Lord North slammed his fist down on the desk. "The French are a treacherous lot of bastards."

"The campaigns in the colonies angered them."

Lord North dragged a hand over his face. "Well, once again they have chosen to champion a hopeless cause. The colonists will not win this war. Not even with Louis's help."

"I hope it is as you predict, sir," Ethan said. "But I fear they've had some success, despite our efforts to quell this madness."

"The naval ship they sold would have bolstered their coffers significantly had they been paid with a legitimate bank draft. There are bound to be more raids on English ships, now that they've realized the potential rewards."

Lord North removed two cigars from a small humidor on his desk. He went to the fireplace and fished a reed from a box on the mantel, holding it in the fire until the tip glowed red. He lit both cigars, handing one to Ethan.

The two men puffed in silence for a while. Then Lord North said, "I gather things went well with the Raven?"

"So it would seem."

"Have you given more thought to the possibility of bringing her into the weapons investigation?"

The taste of the cigar suddenly disagreed with him. Ethan threw it into the fireplace. "I cannot deny that the Raven's services proved useful on this mission. She has a certain practical ingenuity, along with a fortitude that surprised me. But it would take me much longer than a fortnight to develop the level of trust I would need to take her in on this mission, sir."

Lord North raised his eyebrows. "Perhaps a bit more time spent working together will help to promote such trust. I want the two of you to go to Kent. There are rumors that a Prussian operative may be about."

"What is he after?"

"It isn't clear." Lord North threw his cigar into the fire as well. "Her Grace, the Duchess of Canby, will attend a May Day wedding there, as well, and will require protection."

Ethan snorted. "My aunt hardly needs protection. The

woman hurls daggers with her eyes, and can deal a deadly blow with one sideways glance."

Lord North smiled. "I am well aware of Her Grace's arsenal. But this time, harsh words alone cannot shield her. I have reason to believe Sir Ambrose Hollister is after her."

"Hollister?" Ethan shot a look at Lord North. "He wouldn't dare show his face."

"In fact, he did. In the kitchens of Lockwell Hall. Scared a scullery maid near to death. She reported his presence to the duchess, but Hollister was gone before anyone could catch him."

Ethan felt a rush of elation. Hollister was alive. He'd begun to doubt the man would ever surface.

Hollister had tried to strangle the duchess seven months before, and there had been a mad hunt for him ever since. The bounty on his head was tremendous.

But Ethan had his own reasons for wanting Hollister, and they had nothing to do with money, or avenging his aunt.

Hollister had owned half of the shipping company Two Moons, through which the first two weapons shipments had been sent. He could reveal the name of the man Ethan sought.

"I cannot believe Hollister would turn up at Lockwell Hall, after what he's done. I wonder, what is the draw for him? He has to know the danger."

"Interesting, isn't it? Perhaps you can find that out from the duchess while you are in Kent together."

Ethan balked. There was no one better to protect his aunt than himself, he knew. And finding Hollister could prove crucial to the weapons investigation. But to be ensnared on yet another mission with Maris Winter . . .

"I will attend the wedding with my aunt. But I do not want the Raven to accompany us. I am more than capable of protecting the duchess myself, and handling any other business that might arise."

"I do not doubt your competence, Gray. But you cannot be with Her Grace at all times, can you? What if Hollister decides to strike while your aunt is napping? Or dressing? The Raven could attend her everywhere."

"Freddie could do that."

"Freddie can't defend the duchess's life. She's not a member of the committee, and she has no training."

Ethan tried to imagine Freddie fending off Hollister with one of those melodrama novels she carried everywhere. "I suppose you are right. My aunt would be in much better hands with the Raven."

Maris Winter would not hesitate to protect her charge, of that he had no doubt.

"Excellent. I shall write to the Raven immediately."

Ethan donned his jacket. "In the meantime, I am off to find a book."

Chapter 9

Ethan let himself in through the servants' entrance of Lord Shelbourne's town house just after noon.

Having spent many hours with the family under the guise of courting Lord Shelbourne's daughter, Mildred, he knew from experience that the entire household attended chapel between the hours of eleven-thirty and two, as mandated by Lady Shelbourne. It would be at least half an hour after that before the kitchen staff returned to begin preparations for the afternoon meal.

Lady Shelbourne and Mildred would take their daily constitutional in Hyde Park, arriving home by four. Lord Shelbourne himself would not be about, as he would be attending chapel and having the remainder of his meals in Newgate Prison, a result of his involvement in the weapons-smuggling scheme.

Ethan passed Lord Shelbourne's study on the first floor, his mind flitting briefly to his near-encounter there with the peacock.

He didn't waste his time revisiting the place. The papers

in Lord Shelbourne's desk and other personal effects had been seized by the Crown after his arrest, and no other letters had been found.

Instead, Ethan took the rear stairs and went directly to the library on the second floor. The door stood open, revealing volumes situated on shelves that climbed from floor to ceiling on all four walls. The left wall was nearly empty, which might have made Ethan nervous, except that he knew from previous investigation that the wall in question had contained only tomes relating to science and nature.

The right wall held military histories and biographies. The cases on the walls surrounding the door behind him, philosophy and religion. That left the wall directly in front of him.

Still, despite the relatively small size of the room, there had to be at least three hundred volumes on those shelves alone.

He read a few of the spines, hoping the books would be arranged in some sort of order, perhaps alphabetical or by author. No such luck. He would have to go volume by volume until he found what he was looking for.

Pulling a rolling ladder over from another wall, he began at the top left corner, going shelf by shelf, reading each title. Occasionally he would pull a volume from the shelf and leaf through the pages, hoping to get lucky and find something useful.

He searched more than half the shelves, his nerves drawing tighter with each passing minute. It was entirely possible the book wasn't even there.

But in his gut, he knew it had to be.

He checked his pocket watch. Ten minutes to two. He still had a good forty minutes before anyone returned, and even then, those who came home early would almost surely confine their activity to the kitchens.

He searched a shelf of fiction titles more thoroughly. It was the type of reading material Shelbourne was most familiar with, and it made sense that he and the mystery man might use other works of fiction as ciphering devices. From the shelves he pulled works by Pope, Swift, Gay, Johnson, Shakespeare.

And . . . Fielding.

Snagging the spine of *Amelia* with his thumb, Ethan slid the book from its space. A small square of paper fell to the floor, landing faceup on the carpet. Ethan's heart kicked against his ribs. The handwriting matched that on the letter he'd stolen from Shelbourne's desk, and the contents revealed more of the same type of code he'd discovered in the letter.

Numbers revealing pages and paragraphs that would have told Shelbourne where and when arms would arrive at the quays, or where payments should be dropped. But this note contained one thing the other did not. A signature.

Not a full name, but a single letter.

W.

W. Who could it be? His mind ran through the list of names connected to the case that he'd uncovered so far, from gun makers to dock workers to the other two gentlemen indicted in the scandal—Lord Chadwick and Sir Ambrose Hollister. No obvious connection to a W.

The initial had to represent the gentleman Ethan had been searching for all these months. The one about whom he could find no trace.

The one the peacock was determined to keep hidden.

Ethan slipped the copy of *Amelia* back into the space left by its absence.

He checked his watch. Ten minutes after two. He'd have plenty of time to get out of the house—

"Ethan?"

His name, spoken hardly above a whisper, thundered in the silence. He turned to find himself face to face with Mildred Shelbourne.

She seemed as stunned as he, and for a long moment neither one of them spoke.

Lady Mildred's brown eyes were dull and rimmed with red, adding nothing to her equine appearance. She looked like a child's rag doll that had been forgotten, left in a corner somewhere to gather dust. "What are you doing here? How did you get in?" Her tone was harsh. Accusatory.

He was not surprised. She had ample reason to hate him.

"I wanted to see you."

"Really?" Her expression turned hard. "I can't imagine why. You disappeared quickly enough the night of Father's arrest. I waited for you to come to me, but you never did. I think it quite natural of me to assume our courtship was over, after nearly half a year without one word to each other."

"I am sorry, Mildred. Abandoning you that way was unforgivable. That's why I am here. To apologize—"

"Save your breath. It doesn't matter. You were not the only one who stopped coming 'round after that night. All of my . . . my friends, did. And mother's, too." She burst into tears.

He reached for her, but she held out a hand to stop him.

"I've been so lonely since Father's unfortunate circumstance." She laughed, flat and mirthless. "You see, that's what mother has urged us all to call it. His 'unfortunate circumstance.' "

Ethan nodded sympathetically, but Mildred hardly noticed.

"An unfortunate circumstance," she repeated. "As if being jailed for treason could be likened to a broken carriage wheel, or a nasty cough. He's in jail for treason, for pity's sake!"

Ethan said nothing. Indeed, what could he say? It was he himself who produced the evidence that sent Mildred's father to prison.

Shelbourne would have hanged, too, but Ethan's word kept him from the gallows. It was the least he could do. He'd used the man's daughter abominably to get that evidence.

Mildred knew none of this, of course. And if she harbored any resentment toward Ethan for leaving her, it seemed suddenly forgotten.

"Is that for me?" She pointed to the note in his hand.

Ethan hesitated, then slipped the note into his pocket. "It was. I meant to hide it beneath your pillow. But I realize now that to apologize by note would only add to the injury I've done you. I am glad we found each other, so I might issue my regrets in person."

"Oh, Ethan!" She closed the distance between them at a gallop, throwing her arms around his neck, kissing him full on the lips. He allowed it for a moment, out of habit. But when he drew away from her, her tearful smile crumbled.

Her eyes grew dull again, and she fidgeted with the lace on her bodice. "I suppose I cannot blame you for ending our courtship," she said, her lip trembling slightly. "I am certain your family forbade you to see me."

Ethan grasped at the straw she unwittingly offered. "Indeed, they were most unhappy. Father threatened to cut me out of the business should I continue on with you."

She nodded.

"But I had to see you," Ethan continued. "I had to see how you've been managing since the . . . ah . . . 'unfortunate circumstance.' "

Lady Mildred caught a tear with the back of her hand. "Mother and I have been getting by." She looked sadly at the empty bookshelves. "We're selling Father's books. I am sure you've heard."

He hadn't. But he wasn't surprised. Without Lord Shelbourne, Mildred and her mother would almost certainly fall into financial ruin. A twinge of guilt plucked his conscience. It was a pity, but what was he to do? She'd simply been caught in the middle.

Lady Mildred's eyes suddenly brightened. "If I recall correctly, you are a man of books yourself."

"I am."

"Perhaps you might care to purchase some of Father's?"

"Indeed I would. This is a fine collection."

"Father so enjoyed it." Her lip trembled.

A rush of unexpected sincerity washed over him. He took her hand and kissed it. "Dear lady, should you ever be in need of my assistance, please do not hesitate to call on me. And again, I am sorry for the way I behaved."

She smiled a genuine smile that revealed a rather large set of teeth. "Thank you, Ethan. Most sincerely."

She took his arm. "Come, now. You'd best be gone before Mother returns from church. If she finds you here, she might get the wrong impression."

As she led him downstairs, Ethan took note of the empty spaces and bare floors once occupied by fine furniture and carpets. He wondered how long the women would be able to live on the profits gleaned from the sale of family heirlooms.

He made a mental note to have a check drawn up on the morrow, for thrice what Shelbourne's book collection was worth.

Maris tossed the letter from Lord North into the fireplace, and watched until it wasted completely to ash.

She wondered how she would survive another assignment with Ethan Gray. The last one nearly ruined her nerves. However, she took her position as an operative for the Anti-British Activity Committee seriously. She would not deny a request from Lord North.

She headed downstairs in search of her mother. She would have to tell Olivia she was leaving again—a prospect she did not relish. The news would not be received well, of that she was certain.

As she wandered through her home in search of her mother, Maris tried to ignore the shabby draperies, tarnished silver, and fraying carpets. There simply wasn't enough in the coffers to replace it all. And anyway, it took an army of servants to care for such things, and they were lucky to have a mere regiment remaining.

Maris's father had left them much too soon. He'd assumed, as they all did, that he would live forever. Never was there a more strapping example of manhood than Gavin Winter the younger. He worked hard, rode hard, gambled hard, and exercised his great, booming laugh often.

He grew his father's import company into a formidable concern, building into an empire the small business Old Gavin had started. He'd spent most of the profits on horses and the grand home in which they all lived.

But fate had not taken kindly to her father's immortal assumptions. His death had come as a shock to them all. Maris, however, was the only one of them who had known her father was a spy. Her mother and grandfather were simply told he'd been attacked by a thief in Covent Gardens.

Even more shocking than her father's death were the conditions of his will.

Now, thanks to her father's shortsightedness and her mother's stubborn pride, Maris had to find creative ways to keep food on the table and clothes on their backs. It was left up to her, because, truly, who else was there?

Her grandfather, who hardly knew his own name? Her mother, who couldn't see past her own pride to meet the conditions of the will, even to keep the roof from leaking and the lot of them from starving?

No, there was no one.

It had been Maris's idea to take on boarders at the manor house beside the pond, where her parents had lived when they first married. In a stroke of luck for England, the boarders turned out to be well-connected French expatriates. When she discovered the type of information they could give, she realized she could be of help to the very same organization her father worked for. She contacted Lord North, and the Raven was born.

Over the past several years, her boarders, Monsieurs Belange and Toreau, had unwittingly supplied her with a slew of intelligence via conversations and letters they received from relatives in England and France. And most important, from Versailles, where Belange had a cousin who was a minister in King Louis's cabinet.

Maris discovered a letter from him in Belange's desk one day while the gentlemen were off picnicking, which put her onto the discovery of the auction of the British naval ship.

But the rent collected from the boarders never went as far as she hoped. She'd already run through her entire inheritance trying to keep the place together. Working for the committee paid well, but not well enough. At the end of the month the books did not balance, the household coffers were all but empty and, invariably, she had to beg the few servants who still remained with them to stay on for a fraction of their salaries. If things didn't change soon, they'd all be out in the cold by the time winter arrived.

Maris finally located her mother in the conservatory. Olivia sat at an aged harp, plucking the strings of the graceful instrument with assuredness and skill, her expression serene. It was the only time any of these terms might apply to her.

Maris settled in beside her grandfather, Gavin the elder, who watched from a perch on the window seat. She patted his hand.

He smiled at her, and she wondered if he even realized who she was. He'd been losing his faculties for years now, and was nearly completely deaf as well. But Maris imagined he could still hear the music somewhere inside his head. Or perhaps in his heart.

Maris clapped when her mother finished. Olivia beamed, but her smile faded the moment she rose from the worn velvet stool.

Maris met her halfway across the floor and took her hand. "I have some news."

Her mother's expression grew apprehensive.

"I must leave for Kent tomorrow."

"No!"

"It is only for a little while. A week, perhaps."

"But you've just returned!"

"Yes, I know. But a dear old friend needs me. I cannot deny her."

"So you will deny me, and your grandfather? What will we do without you again?" Her mother's wheedling tone put Maris on edge.

"You will manage, Mother, as you always do. As I said, I will not be long. Besides, you have Monsieurs Belange and Toreau. They always offer a distraction, do they not?"

Olivia wrenched her hands from Maris's grasp. "Go on then. Do what you will. I could not care less." She went to Gavin and urged him to his feet. "Come, sir," she said, although she knew he could not hear her.

They left the conservatory arm in arm, Maris's grandfather looking over his shoulder at her, his eyes full of anxious confusion.

Maris sat at the stool beside the harp and plucked a string. A rich, sad note resonated through the empty room. She stopped the vibration with her fingertips.

It was time to go pack her trunk for the trip to Kent.

"Your Grace, you are ethereal, as always."

Ethan's aunt, Charity Markley, Duchess of Canby, was dressed in crisp midnight blue traveling attire that flattered her regal, still-slender frame. Her coif was simple, her hat elaborate, and her expression impatient. A small, white dog trembled beneath her arm.

"Dear boy, let us agree to put all drivel aside for the duration of this trip, shall we?"

The duchess was known for her impeccable manners and gracious conversation among the *ton*, but had never minced words as far as her nephew was concerned. She knew him for the rakehell he was, just as he knew her for the bitch she could be in private.

Ethan held a grudging respect for the woman, who had managed to dupe the entirety of English society, and indeed all of England itself, with her saintly act. She'd gotten the better of Ethan on several occasions as well, a feat very few people had been able to achieve.

Ethan was known for his charm and allure almost as surely as she, and the two understood each other in an often unbearably familiar way. As much as they might hate to admit it, they were kindred spirits.

Ethan knew his aunt held the same grudging respect for him, too. And while spending the week with her in Kent would not prove easy, it would certainly be entertaining.

"Where is Freddie?" the duchess asked.

"She'll meet us in Kent. Mother and Father will be there, as well."

"Wonderful." Her voice was flat, and Ethan knew she

did not relish the thought of seeing her brother. The two had never got on well.

The duchess held her little dog up to kiss its nose before handing it to a servant. "Take good care of her, Mary. Give her anything she wants."

"Yes, Your Grace."

Ethan was hard-pressed to tell who seemed more relieved to see her go, the maid or the dog.

"As long as we've agreed to put the drivel aside," Ethan said as he escorted her from the portico of Lockwell Hall to their waiting carriage, "can you tell me why Sir Ambrose is so desperate to speak with you that he would risk capture and arrest by coming around here?"

"Why do you assume he is desperate?"

"Come now. I thought we agreed to be straight with one another."

"Did we?"

"All of England has been hunting him since the night of your ball last October, when he attempted to strangle you. You do remember when he tried to strangle you?"

Her expression grew sour. "Of course I remember."

"The reward offered for Hollister's pelt, coupled with the fact that he did harm to one of England's beloved pillars of style and decency, makes it risky for him to be about. Do you know what he wants?"

The duchess shrugged. "I cannot pretend to know what goes on in the mind of that lunatic."

Ethan gave an exaggerated sigh. "My dear Aunt Charity. Why do you insist on making everything so difficult?"

"And why do you insist on making something of nothing?"

Ethan handed her into the coach, and climbed in beside her. "I am worried for you," he said seriously. "If you know what Sir Ambrose is after, I wish you would tell me. I want to help you."

For a moment, she looked as if she might say something. But then the carriage lurched into motion, and the moment was lost.

Having agreed to put all drivel aside, left them precious little to say to one another. Thus, they spent the majority of the ride to Baliforte in silence. A silence that gave Ethan time to think about the woman they were on their way to fetch.

He wondered how Maris would fare with his aunt, and decided she would do nicely indeed. Her cool demeanor was a quality his aunt admired. The two would positively freeze each other solid.

Maris watched anxiously from a third-floor window for the duchess's caravan to arrive at Baliforte. It would soon be dark, and they'd been due early that afternoon. Was it possible they'd been attacked by a marauder—or Hollister?

Gray was a skilled operative, well trained to defend himself and others. But there were miles of tree-lined road where Hollister would have cover, and the element of surprise should he attack. She wondered if perhaps she should ride out to see if she could locate them.

As she was about to leave her post by the window, a coach-and-four turned off the road and onto the drive. It bore the Duchess of Canby's crest on the door.

She flew down the stairs. "Riya! Hurry!"

The housekeeper rushed into the hall, her step surprisingly light for a woman of her considerable size. Gold bangles jingled like bells on her wrists and shoes. The gold threads woven into the fabric of her sari shone against coffee-colored skin.

"It looks as if we will have guests for the night," Maris said. "Will you please prepare two rooms upstairs? I am sure there will be servants to bed. And warn Mother, as well."

"She will not appreciate this news," Riya warned, in a tone that sounded more like a song than an admonition.

"It cannot be helped. I am sure the Duchess of Canby won't wish to travel at night."

"The Duchess of Canby?" Riya's face registered disbelief. "Why would a lady of such importance wish to come here?"

"She is the aunt of a friend." Maris shooed Riya from the hall, not bothering to hide her impatience. "Go on."

Riya jangled away just as Maris heard the coach-and-four pull up in front of the house. Too late, she realized that with Riya gone, she would now have to open the doors to the duchess herself.

She stepped out onto the portico, leaving the doors open behind her. Her stomach danced as she watched Gray alight from the carriage. His auburn hair, tied back with a simple black ribbon, ruffled in the chilly evening breeze, brushing his collar and the strong curve of his jaw.

He extended a hand to an arresting woman dressed in dark blue wool piped with black velvet. The black calash bonnet she wore sported a single bright blue feather. Even without having seen her likeness drawn up in the papers, Maris would have known the woman anywhere. She was the very picture of a duchess, her clothing stylish and her manner reserved.

"Your Grace, welcome." Maris curtsied deep on the edge of the drive. "I am Maris Winter."

The duchess nodded, and turned to her nephew. "What a perfectly lovely girl, Ethan. Clear skin. Straight back. Are you certain you've no designs on her?"

"None whatsoever." His words were light, but his voice held an edge of annoyance. It was clear he did not even care to joke about such a notion.

Though she couldn't explain why, Maris felt a twinge of disappointment at his words.

"I hope you met with no ill fortune," she said to the duchess. "It is late to be on the roads."

Gray approached Maris, and bowed before her. "I do apologize, Miss Winter. We were waylaid by a broken wheel."

"Then I'm sorry for your trouble, but relieved it was nothing more serious." Maris looked over his shoulder. "Where is the rest of your party?"

"We sent them off from Lockwell Hall well ahead of us, so they could prepare for Aunt Charity's arrival in Kent."

"My lady's maid included, I'm afraid," said the duchess. "Whatever shall I do without her?"

"Fear not, Your Grace. We shall find someone to take care of you. Do come inside. I've taken the liberty of assuming you would stay the night."

The duchess seemed relieved. "Thank you, dear girl. 'Tis a most generous and welcome offer. My brain has been scrambled by these horrid spring roads."

The duchess and Gray followed Maris inside.

Presented by candlelight, the house did not appear nearly so shabby as it did by day, for which Maris was infinitely relieved. Perhaps they all would leave early enough on the morrow that her guests would never get a decent glimpse of the threadbare carpets and well-used furniture.

"I believe our housekeeper has set a light meal in the drawing room. Shall we go there first, or would you care to wash up?"

"No, thank you," the duchess said. "I just wish to sit for a while on a seat that isn't bouncing or rocking."

"Can you arrange that, Miss Winter?" Ethan asked. "Or do all of your seats bounce and rock?"

"They are quite stable, I assure you." Maris led them to the more intimate of two drawing rooms. Her mother and grandfather were already there, seated at the tea set. They stood when the guests walked into the room.

"Your Grace," said Maris. "May I present my mother, Mrs. Olivia Winter."

Olivia dipped into a shallow curtsy, not bothering to disguise her annoyance at having her evening interfered upon.

"And this is my grandfather, Baron Winter."

Gavin stared dully at the string of pearls about the duchess's neck, his mind clearly absent.

Maris bit the inside of her cheek. It wasn't exactly the reception she'd hoped for, but at least her mother had been civil. Experience told her she couldn't ask for much more than that.

The duchess and Gray sat beside each other on one of the settees, while Maris and her mother occupied the other. Her grandfather shuffled over to his favorite window seat and stared out at the night.

"Shall I pour out?" Maris asked, when it became apparent her mother was not going to do so. She silently thanked Riya for keeping the silver polished.

"Please, do," the duchess said.

Gray gave Maris a look of mild curiosity, which she chose to ignore, as she doled out teacups, sugar, cream and Riya's airy little biscuits flavored with anise.

"How did you and my nephew become acquainted, Miss Winter?" the duchess asked.

Maris was in the middle of handing her mother a cup of tea, and had to put all of her effort into keeping her hand from shaking. "We met some time ago, at the country house of a mutual acquaintance."

"And who might that be? Do I know him?"

Amusement sparked in Gray's eyes. Maris opened her mouth to speak, but Gray interjected, "It's a woman, actually. And for reasons that I hesitate to discuss in mixed company, I'd rather not mention her name."

"Ah," said the duchess, a knowing glint in her eye. "Any

female 'acquaintance' of yours would undoubtedly wish to remain anonymous."

"Quite."

Maris chided herself for not thinking of a plausible story beforehand as to how she and Gray met. They would have to work on that the next time they were alone.

Alone.

The thought made her light-headed.

The last time they were alone, on the ship, she had wanted to kiss him. Very badly. She'd imagined he was of the same mind, but apparently that had been wishful thinking. Gray didn't seem the sort to hold himself back. If he'd wanted to kiss her, surely he would have.

Somehow they all managed polite conversation between nibbles and sips, and when they'd finished, Riya made her usual musical entrance.

The duchess scrutinized Maris's housekeeper as Riya cleared the tea service. Riya's bangles caught the firelight and candle glow, dappling the room with spots of gold, and when she had gone, the duchess leaned in. "What an interesting housekeeper. Is she of India?"

Maris cleared her throat. "My father was with the East India Company briefly. Riya and her sister, Ajala, served him there. When he left India, he brought them back to England to work here. Riya has been our housekeeper ever since."

"And what does Ajala do?" Gray asked.

Olivia's teacup clattered into its saucer. "If you'll excuse me."

Without waiting for a reply, she left the room.

Chapter 10

"Ajala is no longer with us," Maris said. "But Riya is an excellent housekeeper."

"How charming," the duchess said in a tone that made it clear she thought it wasn't.

Maris was accustomed to such reaction. Most English men and women viewed the people of India with suspicion and mistrust. However, in the short time Ajala had been with them she'd been more like a mother to Maris than Olivia ever had. Maris missed her terribly.

Unfortunately, Riya emitted none of the warmth Ajala had. She was an efficient servant, but one who did not approve of close relationships between a servant and master, which was the reason she was still here while Ajala was not.

"Would you care for a distraction, Your Grace?" Maris said. "I could play something for you on the harp."

"A lovely offer, my dear. However, the fatigue of travel has left me quite depleted. I am afraid I would make for a poor audience."

"Of course. I will escort you to your quarters directly."

"I would like to take some air, myself," Gray said, standing. "Will you point the way to the garden?"

"Come," Olivia said loudly from the doorway, startling everyone. "Gavin and I will take you."

Maris wanted to reach out and grab her mother's hand, to keep her and Grandfather from going anywhere near Gray, but decorum would not allow it. She could only send up a prayer that Olivia would not reveal anything of their situation.

"It has been a long time, Mr. Gray."

Ethan strolled beside Olivia Winter in the small garden off the drawing room. Baron Winter wandered behind them, his feet scuffing the pebbles from the walkway.

It had been a pleasant afternoon, but night had given way to cooler air. Maris's mother gathered her shawl more tightly about her shoulders. "I remember the last time you called. It was not a very pleasant day."

"No, it was not." Ethan wondered at her choice of words. Had her husband's death been merely that? A bit of unpleasantness? Even Maris's cool demeanor seemed warm compared to this woman. "I hope you've fared well since your husband's demise."

"Oh, I am not sad over my husband's death," she said. "Only for the life I've lost because of it."

They walked in silence, Ethan unsure of how to respond.

Olivia stopped suddenly. "Do you have designs on my daughter, Mr. Gray?"

Once again, he was speechless.

"I only ask because I recall the way she looked at you when she was a child. Nay, not so much a child as a young woman. She had stars in her eyes. That kind of admiration is a powerful aphrodisiac, no?"

Ethan cleared his throat. "As you've said, she was very young. Her admiration has long since faded."

No, not just faded. Disappeared.

"Once I had hoped she might meet a fine gentleman. But I fear I cannot do without her. *We* cannot do without her. Have mercy on us, sir." She clasped his hands, her fingernails digging into his flesh. Her eyes were wide, the whites gleaming wild in the moonlight. "I beg you, do not take my daughter from me."

"Please, do not lose another moment to concern, Mrs. Winter. I have no designs on your daughter, I assure you. She is to be my aunt's companion for the week, and nothing more."

"Do you swear?"

"I do."

Even as he said the words, his mind unwittingly flashed back to Maris, asleep on the couch in front of the fire, the coverlet draped seductively over her curves.

Olivia released his hands. He rubbed them on his breeches and stuffed them into his pockets.

"Well, then," she said in a flat voice. "Shall we return to the house?" Suddenly, she'd regressed to the sober creature she'd been during supper. "Come, Gavin," she called back to the old man. "Let us get you to bed."

Old Gavin had been staring up at the stars. He looked at her, as if dazed, and nodded.

Ethan followed them into the house, wondering what life had been like for Maris since her father had died, with a mother who cared nothing about her husband's death, and who would beg a stranger to leave her daughter to spinsterhood.

He simply couldn't imagine.

* * *

"Wait just outside this door until I return," Maris said to Riya. The housekeeper frowned, but did not ask the question she so clearly wanted to ask: Why?

Maris did not volunteer anything more, either. She could not tell Riya the duchess might be in danger, and that she had been enlisted to watch over her. Riya knew nothing of Maris's role as a spy for the committee, nor would she. Ever.

Just as her father had hidden it from everyone but Maris, Maris had kept it a secret, as well. From everyone.

Well, from everyone except Samuel.

It hadn't been difficult to keep it from her mother and grandfather. They both lived in a world far away from this one, most of the time. Their only concern was whether or not Maris would be there to care for them, and to handle all the annoyances of daily life.

But Riya was different. Riya was smart. Observant. Maris had to be especially careful around her. Having to hide things from Riya had made Maris an expert in concealing her thoughts and emotions.

She wasn't completely comfortable leaving Riya alone with the duchess, but it couldn't be helped. She had to get her mother away from Gray before she said something about Samuel.

She donned a cape to check the gardens.

The pathways were lit by a bright moon, which hung like yellowed lace in the sky. The shrubs and bushes, so familiar and comforting during the day, took on a sinister appearance in the night. Many were overgrown, and their branches and vines crept out onto the paths like tentacles, awaiting the opportunity to wrap about her ankles.

Gray and her mother were not, to her dismay, within the garden walls. But the gate on the far side, the one overgrown with ivy, hung open. The silhouette of the barn lay beyond it, in stark relief against the moon. The soft glow of a lantern lit the building from within.

The pungent odor of manure and hay drifted out through the door. Maris hesitated. She usually didn't linger over-long in the stables. It reminded her too much of her father. He loved to spend time there, chatting with the hands and caring for his beloved Arabian, Arturo.

She was surprised to find Gray alone inside.

"Mr. Gray?"

He seemed surprised to see her there. "Maris. You should be abed. We'll leave just after dawn tomorrow."

"Where are my mother and grandfather?"

"I accompanied them back to the house a while ago."

"Riya is keeping watch over your aunt until I return. I wanted to be sure you were settled before I retire."

"I'm sorry I left you to watch over my aunt. I thought I would take a short walk. I'm afraid that on occasion, I suffer from sleeplessness."

"As do I."

"I suppose it is a curse of the trade, no?"

"Perhaps it is." She allowed herself to feel a kinship with him for just a moment. She motioned him to one of the horse stalls. "Come, let me show you something."

Her father's stallion, Arturo, still resided there, growing fat from lack of exercise. He spent his days sunning and eating in the fields, as there was no one in the house who could handle him. But her grandfather refused to allow her mother to sell him. The horse seemed to be the old man's only link with reality.

Indeed, to look upon the horse was a bit like going back in time. She imagined her father leaning against Arturo's gate, his knee boots polished to a gleaming black. She heard his laughter echoing off the walls.

Gray went and stood in the very same spot. He spoke to the horse in a low voice, and Arturo answered with an appreciative snort. For a moment, Maris could not speak. Gray reminded her so much of her father standing there, it was like seeing a ghost.

The day she'd learned of her father's death was the darkest day of her life. Gray had come to them—to her, because he knew she'd been privy to her father's profession—and told her of Gavin Winter's demise.

Gray had been covered in cuts and bruises, and even before Maris had received Lord North's letter about how he had had stormed in alone and killed the Spaniards who'd been torturing her father, she'd known.

She had known what Gray had tried to do for her father. And she'd lost a piece of heart to this man before her.

For years afterward, he was the stuff of her dreams. She'd imagined dancing with him. Marrying him. Giving him children. Her eyes filled with tears. How foolish she had been. And how very sad it was to have to give up one's girlish dreams for cruel reality.

Gray came to her and hooked a finger under her chin, tilting her head up so he could look into her eyes.

"Are you . . . are you *crying*?"

"Of course not. I don't cry. I have a reaction to hay, is all. It makes my eyes water."

"I see." He did not withdraw, did not step away.

They stood toe to toe, the heat from their bodies warming the chill air between them.

"The stallion is wonderful. He must have been truly majestic in his day."

"Yes. He was my father's greatest passion."

"I wonder," Gray said, twirling a lock of her hair around his finger. "What is *your* greatest passion, Maris?"

His question caught her off guard. "I . . ." She took a step back, but he matched it with a step forward. "I have no passions, Mr. Gray."

"So you would have people believe. But I don't."

"Don't what?" This, almost whispered.

"I don't believe you have no passion." His hand slid behind her neck, sending a shock of warmth down her spine. His fingers tangled in her hair, and he pulled her close, covering her mouth with his. His lips were warm and sweet, moving over hers in a soft caress. Slowly, at first, as if seeking her approval.

She was too shocked to react. When she showed no resistance, he deepened the kiss, probing gently with his tongue, running the tip of it over her lips, seeking entry. She gasped, opening to him.

He'd chewed the mint leaves Riya had used as a garnish, causing his tongue to taste cool and spicy against her own. She leaned against him and he caught her around the waist, walking her backward until the backs of her thighs hit a barrel. Her arms snaked around his neck, pulling him as close as their bodies would allow. She made a small noise in her throat, igniting his ardor. His kiss exploded with heat.

Maris fought for breath. She'd had lovers, of course—inescapable in her profession—but she'd taken very little enjoyment from her contact with them. She'd never felt this desirable. This provocative.

Gray's fingers played in her hair as he murmured her name against her neck. Maris's fingers found the buttons of his shirt, working them open until she revealed the coarse, curling hair of his chest.

He took her hand to his mouth, caressing the palm with his tongue. A flush spread through her body, turning her to liquid fire and coming to rest between her thighs. She wrapped a leg around his, and felt the hard length of his shaft press against her, seeking her heat.

"I knew," he murmured against her breasts.

"What did you know?"

"I knew you could not be as cold as you pretend to be."

His words dragged her back to reality. She pulled away. "You think me cold?"

"I did. Until tonight."

"But . . . why?"

He loosened his hold on her. "Your feigned disinterest. Your unyielding visage. But it is the reputation of the Raven, is it not? To be cold and calculating."

She removed herself from his grasp. "As much as it is your reputation for whoring for information in the beds of unsuspecting wives, I suppose."

He stepped back, his face carefully neutral as he buttoned his shirt. "I'd venture that was not your first kiss, either, Maris. You'd do well not to throw stones."

She pushed past him and went to Arturo's stall, stroking the animal's nose. He gave her a wise look.

"We should return to the house," she said, her forehead pressed to the horse's. "Morning will come quickly."

"Right." All emotion had left his voice.

And he thought *her* cold?

It was stupid of her to let her long-ago dreams cloud her judgment. She felt an attraction to Gray that time had not diminished. But taking him to bed to slake her childish fantasies would only serve to discredit her skills as a spy, and distract her from her true purpose. She must stay focused on what was important.

She followed Gray back to the house, leaving a good distance between them, dreading the next few days.

Sleep refused to come, and it wasn't because he was attempting to find it on the bench outside his aunt's room.

As benches went, it was tortuously uncomfortable. Hard, wooden, and much too short to contain the length of him.

But it wasn't the bench. It was the kiss.

He hadn't been able to help himself. For a moment, he'd

seen that light in Maris's eyes—the one that had shone so long ago, when she'd looked at him as if he were noble. Heroic.

He'd wanted to douse that light tonight. Convince her he wasn't some sort of knight in shining armor.

Or, a tiny voice whispered in his mind, *did you want to believe you were, just for a moment?*

Maris awoke well before sunrise. Her sleep had been restless, plagued with dreams of Ethan Gray's kisses. She performed a quick toilette before donning her traveling clothes and heading off to the duchess's quarters.

She tiptoed past Gray, who lay asleep on a bench outside his aunt's door, his long legs dangling over the arm rest.

Riya had slept in the room beside the duchess's, in case she was needed in the night.

"Riya, wake up."

The housekeeper yawned and stretched in the small bed.

"Hurry," Maris whispered. "You must help Her Grace with her toilette. Help her dress."

In the hall, Maris poked Gray's shoulder several times before hurrying away, her dreams of him still too close to the surface to face him in the dark.

The travelers took a light breakfast before Maris bid Riya goodbye, handing her a purse containing the last of the monthly budget. She trusted Riya far more than her mother in matters of money.

It was just before dawn when they set off for Kent in the duchess's coach.

The day turned out to be lovely. The horses made good time on the road between Baliforte and the duchess's cousin's home in Rochester. Though Maris hardly looked at Gray, nor he at her, she found her conversation with the duchess stimulating and time passed quickly.

They arrived in Rochester at the home of Lord Tolliver well before dark. Much fanfare was made of the Duchess of Canby's arrival, with servants and guests gathered on the great circular drive of the manor to welcome her. Though obviously fatigued, the duchess stopped to greet a great many of them, which Maris found admirable, but not exactly safe should Hollister be lurking about.

She made a point to stay close to the duchess's side, while Gray greeted a handsome couple she could only assume were his parents. The resemblance between Gray and the older man was undeniable.

Her thoughts were confirmed when their paths intersected—she and the duchess; Gray and his parents—just outside the door to Lord Tolliver's home.

"Felicity. Maldwyn." The duchess nodded at Gray's mother and father.

"Dear sister. So good to see you." The Earl of Maldwyn leaned into a shallow bow.

"What do you make of this wedding?" The duchess asked Lady Maldwyn.

"It is a good match. The groom's family is most excellent. Tolliver's daughter is lucky."

"I quite agree." The duchess looked over the top of her enormous fan at the people crowded about the door to her cousin's home.

"Father and Mother," Gray said. "May I introduce you to a friend of mine, Miss Maris Winter?"

Lord Maldwyn took Maris's hand in his. "Miss Winter. It is indeed a pleasure." His eyes told her he knew who she was, and why she was there.

She curtsied. "The pleasure is mine, sir."

She'd never met the elder Gray, but had heard stories about his reign as spymaster from her father, who had held a great respect for this man. Lord Maldwyn had a reputation for being both quick-witted and unyielding—two traits that had been passed down to his son, along with steely gray eyes and heart-stopping smile.

Maris greeted Gray's mother, a tall, russet-haired beauty with kind eyes, before the Duchess of Canby moved up the stairs and into Lord Tolliver's Tudor manse. As they stepped through the door, they were pounced upon by a young woman with coppery curls piled high atop her head. "Ethan! Come with me. I want you to meet Lady Piedmont."

Gray's smile went slack. "Don't tell me this is part of your endeavor?"

"Naturally!"

Lady Maldwyn brushed a curl from the girl's face with a gloved hand. "What endeavor is that, my dear?"

"I am going to find a wife for Ethan."

Lady Maldwyn looked amused, but her husband did not.

"Perhaps you should concentrate on finding a husband for yourself," Lord Maldwyn said, a hint of exasperation in his voice.

"Oh, didn't Ethan tell you?"

They all looked at Gray, and he shrugged.

"Tell us what, dear?" Lady Maldwyn said.

"I don't plan to marry. I've decided to become an intellectual."

Lord Maldwyn's face ran through several shades of pink before deciding on a color closer to crimson. "An *intellectual*? Like some sort of bluestocking?"

"Exactly." The young woman beamed.

"And with that," Gray said, turning to Maris, "may I introduce you to my sister, Lady Frederica? Freddie, this is Miss Maris Winter."

"Miss Winter," Lady Frederica repeated. "I will call you Maris, and you shall call me Freddie. As most will affirm, I am not much of a lady. Am I, Ethan?"

"Oh, I don't know about that," Gray answered. "Your temperament is certainly changeable enough to qualify."

"Of course you are a lady," Lord Maldwyn snapped. "And it is well past the time you started behaving as such."

"Nonsense, Maldwyn. My niece is lovely in every way." The duchess took Freddie's arm. "Now, walk with me for a while, dear, and tell me of this season's endeavor. Who have you got in mind for your brother?"

Maris felt an inexplicable prick of jealousy at the thought of Gray courting some random woman. Kissing her, holding her, his embrace warm, his lips tasting of mint . . .

She shook the thought from her head. There was absolutely nothing intriguing to her about Gray's personal pursuits.

But when the duchess called over her shoulder to ask if Maris would care to accompany them, she found herself rushing to catch up so she could hear every detail of Lady Freddie's "endeavor."

Ethan yawned into his sleeve.

The feast to introduce Lord Tolliver's daughter and the groom marched on into the wee hours of the morning. The wedding itself would be held on the morrow. And then, he hoped, they could all make a swift departure.

He was anxious to return to London to see what information he could unearth about the mysterious "W" who'd sent Lord Shelbourne the notes in code. He reminded himself to speak to his father about it later, to see if he had any ideas.

He was anxious, too, to be out of Freddie's clutches. He'd underestimated her enthusiasm for finding him a wife. She'd been dragging poor, unsuspecting women to his side the whole night.

To be fair, they were all women for whom he might have held some sort of interest, had he been more inclined to go along with Freddie's plan. And if Maris Winter hadn't been in the room. He couldn't quite understand why her presence mattered to him, but it did.

Next to the women Freddie presented, Maris seemed subdued in manner and unimaginative in dress. But far from fading into the wallpaper, she did just the opposite. Her composure and confidence caused her to stand out. And her air of reserve seemed a challenge, issued to all the men in the room.

Ethan had noticed more than one appreciative glance from the gentlemen who surrounded his aunt and Maris. In fact, there was one gentleman in particular, rather tall and, Ethan supposed, handsome, who seemed intent upon ingratiating himself into Aunt Charity's crowd.

The man had attached himself to Maris's side, taking every opportunity to speak to her, to make her laugh. She had a nice laugh, clear and melodious. He realized that all the time she'd been with him, she hadn't laughed at all.

As he watched them, Maris caught his gaze and broke away from the group, coming over to where he stood.

"Any sign of Hollister?" she asked.

Ethan shook his head. "I doubt he'd show up here tonight. There are far too many people. I suspect he'd make his move somewhere a bit less public."

"In any case, I will be sure not to let Her Grace out of my sight."

"My father will take over for you shortly, and perhaps you will manage to squeeze a moment of enjoyment from this affair. In any case, you have been a superb guard."

She blinked, as if he'd startled her. "I hope your aunt doesn't suspect that I am here to protect her."

"I sincerely doubt it. You've made it all seem so natural, as if you have chosen to become one of her unfortunate ladies-in-waiting."

She laughed. "It isn't all bad. I suspect your aunt is not quite the benevolent noblewoman she presents herself to be in public, but I like her just the same. We all put on a show every now and then, don't we?"

"I suppose we do."

Ethan wondered what part of the Raven was show, and what part was truly her. He wondered if she'd been acting the night before, in the barn, when she'd looked at him with warmth and admiration. Had it been some sort of ploy to flatter him? To gain his trust? To make him feel guilty?

He realized that he had very little idea how her mind worked. That both intrigued him and scared the hell out of him.

"Who is the tall gentleman you've been speaking with?" he asked.

Maris followed his gaze. "That is Mr. Litchfield. He used to sell horses to my father. His family's stables are incomparable. Are you in the market for a new mount?"

"Not at the moment."

"Too bad."

Just then Litchfield caught Maris's attention, and smiled. It was a smile that seemed steeped in intimacy, and Ethan wondered if they had been lovers.

The thought piqued him. But he knew she'd had at least one. Perhaps several. Perhaps dozens. And he felt certain she'd had them all without lifting one little finger to entice them.

That, he realized, was what made her so attractive. She made no excuses for herself, did not try to be someone she wasn't. She did not feel the need exaggerate her merits.

She didn't need a man. Nor, he thought, did she particularly want one, most especially not him.

He'd once thought she lacked mystery. But now he realized she was the most mysterious woman he'd ever met—one who felt completely secure in her own skin.

Suddenly, the room seemed far too warm. He tugged at

his neck stock, wondering how he ever could have considered Maris Winter cold.

Gray gave Maris an odd look. "I'm going to walk around a bit. See what's what."

"What about your aunt?"

"She's in excellent hands."

Maris was flattered that he trusted her enough to keep watch over the duchess without him. But she'd grown accustomed to his constant presence, whether at her shoulder or across the room.

After working most missions alone, feeling as if she could fall off the edge of the earth without anyone knowing she was gone, it was something of a comfort to have a partner at her back.

But it was disconcerting, too. It robbed her of the confidence she'd always taken pride in. In fact, ever since Lord North had paired them for the investigation in France, she'd felt as if she were losing a tiny piece of assuredness every day.

The sooner she and Gray parted ways, the better off she'd be.

She moved to the duchess's side, playing the attentive new friend. She and Litchfield traded gossip, and she learned that several of the Frenchmen who had visited Monsieurs Belange and Toreau the previous autumn would be residing in London for the season. She would advise Gray and Lord North to keep a close eye on them, as she suspected their allegiance to France was much stronger than they let on.

While she and Litchfield spoke, she kept watch out of the corner of her eye, ostensibly for Hollister. But in the back of her mind, she knew she also kept watch for Gray. A man far more dangerous—at least, more dangerous to her.

CHAPTER 11

"I'm through laying beauties at your feet," Freddie snagged Ethan's arm before he was able to get out the door.

"What a relief."

"Don't you want to know why?"

"Why?"

Freddie gave him a knowing smile. "Because you're already smitten."

"I'm smitten? With whom?" he asked, but he really didn't want to hear his sister's answer.

"With Maris Winter, of course."

He laughed. "I'm afraid you are gravely mistaken."

"Oh, I think not. There was a distinct spark of jealousy in your eye when you saw her talking to that handsome gentleman over there."

"Litchfield? You think him handsome?"

"Of course. All the women do. Can't you see how they are looking at him? It's much the same way they look at you."

Ethan watched the women in Litchfield's vicinity. Indeed, they couldn't seem to take their eyes off of him. Was it his imagination, or did Litchfield seem to have eyes only for Maris?

"Admit it, Ethan," Freddie said. "Maris has piqued your interest. And why not? She is exactly the type of woman you need."

He laughed again, more at the notion that he needed any woman than Freddie's proclamation that he needed *that* one. "What type of woman do I need?"

"The type who isn't brought to her knees by your handsome face. The type who can hold her own in a conversation with Aunt Charity. The type who makes you seek her out from across the room."

"I do no such thing."

"You do. And what's more, she does the same."

"She does?" He tried to sound nonchalant, but his sister saw through him.

"Ha!" Freddie laughed. "You *are* smitten! I knew it." She kissed him on the cheek. "I suppose I should be angry that you've ruined all my plans for the season. But I'm just too happy. Now, what should my new endeavor be?"

"Here's an idea. How about having no 'endeavor'? You are forever finding projects for yourself. Why don't you simply enjoy the season?"

"Oh, be serious. No one can really *enjoy* the season. It holds about as much excitement as watching the queen nap at the opera."

He smiled. "Well, then, how about finding a beau for yourself, as father suggested?"

The sparkle in Freddie's eye faded. "I told you, I've sworn off men."

"Have you heard from Captain Blackwood?" he asked quietly.

She shook her head. "Leave him to his boat and his war. I'll not speak of him ever again."

"I think that is a wise decision." He tugged her arm.

"Perhaps I should design an endeavor of my own. Shall I find the perfect gentleman for you?"

"Alas." She sighed dramatically. "I'm afraid he is a mythical creature."

"Who is a mythical creature?" Their mother came up beside them and handed Freddie a cup of Madeira.

"The perfect gentleman," Freddie said.

"What about your father?"

Ethan and Freddie both laughed, until it became clear their mother was serious. "No one is perfect, it's true," she said. "But there is someone who will be perfect for *you*."

"Like Miss Winter is perfect for Ethan?" Freddie said, her expression all innocence.

His mother raised her eyebrows. "Is she?"

"Yes. But Ethan refuses to admit it."

"I approve," said Felicity. "Aside from the fact that she's been keeping your aunt amused, she's also quite an interesting young woman. Did you know she plays the harp? And fences, too, of all things."

"She does?" Ethan glanced at Maris, who, yet again, seemed engrossed in Litchfield's conversation.

"You see, you have many things to learn about your young lady."

"Exactly," Freddie said. "So why are you standing here with us?"

"I couldn't say," Ethan said dryly. "I suppose I've enjoyed the distraction. It isn't often a man gets to spend time with two ladies who have such vivid imaginations."

His mother and sister gave each other a meaningful look as he bid them good night, and headed toward the doors to the large, stone terrace.

Wooden torches illuminated the multitiered terrace that stretched from one end of Lord Tolliver's ancestral home to the other. On the middle terrace a quartet played, the melodic sounds of the strings in harmony with the songs of night birds.

Everywhere, guests mingled in tight groups, ladies with their heads bent together, gentlemen leaning on their sticks. Ethan wandered past the clusters, catching snippets of conversation, watching, waiting for someone to reveal themselves as something more than a wedding guest.

He ran into his father near the quartet.

They nodded to each other, and Ethan felt his usual pang of regret that he wasn't all his father had hoped for. Perhaps if he'd been more careful, more clever, he'd have won his father's respect and the air between them wouldn't seem quite so chilly.

"How is your aunt?"

"Fine. Miss Winter is with her."

"Alone? Is that wise?"

"I feel certain Aunt Charity is in good hands."

"Hmmp." His father looked out over the lower terrace, his eyes constantly searching. Even though he'd retired from the committee, old habits died hard. "Hollister is ruthless."

"Yes. But Maris is capable. I'm more worried that he's at Lockwell Hall, collecting whatever it was he came after in the first place. I cannot lose track of him again. I need to question him about the weapons shipments."

Ethan made a habit of keeping his father informed of committee business. Although he'd given up spying a decade ago—when he'd handed his position as spymaster over to Ethan—he still had one of the sharpest minds in England. Lord North and King George called on him regularly to advise them in all matters related to espionage.

"The weapons had gone through Two Moons Shipping, hadn't they?" Maldwyn asked.

"Only while Hollister was involved with the operations

of Two Moons. But once Randolph regained possession of it, the shipments were moved to another quay."

Randolph was Ethan's cousin, the current Duke of Canby. He'd regained complete control of Two Moons Shipping—which had once been a holding of the duchy—after Hollister had disappeared.

"I've told Lord North you need assistance with this investigation," his father said, clearly exasperated with his youngest son. "I cannot understand your reluctance in this matter."

Ethan steered the conversation away from the uncomfortable subject of his needing a partner. "Lord North believes there is an informant here, collecting some sort of information for the Prussians. Have you seen or heard anything that might be useful in figuring out who it is?"

His father's eyes lit up. "I will keep my ear to the ground."

"Good."

"Now I suppose I must go in and see how the young lady is faring with your aunt."

Ethan touched his father's arm. "Maris is a good agent, sir."

"She's a woman."

"She's nothing like Madeline."

Lord Maldwyn shook his head. "Be careful, son. Don't let the past repeat itself." He climbed the stairs to the upper terrace, and passed through the open doors into the ballroom.

Ethan cursed himself. He should have known better than to defend Maris to his father. Should have known it would do nothing more than recall his mistakes.

Bloody hell. Would he never be able to redeem himself in his father's eyes? What would it take to put Madeline Grenshaw's betrayal behind him forever?

Putting an end to the weapons shipments would surely help.

Ethan looked up at the stars, wondering where Hollister was, anxious to prove to his father, his men, and himself that he could manage all this with an ease he did not feel.

An arm snaked out from behind a potted palm, snagging Freddie's skirt as she passed.

"Guess who?"

As an answer, she spun around and drove her knee up between the man's legs.

He doubled over with pain. "*Jesu!* Lady Freddie, have mercy!"

"Captain Blackwood?" Her heart fluttered madly in her chest.

"Aye." He straightened, wheezing a bit as he stood.

"What are you doing here?"

"Forfeiting my ability to sire children, apparently."

Freddie thrust her chin out. "I refuse to apologize. One simply doesn't grab a lady from behind a potted palm. Not if he expects to receive a civil response."

Blackwood sucked in a breath and straightened. "I apologize profusely. But I wanted only to see you, and as an uninvited guest thought it prudent to keep myself out of sight."

"Don't be silly. There are hundreds of people here. No one is going to notice one extra." She dragged him out from behind the flora by his elbow.

"I'm off to the conservatory," she said, pulling him along with her. "I understand there is an excellent flautist about to present. If you wish to speak with me, you'll have to do it there."

Blackwood fell into step beside her, and she let go of his jacket.

"What do you want?"

"I told you, I wanted only to see you."

She stopped dead. "You wanted to see me? Why, when you think me naught but a spoiled child?"

His mouth twitched. "I know I said so, but I was mistaken, Lady Frederica. 'Twas only after I left that I realized how much I . . . I missed you."

Freddie narrowed her eyes. "I don't believe you."

Blackwood's fingers brushed against hers as they walked. "Is your family here?"

"Yes. And you'd best hope that my brother doesn't catch sight of you."

"Why?"

"Because he was extremely unhappy to hear that you treated me so poorly. He threatened to thrash you within an inch of your life."

"I shall make a point of avoiding him, then." He linked her little finger with his.

She snatched her hand away and stopped walking, not giving a boiled fig who might overhear them. "Honestly, Mr. Blackwood. I cannot understand why you are here. You made it quite clear the last time we met that you wanted nothing more to do with me."

"I was wrong."

"So I am simply supposed to accept your apology and pretend we are the best of friends?"

"I wish you would."

Freddie entered the conservatory and settled into one of the chairs arranged in a semicircle around a music stand in the middle of the room, burying her trembling hands in her skirts. Blackwood slid onto the seat beside hers.

"Very well," she said. "As a lady, I accept your apology. But I cannot pretend we are friends."

Blackwood looked wounded. "But why?"

She lowered her eyes. "Because you hurt me, Josiah,"

she said quietly. A tear borne of frustration slid, unbidden, from the corner of her eye.

Blackwood withdrew a handkerchief from his sleeve and handed it to her. She swiped the errant tear away.

"I care for you Freddie. A great deal. Please know that," Blackwood murmured. Then he slid from his seat and pushed through the burgeoning crowd, leaving her. Again.

How audacious! How utterly crass! A man did not speak so to a lady who had just rebuffed him. She wished never to see Blackwood's face again. Never!

And she planned to tell him so, that minute.

She rose to follow him, but just then the flautist took his place at the music stand, and a fat priest pushed his way to Blackwood's empty seat, his large belly blocking her in.

She attempted to push past him, but the priest's girth effectively plugged up her exit. He smiled and nodded to her.

Freddie plopped back into her seat, cursing the generous buffets that had led to the man's bulging belly, and watching Blackwood's back as he threaded his way through the crowd and out the door.

Ethan was heading back up to the house after an unsuccessful search for both Hollister and the Prussian agent, when he spied Maris on the other side of the terrace. She stood beside a life-sized marble likeness of Lord Tolliver, her back toward him.

He set off toward her, but before he could get too close, a gentleman's arm emerged from the shadows of the statue to enfold her in an embrace.

Litchfield? Ethan was certain of it.

His hands curled into fists. He turned on his heel, tempted to go find Freddie and tell her how mistaken she was about the object of Miss Winter's affection.

* * *

"Go on," Maris said, as Samuel released her from his embrace. "Get out of here before someone sees you."

Samuel flashed her a grin. "Too late."

"Samuel, why do you do this to me?" Tears of frustration filled her eyes. "I cannot protect you anymore. I am tired. So tired."

His smile vanished. "I never asked you to protect me. Why do you do it?"

She shook her head. "You know why I do it. Because I love you."

"And I, you. But you are wasting your time, and putting yourself in danger."

She sighed. "If you don't want my help, why do you keep appearing everywhere I am?"

"This is hardly everywhere."

"I saw you in Boulogne."

"I saw you, too." He shoved his hands in his pockets. "You seem to be getting quite cozy with the Wolf."

Maris ignored the barb. "Why did you risk coming into our room? He might have caught you."

Samuel smiled. "He'll never catch me." His face grew serious. "I wanted to warn you to leave there. You would have been in great danger if anyone had figured out who you were."

"What is your connection to the stolen ship, Samuel?"

He looked away. "You and the Wolf violated the auction. I should have killed him. Next time I will."

"You cannot. After what he did for Father—"

"I have let him live up to now for your sake, Maris. But do not underestimate my dedication to this cause."

"You don't understand, Samuel. You are treading on dangerous ground."

"No, *you* are the one treading on dangerous ground. And

you'd best wear your shoes, because it is bound to grow more treacherous by the day." He bent to kiss her cheek, and then he was gone.

Maris massaged the crick in her neck. She'd found little comfort and no sleep in the small maid's closet beside the Duchess of Canby's room.

She sneaked back to her own room and woke the duchess's maid, Ivy, who lay snoring upon the comfortable bed Maris should have occupied. She'd promised to pay the girl well to change places with her, so she could be closer to the duchess through the night.

Although Lord Tolliver had guards walking the hallways of the guest wing all night to discourage thievery by the house staff and anyone they might let in, Maris would leave nothing to chance. Gray's room was two doors down, and Lord Maldwyn and his wife were on another floor completely.

The maid opened her eyes and stretched, then popped up as if startled to awaken in such a fine bed.

"Did you sleep well?" Maris asked.

"Oh, yes, mum. And you?"

"Not so much."

Ivy nodded sympathetically. "Them closets ain't the best."

"Well, you shall have the bed again tonight."

"Thank you, mum." The girl hopped from the bed. "Shall I get ye some warm water for washin' up?"

"That would be wonderful, but I think you ought to get back to the closet in case Her Grace awakens."

"Yes, mum." The girl hurried to the door.

"And Ivy?"

"Yes mum?"

"As we agreed, you'll not get your money if you tell anyone about our arrangement."

"Wouldn't dream of it, mum." She disappeared through the door.

Maris waited until a decent hour before summoning one of the house servants to bring some water and help her dress. By the time she was ready, Ivy had come to fetch her to accompany the duchess to breakfast.

Dozens of people milled about the long dining hall, the excitement over the wedding growing. Gray's parents were there, as was Lady Freddie. But thus far, there was no sign of Gray himself.

A table laden with stewed fruits, meats and fragrant breads—meant to hold the guests over until the formal meal after the wedding—beckoned.

"Shall I make a plate for you, Your Grace?" Maris asked.

"Please do. We shall sit on that bench by the windows."

"Very well. I will meet you there."

The duchess and her entourage set off for the bench, while Maris filled a plate with venison, scones, honey, miniature tarts, apricots, and figs.

Lady Frederica appeared at her side. "Good morrow, Maris. Is my brother about this morning?"

"I haven't seen him."

"Perfect. Then we can speak freely about him, can't we?"

"I suppose so," said Maris, both amused and wary. Lady Freddie seemed in an exceedingly good mood, and Maris wondered at the cause.

The young woman followed her down the length of the table, loading a plate with food. "How long have you known my brother, Maris?"

"It's hard to say, exactly. I suppose I heard about him long before I actually met him."

Lady Freddie pursed her lips. "His reputation does precede him, doesn't it?"

"A bit."

"Well! No matter. I am here to dispel any rumors you may have heard. Unless they are good ones, of course."

Maris gave her a questioning look as the two headed off for the bench with their plates.

"My brother isn't anything at all like most people believe," Lady Freddie said. "He's been somewhat of a rake, I admit. But he has a good heart."

"Hmm."

"He does! He is simply . . . well, he's cautious with it."

Maris felt a twinge of nerves. "And what does that have to do with me?"

Lady Freddie looked truly surprised. "Why, because you've captured his fancy, of course."

Maris nearly dropped her plate into the duchess's lap. "Lady Freddie, I don't think—"

"Don't tell me you haven't noticed? He cannot keep his eyes off you, Maris. Have *you* noticed, Aunt Charity?"

The duchess took her plate from Maris's hand. "Quite. Miss Winter, I've never seen my nephew so bewitched by a woman."

Maris set her own plate on the bench, afraid her trembling hands would give her away. "I am sorry to disappoint you, Freddie, but your brother and I are merely friends."

"Oh, dear." Lady Freddie pointed over Maris's shoulder with an apricot she'd speared on a fork. "I'm afraid I'm not the only one who will be disappointed to hear it."

Maris turned around. Gray stood in the doorway, his gaze searching the room. When it lit upon her, he gave her a deadly smile.

Maris crossed an arm over her stomach, trying to quiet the butterflies that had suddenly sprung up there. Oh, lord. This was not good.

Not good at all.

Chapter 12

The guests followed the bride and groom out of the darkness of the church, squinting against the bright sunlight.

The party walked en masse along the River Medway, through the center of town. In the square, Sweeps Day—the one day of the year when the chimney sweeps set down their brooms—was in full swing. Dancers, jugglers, acrobats, and horses dressed out in colorful silks crowded the streets. The May Day celebration was a joyful sight, the perfect backdrop for a newly married couple to begin a life together.

The wedding guests would return now to Lord Tolliver's home for the nuptial feast and a toast to the bride and groom, and then they would be free to join the celebrations throughout the town.

"Do let us hurry. I am anxious to get out of this infernally stiff gown." The duchess gathered up her skirts and urged her entourage on.

Maris was uncomfortable in her formal wear, too. She was dead tired, and her feet throbbed in the impractical spool-heeled shoes, which matched her finest gown.

The clothing had been a luxury she could ill afford, but she'd needed something to wear to parties and events such as this. It was an absolute necessity to keep up appearances. She only wished she could go barefoot beneath.

Mr. Litchfield hurried up from the rear of the group and fell into step beside her. "Did you enjoy the ceremony?"

"Quite. And you?"

"My soul rejoiced to see such a love match. A feeble old man such as myself could not hope for such happiness."

Maris laughed. "You are hardly feeble."

"Ah, but you do think me old!"

"Nay!" Maris laughed. "You are practically a babe. And a handsome one at that."

Litchfield's eyes sparkled. He took Maris's arm and gave it a squeeze. "Then perhaps there is hope for me yet, eh?"

"Oh, I am sure of it."

Over her shoulder, Maris caught Gray staring at them, a strange look on his face. She excused herself from Litchfield's company, but before she could reach him, Gray hurried ahead, and Maris's poor feet couldn't hope to catch him.

When the wedding feast was over and the young couple had been toasted to near exhaustion, Maris trailed the duchess upstairs. If the elder woman had any suspicions about why her new friend seemed to follow her everywhere, she didn't let on. She seemed grateful for the company, and Maris got the impression that she'd officially been enlisted to serve as a buffer between the duchess and the rest of the world.

Gray followed them a discreet distance behind, watching until Maris gave the "safe" signal before he disappeared into his own quarters two doors down.

Maris entered her own room, but waited in the maid's closet while the duchess napped, using the quiet time to think and meditate. The practice, which she'd learned from Riya, never failed to reinvigorate her. So when the duchess awoke, Maris was ready once again to face her demons—Gray, Samuel, and even Hollister, should he make an appearance.

With Ivy's help, the women dressed quickly, then made their way downstairs to meet up with their group, which included Lady Freddie, Litchfield, Lord and Lady Maldwyn, a few other ranking members of the *ton*, and a half-dozen footmen who had the unenviable job of carting the necessary accoutrements—chairs, refreshments, awnings, lap blankets, and such.

Once on the streets they were swept immediately into the May Day celebration. They located a spot between two grassy banks, and the servants quickly erected a bright yellow awning. The party settled in to watch the spectacle unfold about them.

Morris dancers, with blackened faces and bells on their knees, weaved amongst each other in a riot of color and noise, shouting and clashing sticks. Hawkers, musicians, and revelers swarmed around them.

"Isn't it exciting?" Lady Freddie exclaimed.

"It is," Maris agreed, clapping in time with the music of a fife. It had been a long time since she'd done something so frivolous as attending a faire. Beneath her gown, she slipped her feet out of her shoes and breathed a sigh of relief.

"Wouldn't it be wonderful to dance in the streets with someone special?" Lady Freddie's eyes sparkled.

"I suppose. Have you anyone who fits the bill?"

Lady Freddie's smile faltered. "Me? No, I do not. But I shan't let that spoil my pleasure. Women are far better off without men, isn't that so, Aunt Charity?"

"Absolutely." The duchess opened her fan with the flick of her wrist, waving it beneath her nose in an attempt to ward off the growing heat of the day.

Maris wondered what young man had won Lady Freddie's heart—or broken it—for that could be the only explanation for the girl's obstinate refusal to notice the other men clustered about her.

"Good afternoon, Your Grace. Ladies." Gray ducked beneath the awning, cutting a striking image in fawn-colored breeches, a crimson waistcoat, and midnight-blue jacket. "Freddie, I have a surprise for you. Look who I found at the wedding."

"Lord Staunton! How wonderful to see you." Lady Freddie flashed a dazzling smile to a portly young man who peered at her over Gray's shoulder.

Lord Staunton turned as red as an apple. "Lady Frederica, my pleasure knows no bounds." He bowed, knocking his forehead on one of the poles that held the awning aloft.

Lady Freddie laughed. "You've always been such a clown, Staunton."

If possible, the man turned a deeper shade of red.

"Oh, Mr. Litchfield," Lady Freddie said, giving her brother an impish look. "Miss Winter just confessed to me how much she would enjoy a dance."

"Would you?" Litchfield, never more than a few steps away, came forward. "May I accommodate—"

"Sorry." Gray stepped between them. "I believe she's promised this dance to me."

Gray took Maris by the hand and attempted to lead her into the revelry.

She shook her head.

"Did you not just say it would be wonderful to dance in the streets?" Lady Freddie said.

"Yes, but I—"

"Come, then. I shall dance with Staunton, as well." Lady Freddie grabbed Lord Staunton's coat sleeve and tugged him into the crowd.

Gray looked at Maris, eyebrows raised.

"We must stay near your aunt," she said.

"We won't go far. And my father is here."

Before she could refuse him again, they were jostled into a group of passing dancers and swept out onto the cobblestones. To Maris's horror, her shoes were left behind.

A dozen beautiful women bedecked in green ribbons and lace soon surrounded them, each holding a garland arch of white flowers. The women turned to face each other, raising the arches up to create a fragrant tunnel. Maris stepped lively, attempting to keep her bare toes out from beneath their shoes.

"Run through," one of the women shouted to Maris over the music. The others nudged Ethan. He took Maris's hand and pulled her under the arch.

Before they could reach the end of the tunnel, the dancers broke formation and surrounded them, trapping them in a moving circle of flowers.

"Kiss for luck," they urged. "Kiss! Kiss! Kiss!"

Maris froze to the spot, mortified. Gray laughed. The dancers closed ranks, giggling and pushing her ever closer to Gray.

"Kiss! Kiss! Kiss!"

The crowd at the edge of the street chanted along, clapping their hands to the rhythm of the dancers' feet.

Maris felt slightly dizzy. The dancers moved about them like clouds, their garlands a swirl of white against the blue sky above.

Suddenly she was trapped in the circle of Gray's arms. He hooked her chin with his finger and tilted her head up, lightly touching his lips to hers.

Maris closed her eyes, blocking out the chanting and the women and the crowd. She breathed him in, feeling as if she were floating high above the streets of Rochester. For a moment, it was only her and Gray alone, suspended and weightless in the sweet, lingering kiss.

A chorus of rowdy cheers broke the spell.

The circle of garland opened, and Gray pulled her from the middle by the hand. They made their way back to the awning, laughing.

Everyone beneath the awning was laughing and smiling, with the exception of Litchfield, who looked a bit dispossessed, and Lord Maldwyn, who flashed his son a dark look and stalked off.

Lady Freddie clapped her hands. "Now you both shall have good luck for the rest of the year. Oh, Staunton. I wish that had been us!"

Lord Staunton blushed again, clearly besotted. At least, it was clear to everyone but Lady Freddie.

"I—I must be going. Lady Frederica, may I call on you sometime? As a friend, of course," he said quickly.

"I will look forward to it," Lady Freddie said warmly.

Lord Staunton took his leave, and shortly thereafter the duchess professed a desire to return to Lord Tolliver's for a rest. "It shall be a long night, I'm afraid."

The servants gathered up the awning and chairs, and the group lurched into motion like a great, lumbering beast.

"Miss Winter, wait." Gray snagged her arm, giving her a serious look.

She turned to him and he leaned down, pressing his mouth to her ear. His breath sent an army of goose pimples marching over her arms.

He whispered, "Your secret is out."

Her breathing quickened. Her secret! What secret did he speak of?

"I would wager these are yours." He held out his hand. Her shoes dangled from his fingertips.

The goose pimples turned to heat, which climbed her neck and flared across her cheeks. "I'm afraid you would lose that wager, Mr. Gray."

She turned and strutted across the cobblestones, thankful

her back was to him so he couldn't see her wince each time she took a step.

"Any sign of Hollister?"

Ethan and his father strolled the grounds of Tolliver's estate, taking a bit of fresh air after hours of cramped quarters at the mile-long supper table.

"No. I don't think he's followed Aunt Charity here. It wouldn't be smart."

"He's never been particularly smart," his father said. "He attempted to choke my sister in her own home, with hundreds of people down the stairs at a ball."

"True. But I suspect he's not the only one who has been tempted to strangle her."

"Myself included." His father chuckled, and then grew serious. "It would seem Hollister is desperate, to take such a risk."

"He would have to be desperate to return to Lockwell Hall."

"He wants something. And if Charity doesn't carry it on her person, then perhaps Hollister is still somewhere near Lockwell Hall."

"I have half a dozen men watching the house. But I think whatever it is he wants, Aunt Charity holds the key. I suspect he'll try to get to her when she's least protected," Ethan said. "Unfortunately, the Raven and I won't be able to stay with her much longer."

His father stopped at a stone bench in a small enclave of the garden. "What do you think of her?"

"The Raven?"

"Of course."

Ethan didn't know how to answer.

Whatever he said, his father would read far more into it

than Ethan intended. He would be suspicious, and perhaps he had a right to be.

Maldwyn abhorred fraternization between male and female operatives, in large part because of what had happened between Ethan and Madeline. He'd warned Ethan not to get involved with the Sparrow on a personal level.

But the shame was Ethan's own. And if *he* could get past it and develop an appreciation for a competent operative—even a female—his father should be able to do the same.

"The Raven is a skilled agent," he said, joining his father on the bench. "I underestimated her in the beginning. I've come to respect her abilities."

"So you trust her implicitly?"

"Not implicitly, no."

"Good."

Ethan sighed. "Perhaps I will never be able to fully trust a female agent again."

His father nodded. "Despite what happened with Madeline, you have excellent instincts, son. Don't push them away."

Ethan should have been pleased at this rare bit of praise, but somehow the thought that he'd earned it by mistrusting Maris seemed to leach all the pleasure from it.

They sat in silence for a while. Ethan ground his shoes into the pebbles beneath his feet. "Freddie likes her."

"As do your mother and your aunt. But that doesn't mean much, does it?"

"Haven't you heard that a woman's instincts are rarely wrong?" Ethan said, only half-joking.

His father smiled. "So your mother tells me, time and again."

Ethan grew serious. "Do you trust Mother?"

"Of course."

"How did you know you could?"

His father considered the question. He said, "I supposed I didn't know. Not implicitly. I simply had to go on instinct."

They were silent for a while, then Ethan said, "There is another matter I wished to discuss with you."

He updated his father completely on the case of the arms shipments, explaining that every lead had been somehow obliterated from any formal records.

"Shipping records, bank records, tax records?"

"Yes."

"Have you questioned the gun makers? Asked them who placed such large orders?" His father asked.

"No, I haven't. I can't be sure who is involved. If I question the wrong person I will tip my hand, and we both know how dangerous that could be."

His father rubbed his chin. "What about warehouse records?"

"Destroyed."

Maldwyn snapped his fingers. "Have you checked the office of His Majesty's Treasury?"

"The Treasury? Why?"

"We find ourselves at war, no?"

"Yes."

"There is a little-known law that states that in a time of war, all weapons made to be shipped overseas must be registered with the Office of the Treasury."

"But it makes no sense. The Treasury is a domestic taxing department."

"I believe the law came about so that in wartime, weapons could be taxed both at manufacture and at shipping. The information is reported by the gun maker, not the shipping company. However, the law is rather obscure, so whoever has destroyed the information elsewhere may not know about these records."

"Brilliant." A rush of excitement propelled Ethan to his feet.

His father smiled. "I remember that feeling well. I miss it." He stood. "We should return to the house. Your mother will wonder where I am. She worries about me, you know."

"I know."

Not for the first time, Ethan wondered what it felt like to have someone waiting and worrying.

"What is your connection to Lord Tolliver?" Maris stood beside the duchess at a marble fireplace in the grand salon, above which a portrait of the man in question hung.

"We are cousins by marriage," the duchess said. "His mother and my late husband's mother were sisters. Lord Tolliver and my husband shared a love of falconry." Her eyes welled with tears. "My son inherited that love."

On impulse, Maris took her hand and patted it. "I was so sorry to hear of his demise."

The death of Charity's eldest son, John Markley, Seventeenth Duke of Canby, had spread shock and sadness through all of England. He'd been presumed dead for years, and then had escaped a French prison to return to England in an amazing resurrection, only to be attacked by a highwayman a few weeks later, and killed.

The duchess smiled through her tears. "Did you know Canby?"

"I'm afraid I never had the honor."

"He was quite handsome."

"Yes. I saw his likeness once, in the papers."

"He was a good man, too." She sighed. "He and I never got on well, but I loved him dearly. I cannot believe he is dead."

"It must have come as quite a shock, especially since he'd just returned home."

"There were so many things I did not know about my son, and I shall never know." The duchess stared at the painting, but Maris could tell she wasn't seeing it. "He found a home without me elsewhere. There are many secrets hidden there. Secrets that will never be discovered now."

"Secrets?"

The duchess snapped out of her reverie. "Never mind. Enough about things that cannot be fixed. Now, tell me child, what about you?"

Maris shrugged. "There isn't much to tell, I'm afraid. I live in relative peace with my mother and grandfather. On rare occasions, I am able to visit friends or take a turn about London. But since my father passed, my mother has become . . . uncomfortable . . . being alone."

"But what of marriage? Surely she cannot expect a decent husband will just come knocking on the door."

Maris smiled. "As you can see, I am well past the age. Besides, as someone once told me, I am much too disagreeable to make a proper wife."

"Disagreeable?" The duchess raised her eyebrows. "Sometimes a woman can find her way in the world without an escort of the male persuasion. In fact, sometimes she can find her way better than a man could." Her eyes swept the room, settling on Mr. Litchfield. "But then again, sometimes a bit of company wouldn't hurt."

Maris followed the duchess's gaze. Could it be possible that Her Grace was interested in Litchfield?

"Would you mind terribly if I invited Mr. Litchfield to sup with us?" Maris asked. "The last I heard, he was stuck between those awful Pelham sisters. They shall talk his ears numb. I am sure a word from you could rescue him. Have him relocated to our table."

The duchess raised a brow. "Lady Tolliver is just over there, near the window. Will you fetch her for me?"

"Of course. And on my return, shall I report the happy news to Mr. Litchfield?"

"Do."

Maris did as the duchess bid, and sent Lady Tolliver over before locating Litchfield among a sea of women who ranged in age from sixteen to sixty.

Litchfield waved Maris over, his smile growing even brighter. "My dear, you are lovely tonight."

"Thank you, sir. And you cut quite the dashing figure."

"If I did not know you since you were a child, I would think you were flirting."

"And if I didn't know you since I was child, I might be."

Litchfield laughed. "Touché."

"Actually, I am here on an errand. I am to request your presence between myself and the Duchess of Canby at supper."

Litchfield gave her a curious look.

Maris lowered her voice and leaned closer. "I could be wrong, but I believe Her Grace has developed somewhat of an attraction for you."

Litchfield grinned. "You jest."

Maris shook her head.

"In that case, I would be honored to join you."

Maris smiled. "Good! Shall we . . . ?"

Litchfield offered his arm, and when Maris looked up, Gray had stopped dead in his tracks just a few feet from them. His expression turned dark as a storm cloud.

Maris opened her mouth, but before she could speak to him, he turned and stalked away.

"It would seem your Mr. Gray is angry about something."

"*My* Mr. Gray?"

"Well, isn't he?" Litchfield seemed genuinely surprised. "The way you both keep one eye pasted on the other, I'd just assumed—"

"He's not. I am not," Maris said quickly. She took a moment to regain her composure. "What I mean to say is that I have no interest in Mr. Gray, and he has no interest in me."

"I see." Litchfield regarded her for a moment. "Perhaps someone ought to inform the gentleman."

Hours after the dinner party had ended, Maris tossed and turned in the tiny bunk in the maid's closet, trying to find comfort. Impossible when her head touched one wall, her feet another. And when her mind would not be still.

Litchfield's words bounced about in her mind, leaving her restless and annoyed. Her old friend had a vivid imagination. She propped her pillow up against the wall at her head, and attempted to sleep sitting up without cracking her skull on the bunk above her. How ever were three grown women expected to fit in this tiny room?

She'd just about drifted off when a piercing shriek awoke her.

She burst from the closet into the duchess's room, only to find Her Grace snoring loudly in her bed, oblivious to the noise coming from the other side of the wall.

It was then Maris realized the screams were being issued by Ivy, the maid. From *her* room.

She raced back into the maid's closet and through the connecting door to her own quarters. Ivy continued to shriek, but now Maris heard another, deeper voice, attempting to calm her.

Urgent pounding at the door gave way to one of the hallway guards, wielding a candle in one hand and a stick in the other.

He shone the weak light across the room to reveal Ivy standing in her shift beside the bed. And on the opposite side, clad only in a pair of breeches, stood the reason for her hysteria.

Ethan Gray.

Chapter 13

Gray clutched his elbow. "She hit me with the bloody candlestick!"

Maris hurried over to Ivy. "Do not make a fuss," she whispered. "He was looking for me."

Ivy's eyes widened, and Maris nodded. Better to have one maid think a man was seeking her bed, than have a dozen servants and guests know that she'd been sleeping in the maid's closet.

Soon a small crowd of servants, guards, and guests had gathered in the doorway. Realizing she was in no danger, Ivy stopped shaking.

Maris stepped forward. "Mr. Gray, you've obviously mistaken this room for your own. Yours is on the opposite side of the duchess's quarters."

Gray stumbled over to her, leering. "So sorry," he slurred. "Perhaps I can share yours for tonight?"

The group in the doorway tittered.

"You insult me, Mr. Gray. But for the sake of Her Grace's friendship, I shall ignore your discourteous comment."

"Why, he's bloody pissed!" someone said from the doorway.

Gray's expression turned indignant. "Who said that? I am *not* pissed!"

The guard with the candle approached. "Of course you're not, sir. Shall I help you find your room?"

"Yes, please." Gray stumbled, reaching out for Maris and grabbing onto her. "My room. Fifteen minutes," he whispered, too low for anyone else to hear. There wasn't a hint of liquor on his breath.

She made a show of pushing him off. "Really, Mr. Gray. Collect yourself."

He hitched up his breeches and clapped a hand on the manservant's shoulder. "Lead the way, good man."

The onlookers parted to allow the two men through the door. Maris shooed the rest away. "Be off with you, the excitement is over," she scolded. "Let us be abed."

Maris hoped none of them had realized that it was Ivy who'd been asleep in the bed instead of her. In the darkness, there was bound to be some confusion. Still, Maris cursed herself for not informing Gray that she'd switched beds with the maid. He'd undoubtedly come looking for her.

But why? The question danced through her mind.

More than one answer she considered gave her the shivers. She donned a heavy wrapper and sat on the edge of the bed for a quarter of an hour, trying to keep her nerves from running away with her good sense. She closed her eyes, breathing slow and deep.

Perhaps he'd seen her talking to Samuel.

Or perhaps he had news of Hollister.

When all movement in the halls settled, she opened the door a crack. She waited until the guards made their pass, then hurried past the duchess's room to Gray's door. Her knock was soft, but urgent.

Gray must have been waiting just inside the door, for it swung open immediately. He pulled her inside.

"Did anyone see you?"

"I don't believe so. But it hardly matters, does it? I couldn't have been nearly so obvious as you were."

He let loose a string of expletives. "Who was that in your bed?"

"Ivy, your aunt's maid."

"Her *maid?* Why was she in your bed? Where in the hell were *you*?"

"I was in the maid's closet."

"You were sleeping in the maid's closet?"

"Not really."

"Not really?" Gray echoed her answer as he paced before her, rubbing the back of his neck. "What were you doing in the maid's closet, then?"

"I wanted to be closer to Her Grace's room. If Hollister tries to get to her while she sleeps, I will be better able to protect her."

"But there are guards patrolling the hallway, and her window is much too high for Hollister to get to."

"I want to be certain she is safe."

He prowled about her like a caged beast. He was close. Too close. "Do not lie to me, Maris. I know where you were."

She put her hands on her hips. "Where else might I be in the middle of the night?"

He was silent. Suddenly, she understood.

Her face burned, and she was thankful for the dark. Once again, he was taking issue with her morality. "I take my responsibility to guard the duchess very seriously."

"I saw you, Maris. I saw you with him."

The sound of her pulse rushed in her ears. "With who?"

"Litchfield."

Maris expelled a breath. "Are you suggesting that I am having an affair with Mr. Litchfield?"

"I've seen the way he looks at you."

Maris laughed. "You ass. *I* am not the one who has an interest in Litchfield. And do you truly believe that I am such a ninny I would forsake your aunt's safety to meet with him?"

"Yes. No." He raked his hair. "Damn it, I don't know. I cannot pretend to know what is in a woman's heart."

"Promise me you'll not try to guess. You might injure yourself."

She hoped her caustic tone masked her true emotions. He'd hurt her. How little he knew her, to believe these things despite the fact that they'd put their lives in each others' hands. Despite the fact that he was a man known for his keen observation, deductive reasoning, and ability to put himself in the minds of those he sought.

It was clear he knew *her* mind about as well as he knew her heart. Litchfield, indeed!

She supposed his assumption shouldn't upset her. She should be pleased he had no insight into her mind. He most certainly would not like what he found there.

Yet, inexplicably, it *did* upset her.

"Mr. Gray, what were you doing in my room tonight?" she asked quietly.

"I came to tell you that we are leaving tomorrow afternoon. I must return to London as soon as possible. And my aunt will be safer at home."

"You could have told me those things in the morning."

"I could have. But—" He stopped pacing before her, pressing both palms against the wall, trapping her between his arms. "By God, Maris, I could not help myself. I wanted to see you in your bed, with your hair loose. I wanted to see you free of your ghastly high collars and your disapproving looks. I wanted to see you soft with sleep, like you were in Boulogne, your skin warmed by the fire . . ."

He leaned closer and closer, until his lips brushed her cheek as he spoke.

"Mr. Gray—"

"Ethan."

"Ethan . . ." she breathed.

He captured her earlobe between his teeth, teasing it with his tongue before tracing the curve of her ear, his breath hot and wet.

"A-ahh." The sound escaped her before she could stop it. Her entire body erupted with the shivers.

As he ravaged her ear, his body drew closer, backing her against the wall. His hands slid down the wallpaper, tracing the outline of her body before coming to rest near her elbows, trapping her even further. The only escape for her arms was to raise them up to rest on his shoulders.

The muscles there were solid and tight, flexing beneath her hands as he moved his mouth from her earlobe down to her neck. He dipped his tongue into the hollow of her throat, tasting her. Measuring her pulse beneath his lips.

Tempted by the silky brush of his hair, her fingers slipped into it and she pulled him closer, fighting to catch her breath. She closed her eyes.

Ethan caught her hands, twining his fingers with hers. He raised her arms above her head, trapping them against the wall with one hand as he captured her mouth with his. Their tongues locked in heated contest.

With his other hand, he loosened the ties on her wrapper and it fell open, leaving only the thin barrier of her soft linen shift between them. Ethan moved his mouth down to her breasts, exhaling a blast of heated breath onto her nipple. Fire leapt in her belly, consuming her insides.

Soon, very soon, she would lose her mind. She'd lose the ability to control herself. And she mustn't.

Demanding almost more effort than she could manage,

she pushed him away. He stood panting before her, surprise mixing with desire in his eyes.

"I must get back to the duchess," she said, her voice uneven. She ducked out of his embrace and escaped out the door. Had he followed her, she wouldn't have known what to do.

He did not.

She passed the guards outside the duchess's door, ignoring their leers. She arrived back in her room, horrified to find that it was nearly dawn. As she opened the shutters on her window to let in a stream of pale pink light, there was a soft knock at her door. Soft, but urgent.

Gray.

She hurried to the door, and then hesitated, bracing for the physical onslaught of his presence, but no one was there.

She looked out into the hall. Empty.

Then the knock came again, and Maris realized it had come from the door that led into the maid's closet.

She pressed the panel in the wall, unhooking the latch, and the door swung open.

"Miss Winter, hurry," said Ivy. "The duchess—she's gone."

"Gone!"

The two women dashed through the closet and into the duchess's room. Indeed, the drapes were pulled back and the bed was empty. The window stood open.

"Go fetch Mr. Gray at once!" Maris commanded.

She darted back to her room and pulled on the traveling clothes that hung in the chifforobe. Ivy returned in minutes, quickly fastening the hooks and buttons on her gown. Maris arrived back in the duchess's room via the maid's closet just as Gray came in through the door.

"Is anything missing from this room?" he asked Ivy.

"I don't know, sir. I'd have to look."

"Be about it, then."

Hands shaking, Ivy opened one of the duchess's trunks and rifled through it. "Shoes. A yellow pair. They were at the bottom of this trunk."

"Anything else?"

The maid opened another trunk and rooted through it. "Her nightclothes, they are here—"

"What, exactly, do you think you are doing?"

The Duchess of Canby stormed into the room and slammed the lid of the trunk shut, narrowly missing Ivy's fingers. Maris noticed that the fichu she wore was half untucked from her bodice.

"Your Grace!" The maid hopped to her feet and curtsied repeatedly, like some sort of broken mechanical figurine.

"Where were you?" Gray snapped.

The duchess raised her eyebrows at his reproachful tone. "Impertinent boy! Why would I tell you?"

Gray smoothed his features and lowered his voice. "I am sorry, Aunt Charity, but we were worried. Where did you go?"

The duchess shrugged. "There was some sort of commotion in the middle of the night. Once I awoke, I found I could not fall back to sleep. At my age it happens quite often, you know. So I decided to take a turn about the garden."

"By yourself?" Gray asked.

"Of course."

Gray shook his head. "Thank you, Ivy. You may go. And you, as well, Miss Winter."

The maid gave a quick curtsy and disappeared.

"Maris may stay, Ethan," said the duchess. "You, on the other hand, are excused."

Gray gave Maris a pointed look. "My aunt will find you later, Miss Winter."

"Of course," she said, lowering her eyes, aware that it

would not be smart to let the duchess know that she'd been there to protect her all along. "Your Grace, shall we take breakfast together, later?"

"That would be fine." Gray answered for Charity, who shot him another disapproving glare. "And please, Miss Winter," he said, "be sure to have someone pack your things. We must say our farewells and leave for home as soon as possible."

"Exactly what were you thinking?" Ethan tried to keep the anger and incredulity from seeping into his voice, without success.

His incredulity was aimed at his aunt. He couldn't believe she'd leave her rooms to wander, unescorted, through all but dark gardens. The stupidity of that was staggering.

But his anger was directed solely upon himself. He'd allowed petty jealousy and the lure of Maris Winter's lips to distract him from his purpose—and hers—which was to protect his aunt, day and night.

Charity strolled to the window and gazed out over the garden. "You've given me the megrims, Ethan. Please leave."

"Not a chance. I would like to know why you decided to risk your neck by leaving here unaccompanied, when you know quite well that Ambrose Hollister could be lurking anywhere, waiting for you."

Charity waved him off. "I'm growing awfully tired of all this, Ethan. I cannot live like some sort of caged beast."

He snorted. "You've hardly been caged. You've been free to travel, to partake of the wedding and the May Day festival. You go riding, and shopping, and promenading. I simply wish you would show a bit of sense when it comes to protecting yourself."

"Oh, for pity's sake. There was no need to worry. I wasn't alone."

Ethan raised his eyebrows. "You weren't?"

"Of course not. Do you think me daft?" She fussed with the trim on the sleeve of her gown, avoiding his eyes.

"Where were you, really?"

"I'd rather not say."

"Ah."

It was difficult for Ethan to think of his aunt having interest in a gentleman. Since his uncle had died, she seemed to have absolutely no use for men. In fact, her comments were generally hostile when it came to discussing the merits of the opposite sex.

He sighed. "Be careful, will you? Hollister is a dangerous man."

Charity smiled wearily. "All men are dangerous."

Ethan shook his head. "Whatever you've got over Hollister, I certainly hope it's enough to save your neck." He walked to the door. "Make sure you are ready to leave at noon."

They spoke little on the drive home. Their carriage rumbled along between one that carried the luggage in front and one that carried the servants behind. Each of the drivers were armed, providing some measure of protection on either end.

Ethan scanned the woods for attacking marauders, though he highly doubted Hollister would make an appearance on the road. He noticed Maris did the same, all the while scrupulously avoiding his gaze, as he was hers.

The duchess leaned back into her seat and opened her fan. "Yet another couple has united in nuptial bliss. I hope they find it meets their expectations."

"Does marriage ever meet one's expectations?" Ethan muttered.

" 'Tis doubtful," Maris said.

Ethan looked over at her, surprised. He would have thought Maris Winter to be a staunch supporter of matrimony, and all it entailed. Surely, her proper nature championed the chaining together of a man and woman to suffer each other's company for all eternity.

Not for herself, though, of course. She was much too independent.

He wondered if she harbored the same concerns he did. Who could possibly accept the kind of lives they led? Although, marriage would certainly be different for Maris than it was for him. If Maris married, she would naturally give up spying. A woman couldn't run about killing Swiss Guards when there were a husband and children involved.

He studied her out of the corner of his eye.

Her cheek rested against the window frame of the coach as she watched the countryside pass. Her eyes were clouded with some emotion that he could not readily identify, and he wondered what she was thinking of.

Was she thinking about last night? Did she wish it had never happened? Or did she wish it had gone further?

He shifted uncomfortably in his seat.

Under different circumstances, he and Maris might have been good for each other. Despite the previous night's moment of insanity on both their parts, they worked well together, and he could say that about precious few of the partners he'd worked with in the past.

Unfortunately, though, it would all have to end. The attraction that had grown between them made it too dangerous to continue on as partners. When he met with Lord North on the morrow, he would put an end to his alliance with the Raven, and quash any suggestion about her working with him on the weapons investigation, or anything else.

As they grew closer to Baliforte, Maris grew quiet and pale. Ethan thought he understood why. Her mother seemed fragile and needy, while her grandfather had clearly parted with this world some time ago, even though the husk of the man remained.

He'd seen only a few servants, and wondered how Maris amused herself all the day, with no one about to talk to.

He disembarked the carriage with her, and walked her to the closed doors. "Is there no one to greet you? No servants?"

"Perhaps no one saw us arrive. But if your footmen will leave my trunk on the drive, I shall have someone fetch it posthaste."

"Of course."

He wanted to speak to her about the previous night, in his room. He wanted to apologize, but he didn't know how to broach the subject.

Maris drew the pins from her traveling bonnet and removed it, her pale hair burnished gold by the sun. "Your aunt invited me on to Lockwell Hall."

"She mentioned to me she would. Are you of a mind to accept her offer?"

She hesitated. "I will go, if you need me there."

He shook his head. "I will stay at Lockwell Hall tonight. My father and mother and Freddie will be there tomorrow. She will be safe with Father."

Maris looked relieved. "Very well. I have some matters here that I really should attend."

"I understand. But I thank you for making this trip with us. My aunt was in excellent hands."

She looked up into his eyes. "About last night—"

"We'll not speak of it. I was a bounder. I pressed myself on you—"

"No. It was a mistake, on both our parts."

"But it is over."

She nodded. "Would you and Her Grace care to come inside for some refreshment before you continue on?"

"No. We really should be off if we hope to make Lockwell Hall before nightfall."

"Of course."

She stepped around him and opened the door. "Take care, Mr. Gray."

"Ethan."

"Ethan, then."

He smiled. "It was a pleasure to work with you, Maris."

"Likewise. Perhaps we will work together again, someday."

She smiled at him, and his heart lurched. Then she disappeared into the house.

Ethan stood before the door for the longest time, wondering why he suddenly felt so empty.

Maris leaned against the inside of the door and closed her eyes, fighting to swallow the lump that had formed in her throat. She wished she could say it was a relief to leave Ethan Gray on the other side.

It wasn't.

She couldn't quite pinpoint when her anxiety over being with him had turned into anxiety over *not* being with him.

She was so accustomed to being the protector—of her mother, her grandfather, even Samuel—that having someone look out for *her* was a welcome change. No one had done that since her father had died.

Having Gray at her back gave her a great sense of security. And while she certainly didn't believe that women were merely decorations for men, she had to admit feeling soft and desirable on occasion was a delightful deviation from the standard.

"Miss Maris, you have returned." Riya jingled past, carrying a tray of dirty dishes.

"Where is Mother?"

"In her room, napping. She has a severe headache."

"Again?"

Riya nodded. "Your grandfather is in the stables, with the horse."

Maris sighed. Her grandfather had been spending more and more time there. It was almost as if he were slipping further into the past. "He still misses Father, after all these years."

"Apparently."

Maris followed the servant into the kitchen, where she sliced a thick piece of bread and slathered it with butter. She sat on a stool beside the oven and watched Riya begin preparations for their supper, just as she used to watch Ajala from that very stool when she was a child.

The cook would arrive soon, to take over. But Riya insisted on planning the menus and gathering the ingredients herself, just as her sister had. It was their way of making sure the family was served only fresh, healthy food.

Maris was grateful. She'd once caught the cook slicing moldy turnips into a pot. When Maris confronted her, she complained that she hadn't enough money to spend on proper ingredients.

After that incident, Riya expanded the kitchen garden and tended it herself, making certain there were always fresh vegetables and herbs for cooking. She was a good housekeeper, and if it weren't for Riya's stubborn belief that Ajala had gotten what she deserved, Maris might have let herself become friends with the woman.

Maris finished the bread and brushed the crumbs from her skirt as she slid from the stool. "I'm going to find Grandfather."

She exited the house through the kitchen door, walking past Riya's vegetable garden as well as the spring house and the smokehouse before she reached the path to the stables.

Shadows grew long across the walk as she slipped through the gate.

Her grandfather was there, just as Riya said, sitting quietly on the bench outside Arturo's stall. He looked up when Maris entered, and smiled.

"Hello, Grandfather." She spoke loudly, but he just nodded, not really hearing the words.

"Did you see Samuel?" he asked.

Her heart leapt. "Samuel? Was he here?"

Her grandfather just smiled.

"Was Samuel here?" she yelled.

"He'd best not have been."

Maris nearly jumped out of her skin. Olivia stood not ten feet behind them, her eyes dark as thunderclouds.

"Mother. Where did you come from?"

"I came to see you. I was so happy when I learned you were home. But then I hear you speaking *his* name."

"Mother, I understand your feelings. But you cannot keep me from caring about him. Samuel is—"

"That name shall not cross your lips again, ever. If it does, I will not hesitate to put you out."

Maris looked to her grandfather, but she knew she'd get no support from him. The poor, dear soul had not a clue what was unfolding between the two women.

The truth was, Maris wouldn't have cared a bit if her mother put her out, if it weren't for her grandfather. He needed her here. So did Riya, and the rest of their small staff. No one wished to be alone with her mother.

Nor should they have to be. Olivia was Maris's cross to bear alone.

Besides, if Maris left Baliforte she would no longer be able to cull information from Monsieurs Belange and Toureau. Information that could save or destroy many lives, including Samuel's.

"I'm sorry." Maris went to her mother and gave her a

peck on the cheek. "It was thoughtless of me to speak of him."

As quickly as it had come, Olivia's dark mood receded. She donned a bright smile. "There! It is not so hard to put someone out of your mind, now, is it?"

"No." Maris swallowed the lump in her throat. "No, it's not."

"Good. Then come along. We must change into our best gowns. Monsieurs Belange and Toureau have informed me they will be bringing a guest for supper."

CHAPTER 14

"Ho!" Ethan called out to the man on horseback from the end of the drive at Lockwell Hall.

He'd seen the rider coming up the lane from the vantage point of a window on the upper floor of the manse. He recognized, by virtue of the courier's colors, that he'd been dispatched by Lord North.

The lad clattered to a stop beside him, breathing heavily. "Ethan Gray?"

"Yes."

Ethan took the letter proffered by the special courier. He handed up a few coins. "For your trouble."

"Thank you, sir."

Ethan did not wait until he reached the house, but opened the letter there on the drive. It was a copy of the list from the Treasury Office that his father had suggested he check. The list containing the names of all persons ordering weapons for export.

There were seventeen names on the list.

Ethan eliminated six of them immediately, as the

weapons they purchased were ordered from manufacturers in London instead of the Birmingham gun quarter, where he knew the weapons he sought had come from. That brought the number down to eleven.

Of those, four of the names contained a "W."

It was conceivable that one of the people whose name did not include a "W" might have signed that initial anyway, perhaps signifying some sort of nickname or code. But Ethan decided to start with the four obvious choices. In his experience, the more obvious of choices was typically the right one.

He read:

David A. Winchester of Leeds. Sir Walter Godfrey of Lincolnshire. Lord Wentworth of Derby. Baron Wetherly of Battensborough.

Ethan knew Lord Wentworth personally, and highly doubted he was the "W" in question. The man was close to eighty, rich as Croesus, with no heir. He was once an avid fox hunter who frequently made gifts of fine hunting rifles to friends and even mere acquaintances. He traveled often, and had probably ordered a stock of rifles to have on hand should he feel compelled to give one away to a Cornish bootblack or the woman who laundered his neck stocks in Belgium.

Ethan folded the list and tucked it away. As soon as his father arrived at Lockwell Hall to keep watch over his aunt, he would pay a visit to the three most likely candidates on the list.

He worried that time was running short. If his calculations were correct, there would be another shipment of weapons ready to go in a fortnight. Three weeks on the outside.

He had to find the mysterious "W" before then.

Included with the list North sent was another missive, as well. A small slip of paper, written in code, which Ethan recognized as the hand of an operative named Badger working out of London. It read, BEEN TO GREEN DRAGON. NEWCOMB OFFERING HUGE SUM FOR HOLLISTER'S HEAD.

The Green Dragon was a quayside pub where a man's every need could be filled—from drink and women to larceny and murder—as long as he dared to enter the place.

More than one man had walked into the Green Dragon on his own two feet, and left dragged out by his ankles, either alive or not. Some—including several of his agents—had been crippled, blinded, or relieved of a body part or two in one of the frequent fights that erupted.

But the information one found there was usually accurate. If Badger had heard that Newcomb had put Sir Ambrose Hollister's head on the block, it was likely true. And if Hollister knew he was being hunted by Newcomb, he was undoubtedly a desperate man.

According to the men Ethan had posted at Lockwell Hall, Hollister had again tried to gain entrance while his aunt was in Kent, confirming to Ethan that there was something Ambrose wanted there.

And he was betting that something involved Thomas Newcomb.

"What is it that you do, sir?" Olivia's voice was breathless. Her eyes glittered in the candlelight.

Maris cringed at her mother's overexuberance. Tonight Olivia was far from the sullen, overcast woman who had taken tea with the Duchess of Canby. Tonight she was the frantic hostess, determined to make everything perfect for her guests.

Each Thursday evening, the family supped with their boarders who, more often than not, brought a friend. Maris might have enjoyed these suppers, both for their distraction and for the information they often imparted, if she didn't have to worry about what her mother's disposition might be.

Maris supposed they all should be grateful for Olivia's elevated mood, but truthfully, her highs were more annoying than her lows. Whether sullen or excitable, Olivia's extremes played on Maris's nerves like the sound of a cook's saw through a mutton bone.

Their guest was apparently of like sentiment.

The man suffering Olivia's barrage of questions, Mr. Thomas Newcomb, smiled at her, but his annoyance at having his meal interrupted with her questions was clear. He pressed his napkin to the corner of his lips before speaking.

"I suppose you could call me a broker, of sorts."

"A broker, indeed? And what do you broker, sir?"

Newcomb's smile faltered. "All manner of things. Business transactions and the like. Mostly, I am an employment broker. I find men work so they can care for their families and themselves. In return, they pay me a small percentage of their wages for my efforts."

"A noble profession. I am sure you have helped a great many people," Olivia exclaimed.

Maris highly doubted it. Mr. Newcomb seemed the type of man who would take far more than he gave. Though she'd never before met him, she knew him by reputation. Thomas Newcomb was a ruthless customs officer who controlled the lion's share of illegal activity at the docks in London.

"How ever did you become acquainted with our dear friends and boarders, Mr. Newcomb?" Olivia asked.

Maris was curious about that, as well. She couldn't imagine Monsieurs Belange and Toureau befriending such a man. Despite the fine cut of his clothes, Newcomb was ill-mannered and rough, not at all the type of person their two boarders would choose to spend time with unless they'd been pressed to do so.

Newcomb stared at Olivia with dark, deep-set eyes. For a moment, Maris thought he might not answer the question.

He belched, and said, "We have mutual acquaintances in both France and London."

"I see," her mother replied brightly. "Well, we are happy to have you at our table. Riya, haven't we any more lamb?" Olivia poked at the bare bone on the platter beside her.

"No, madam. I am very sorry, but I dropped the second leg while removing it from the oven. Please forgive me." She gave Olivia a pointed look before bowing her head.

Olivia's cheeks flushed. "I am extremely disappointed with you, Riya. Please see that it doesn't happen again."

"Yes, madam." Riya cleared the table of an embarrassing multitude of empty serving dishes as Olivia pressed conversation onto the guests. Maris recognized this as an attempt to draw attention away from the fact that there wasn't quite enough food. She doubted the ploy's effectiveness.

Newcomb made no attempt to hide his displeasure with both the lack of food and the bounty of conversation, and Maris wondered again what business he had with the two Frenchmen. From all accounts, Newcomb was a dangerous man, one not to be trifled with.

Although she shamelessly culled information from Belange and Toureau, thus far she'd seen no evidence that they were directly involved in any wrongdoing against England. In fact, she had grown to care for the two middle-aged gentlemen who held such an obvious and open affection for one another. She truly would hate to see them embroiled in something that might put them in harm's way.

"Is Samuel coming to dinner?" Maris's grandfather spoke for the first time that evening.

Olivia's fork clattered to her plate. She glared at Gavin. "I am going to see what is keeping Riya with the dessert. Please excuse me." She hurried from the room.

Newcomb perked up at this sign of discord. "Samuel?"

"He is a figment of the old man's imagination, no?" Monsieur Belange directed the question to Maris in a sympathetic voice, tapping his temple with his forefinger.

Gavin shouted, "He is real! Tell them, Maris. He is real."

"Of course he is, Grandfather," Maris said quietly.

"He is the great captain of a ship. He is Baron Weth—"

"Shh!" Maris patted his hand. "You must calm yourself. Too much excitement is not good for you."

Gavin took quick, shallow breaths, and glared at Monsieur Belange.

"Perhaps we should be going," said Monsieur Toureau, shifting anxiously in his seat.

"Yes, it is late," said Monsieur Belange, rising.

Newcomb caught Maris's eye, and gave her a smile that chilled her to her toes, as if he suddenly knew something she wished he did not.

"I am sorry, gentlemen," Maris said. "But perhaps it *would* be best if you left. As you can see, my grandfather has become distraught. I must give him his remedy and take him to bed immediately."

"But of course." The Frenchmen bustled out of the dining hall, professing their gratitude for the meal and promising to call on Maris soon. Newcomb followed, somewhat reluctantly it seemed, in their wake.

He gave Maris a lingering glance before he, too, was gone. Maris rubbed the chill from her arms.

"I didn't like that one," her grandfather said. He looked small and frail in the high-backed dining chair.

"Nor did I." Maris helped her grandfather to his feet. "Grandfather, how many times must I remind you not to speak of Samuel in Mother's presence, not to mention that of guests?"

"He should be here, where he belongs," Gavin said stubbornly.

Maris sighed. " 'Tis largely of his own making that he is not."

"He should be here," Gavin repeated.

For the first time, Maris wasn't certain she agreed.

A quarter of an hour later, Maris crouched within a sprawling bush beside the old manor house at the pond, her favorite hiding spot when she wished to watch the two French boarders.

She sat there for more than an hour, waiting for some unknown event that might or might not occur, with nothing but a sense that something useful would happen.

The wait wasn't so terrible. The flowers on the bush smelled sweet, and the thick leaves provided excellent cover when she sat in the center of it. If she wore the right colors, she could peer out through the branches and look straight into the window of the small sitting room.

This evening she wore the dark breeches and shirt she'd stolen from a groom—the ones she'd painstakingly altered for herself. It hardly mattered, for it was already nighttime. Through the Frenchmen's window, she could see them speaking with the unpleasant Mr. Newcomb.

Monsieur Toureau left the room, returning with a thick envelope, which he reluctantly handed to Newcomb. The Englishman tucked it under his arm before donning a hat. He said something to Belange and then left the room.

Moments later, Maris heard the sound of horse's hooves pounding away down the lane. She cursed her decision to sell her fastest mount a few weeks before, but they'd needed the money. The two old mares that remained were fine for pulling a carriage, but they'd never catch up with Newcomb's horse.

As it was, she would just have to wait until the two

boarders retired and then see what she could find in the manor house.

Fiddling with the keys in her pocket, she settled into the bush for a long wait.

Belange and Toureau doused the lamps in the drawing room long after the moon had risen. Maris emerged from her hiding spot and stretched her cramped legs, waiting a few minutes until she saw a candle in the window on the second floor of the house go out as well.

The Frenchmen's two servants, a local man and his wife, had gone back to their home in a nearby village several hours before, and would not return until sunrise.

Maris entered the house through the front door, it being the closest to the small room that served as both library and study, and the place where the men maintained their correspondences. If there was any information to be found, she would find it there.

The door to the room creaked slightly as she entered. She went still, listening. No one stirred. She would have to remember to bring a small bottle of oil and a feather next time, to oil the lock and hinges.

The smell of books conjured an errant thought of Ethan Gray, which she immediately pushed from her mind, annoyed that anything could distract her from her purpose. She shook it off, and focused on the task at hand.

First she searched Toureau's small, elegant desk beneath the window. The scalloped pigeonholes were stuffed to overflowing with letters from family and friends, most from France, but some from Bavaria, Spain, Greece, even Saint Kitts.

She found absolutely nothing of note, and moved on to Belange's larger, but far less graceful bureau. Here, recent correspondence was stacked neatly in a corner of the desk, in two piles.

She leafed through both piles, looking for familiar names, familiar titles, until she came across a letter stamped with a seal from Belange's cousin, the Viscount Rousse, a minor assistant to King Louis's secretary. Taking care not to allow the already-cracked seal to crumble away, she opened the letter and read it.

Rousse had sent an envelope to be delivered to London. The missive stressed the confidentiality of such package, and the fact that Belange should, under no circumstances, open it himself, under the threat of death at the hands of the intended recipient.

It was exactly the information she'd been searching for, but unfortunately there was no way she could pass it on to Lord North.

Not when the package was destined for Samuel's hands.

Chapter 15

Baron Wetherly's estate, Battenborough Hall, was the last of three stops on Ethan's list.

As soon as his father had arrived at Lockwell Hall to watch over the duchess, Ethan had ridden straight to Lincolnshire to find Sir Walter Godfrey, who turned out to be the owner of a gun shop there.

Ethan perused the man's shop, which contained a generous amount of weaponry, and took note of the markings and numbers on several guns so he could check them against the ones he hoped to find in a warehouse somewhere near the quays. However, Godfrey did not strike Ethan as the smuggling sort. His round face held an honest look that would have been difficult to fake. Ethan's gut told him there was scant hope Godfrey was the man he sought.

If possible, David A. Winchester of Leeds seemed even less the sort. A frail man who'd been bedridden for nearly half a year with rheumatism, he'd been a weapons dealer all his grown life, dealing primarily with African buyers.

He hardly seemed energetic enough to arrange a tea party, much less an intrigue of such proportions.

Which brought Ethan to Baron Wetherly.

He'd never been to Battenborough, an out-of-the-way village that both time and prosperity seemed to have forgotten. Though it was not yet two in the afternoon when he arrived there, many of the shops had already closed for the day. Men sat outside their doors on wooden chairs, content to while away the hours napping in the sun, or chatting, or smoking pipes.

Ethan passed through the square with no more than a few curious stares. It was but a short distance from the village to Baron Wetherly's estate.

Battenborough Hall was a sprawling, dark stone affair that resembled a grim fairy-tale castle, the corners of its parapets punctuated by leering gargoyles.

Ethan approached the main entrance on horseback, passing a large, empty fountain on his way up the lane. Cracks tufted with grass and weeds crisscrossed the bottom. A sculpted angel hovered over the basin on a pedestal, its eyes claimed by erosion, leaving it with an eerie blank stare.

Ethan summoned the occupants of the house with a plain iron knocker, which made a dull thump against the wooden door.

It swung open to reveal a man in a gray suit of clothes, with a stringy fringe of gray hair hanging down over his ears. His breeches sagged at the knees, his waistcoat sagged at the buttons, and his jacket sagged at the shoulders, giving him the appearance of a scrawny elephant.

"Good afternoon," Ethan said. "I am here to speak with Baron Wetherly. Is he available?"

"Very sorry, sir," the man said in the lilting burr of a Scotsman. "The master is not about."

Ethan removed a calling card from his pocket and

proffered it to the man he could only assume was the butler. The servant stared at the card as if it were a novelty, but did not take it.

"Can you tell me when your master will return?" Ethan said. "My business is urgent."

"I really cannot say, sir. He is rarely about. In fact, he's never about, really."

"What do you mean, he's never about?"

The butler hesitated, perhaps debating the merits of discussing his master's business with a stranger. He must have decided it did not matter, for he finally said, "I've never seen him, sir. In fact, none of us has."

"Well." Ethan tucked his calling card back into his pocket. "Might I come in?"

The butler frowned, but moved aside, and Ethan stepped into the cool interior of Battenborough Hall. The place was as somber on the inside as on the out, with ebony furnishings and a dark parquet floor in the foyer.

"It is imperative I speak with Baron Wetherly as soon as possible," Ethan told the butler. "He stands to lose a great deal of money if I don't."

The butler snorted. "If he's got a 'great deal' of money, that'd be news to us."

Ethan did not show his surprise at the man's lack of diplomacy. "Sorry?"

The butler shook his head. "I spoke out of turn. But in all honesty, sir, we are sorely frustrated by the new master's lack of interest in this place. 'Tis fallin' down about us, it is."

"The *new* master?"

"Aye. The old Baron's dead these past two years, now. His nephew inherited. He was the only livin' male relative, I understand."

"And the nephew isn't interested in Battenborough Hall?"

"Hardly. He sends enough to pay the staff and keep the house standin', with none to spare. And he's never been here. Not once."

"Not even as a child?"

The butler shook his head. "Nay. Only returned to England after his uncle's death to claim his title. He grew up in the colonies."

Ethan's pulse leapt. "What is his name?"

"I'm not to divulge that information, sir. 'Tis a strict order."

"I don't understand. You cannot name your master?"

The butler gave a sheepish shrug. "To be honest, we aren't privy to that information."

"You don't know the new Baron Wetherly's name?"

The butler shook his head. "Anything we need comes directly from his barrister. Money, and the like."

"Well then. Can you tell me, who is his barrister?"

The butler tugged at his neck stock.

Ethan exhaled. "My partners and I wish to offer him a considerable sum of money for some property the baroncy holds in the south. He stands to make a great deal of money. But if we cannot find him . . ."

The butler still looked uncomfortable, so Ethan pressed on. "Your master will be greatly pleased with this offer, I assure you. It might even prompt him to send a bit more for the care of Battenborough Hall."

The butler nodded. "I don't recall the name offhand, but I believe the housekeeper mentioned that a letter arrived from him yesterday. I will fetch it."

It seemed like an eternity until the butler reappeared, letter in hand, to the gloomy foyer. Ethan took the missive to a window to study it in the light. He smiled at his own good fortune.

He and Baron Wetherly's barrister, Lord Popper, were old acquaintances.

* * *

"I don't need anyone watching over me, least of all my brother. I'm not a child." Charity held her cards in one hand, and with the other stroked the little dog in her lap.

"But you *are* in danger," said Randolph, her youngest son and the newly named Duke of Canby. "Sir Ambrose has been spotted on the grounds twice in the last two weeks."

Charity waved her hand impatiently. "We shall find someone else to provide protection, then."

"No, you will not." Lord Maldwyn glowered at her from the doorway of the game room, filling the space with both his height and breadth. His shoulders were still wide and his legs powerful. Even his abundance of gray hair and the slight stoop of aging couldn't diminish the strength he'd always projected.

How Charity resented that strength.

A man was born with so many advantages. Wealth. Title. Position. Just once she would have liked to be the strongest. The smartest. The best. The one who'd received the attention and praise—especially from their parents.

But it had always been her brother who'd been the favored child. Even when Charity had done the impossible and attracted the suit of the Duke of Canby, her new position as duchess failed to impress her mother and father. By that time, Maldwyn had married, had three children, and had risen to the highest ranks of the Royal Navy, garnering more than his share of honors.

All Charity had was a pretty face, proper manners, and the sense to stand behind her husband in quiet servitude, allowing him to steal her ideas and present them to the world as his own. For God knew, Kellam Markley, the Sixteenth Duke of Canby, had never labored over an original thought of his own.

Charity threw her whist hand on the table, the cards

scattering across the polished surface. The dog jumped from her lap and ran to hide beneath the settee. She scowled at her brother. "Why don't you take Felicity and Freddie home? I can manage here on my own."

"Absolutely not." Maldwyn crossed the room and gave Randolph a pointed look.

The young man folded his hand of cards and set them neatly on the table. "I believe I shall go for a walk."

Charity rose. "I'll come with you—"

"Sit down." Maldwyn took the seat that Randolph had vacated and stared across the table at her. "It's time we mended our fences, sister."

Felicity and Freddie, who'd made up the other two parts of the whist foursome, murmured their excuses and followed Randolph from the room.

Charity glared at her brother. "What is this sudden need for civility between us? We haven't spoken ten words to each other in nearly a decade."

"Exactly." Maldwyn's voice softened. "We used to be the best of friends, don't you remember? Why this acrimony? What is it all about?"

Charity left him and wandered over to the chess table, toying with the alabaster queen. "It's about power. Respect. And why you've always had it, and I have not."

Maldwyn laughed aloud. "You must be joking."

"Not at all."

"You're the Duchess of Canby, for pity's sake. Men strive to be worthy of you. Women wish to *be* you. How can you not construe that as power and respect?"

"That is influence, not power. Emulation, not respect. For as much influence as I have, I have very little power. I cannot send a hundred ships to sea. In fact, I cannot send even one. I cannot possess the things that mean the most to me. This place, for instance. It belonged to my husband,

and then to my eldest son, and now to Randolph. But never to me, for I am merely a woman."

"You underestimate the power women have," Maldwyn said seriously.

"Everything Father had, he gave to you. He could have left something to me. It was the only chance I had of ever having something for myself."

"I am sure Father believed you were well taken care of. After all, you are a duchess."

"All of Kellam's holdings went to our sons, naturally. I have a small stipend and my title. Tell me, dear brother: How would you feel if your entire life depended on the generosity of others?"

Her brother was quiet for a few moments. "I'm sorry. I know it must be difficult for you. But I have little control over the ways of the world, and I wish you would not resent me so. I just want to protect you."

"I don't need your protection."

"You do. I understand Hollister tried again to enter Lockwell Hall while you were in Kent. I wish you would tell me what he's after."

Charity shook her head. "I really haven't any idea."

"Did Ethan tell you there's a bounty on Hollister's head?"

"There has been a reward for him, since he tried to—" She touched her neck. "Since the incident."

Maldwyn shook his head. "Not that pittance. A *real* bounty, offered up by a very nasty man."

"How would Ethan know that?" Charity said, narrowing her eyes. "That doesn't sound like information that would be bandied about the club."

Maldwyn ignored her question. "This bounty will make Hollister a desperate man. He will live in fear. If you tell me what he wants here, perhaps we can use it to lure him out of hiding."

Charity pressed on. "How would Ethan know about a bounty, and why would *you* be here protecting me? Surely there are others who are infinitely more qualified than you."

"I am your brother. I am concerned for your safety."

"Frog ears. You haven't been concerned for my safety since . . . well . . . ever."

Maldwyn frowned. "The danger to you is real, Charity. And whether you like me or not, I intend to stay here until Hollister is captured by the authorities, or until he's dead."

"Well, then," she said. "If I ever expect to get rid of you, I suppose I ought to be thinking about ways to kill him, shouldn't I?"

Lord Popper's suite of offices was locked up tight in the middle of a Wednesday morning.

Ethan knew this was not typical. Lord Popper was a creature of habit who rarely varied his daily routine, and that routine had included Wednesday morning working hours for as long as Ethan had known the man. At the very least, Popper's secretary should have been present.

He went into the offices next door, finding a man sorting documents behind a desk that seemed much too large for him, like a boy playing in his father's study.

"Do you know if Lord Popper is about?" Ethan asked.

The man didn't bother to look up from his papers. "Went up to Bedford for the reading of a will. Took his secretary with him."

"Do you know when he'll be back?"

The man pushed a pair of flimsy wire spectacles up the bridge of his nose and gave Ethan a peevish look. "It's not my turn to keep watch over him, is it? But if ye broke my arm, I would say maybe tomorrow. Maybe the day after."

"Very well. Thank you."

The man went back to his documents. Ethan went back

out to the street and summoned his carriage, wondering where to go from there. There wasn't much sense in returning to the country before he spoke to Lord Popper. And his father was more than capable of keeping watch over his aunt.

He decided to use this time in London to catch up on gossip and check in with his web of operatives based there. He also wanted to see if there was any news of a new weapons shipment. It meant paying a visit to the Green Dragon, which Ethan did not relish, but it was the best way to find out what he needed to know.

Ethan had a contact who all but lived in the pub—a port master's assistant by the name of Gerald Quimby who was forever in need of a quid or two, so he'd be eager to answer Ethan's questions. Perhaps he'd even met the elusive Baron Wetherly. If the man had spent any time at all at the docks, Quimby would know him.

Chapter 16

The Green Dragon was every bit as crude, dirty, and loud as it had been the last time Ethan was there.

Drunken dockworkers, whores, thieves, and charlatans called it home. Respectable patrons avoided it at all cost, if they wanted to come away with their wallets, teeth, and limbs intact.

Ethan's disguise was minimal but effective. He didn't move within these circles often, and the odds of anyone recognizing him were slim. Still, he'd donned the rough garb of a docker, blackened a few teeth, and greased his hair, simply to blend in with the crowd.

In his waistband he sheathed a knife, which he didn't bother to hide. It was standard fare at the Green Dragon. In his boot he carried a small pistol, though if a fight broke out, he doubted he'd have time to reach for it. Altercations at the Green Dragon were often quick and nasty, the loser carried out within moments to bleed in the street.

Ethan spotted Quimby slumped against a wooden beam

on the far side of the room. He cursed under his breath. The sot had better be sober enough to hold a conversation.

He took a circuitous route around the pub until he ended up beside Quimby.

"Bloke."

Quimby slid his gaze to Ethan, his face registering a momentary flash of recognition. "Unh."

"You be in need of a drink?"

Quimby's eyes lit up. "Aye. You be buyin'?"

"Aye. But I need some information first."

"What kind of information?"

"About a man called Baron Wetherly."

The eagerness in Quimby's eyes vanished, and his face clouded over. "Sorry. Never 'eard of 'im."

"What about a skim of weapons? Hidden in a warehouse, set for the colonies?"

Now Quimby paled. "I don't know what yer talkin' about."

Ethan pressed a five-pound note into Quimby's palm. " 'Tis a pity. If you could help me, there would be three times this in your pocket."

Quimby glanced down at the note in his hand, and then back up at Ethan. His Adam's apple bobbed furiously, and Ethan could see him calculating the amount of drink and companionship he could buy with fifteen pounds. Ethan doubted he made such an amount in a year, including the rake-off he took from the docks.

"Not here," Quimby said, his eyes darting about. "Meet me at Southside Dock in an hour. Next to the old customs house."

"You'll not run off with the money I gave you?"

"Ye promise two more like this?"

"Aye."

"Then I'll be there."

* * *

Gerald Quimby rejoiced at his good fortune. Fifteen pounds. Fifteen! And for nothing more than selling a bit of information.

He didn't care to think about what would happen should anyone find out *what* information he was selling. It could get his head separated from his neck. Baron Wetherly wasn't the forgiving sort, or so Quimby had heard.

He slowed. On the other hand, Wetherly might be the rewarding sort. He might look kindly upon an old portmaster's assistant who warned him of certain treachery. And his thanks might be worth far more than a measly fifteen quid.

It was worth the gamble. Think what he could do with all that brass.

Gerald Quimby wasn't a great believer in saving for a rainy day. He imagined strutting down Fish Street in a new coat and breeches, straight to his favorite whorehouse, and being able to have any woman there—even the pretty one. Afterward, he'd head on to Smithy's Pub for a snort. No Green Dragon for him. Not in his new clobber. He'd ruined more than one coat in there.

Quimby didn't even break his pace when he reached Southside Dock. Instead, he headed directly for the quay where Wetherly's ship was moored. Though he'd never met the baron in person, he'd had dealings with the man's secretary, a bloke named Samuel Pardee.

Pardee didn't seem like the patient sort, but Quimby wasn't looking for patience. Just a bit of appreciation.

Appreciation and, of course, generosity.

Maris shinnied up a mooring line of Samuel's ship and dropped over the high blue gunwale.

Taking care to stay out of the light of the moon, she

moved, silent and low, over the scrubbed deck. Maris knew Samuel was preparing to leave England soon, and that most of the crew would be spending their last free nights in the pubs and cathouses before setting sail.

Two sailors emerged from the gangway, arguing with one another as they skirted the wheel and stopped beneath the mizzenmast. Maris ducked behind a cannon mounted at the stern, readying herself for a fight. But the men soon left, too embroiled in their argument to notice her.

As she waited for her heartbeat to return to normal, voices arose from an open skylight a few paces away. After a few moments, she realized the skylight lay directly above the captain's quarters—Samuel's cabin. Maris dropped to her hands and knees and crawled over to it, angling her head closer to the wooden cover tented over the hole. The cover was propped up with a stick to allow fresh air into the cabin.

A low murmur drifted up from below. She lay on her belly, peering through the crack of the skylight with one eye. Below her, Samuel sat at his tiny desk, his dark hair tied back with a blue ribbon. He'd rolled his shirtsleeves up to his elbows, which were propped on the table. Across from him, his dirty face illuminated by the lantern, sat Gerald Quimby.

Maris strained to hear their conversation.

Quimby's wheedling voice drifted up through the skylight. "Sorry to bother you, sir. But I've a bit of information for the baron he might find interestin'."

"Oh? What's that?"

Quimby belched. "P'raps I should be speaking directly with Wetherly."

Samuel slapped a coin onto the table between them.

Quimby scratched his head. "The information I 'ave, the baron'll find more interestin' than a single quid. *Much* more interestin'."

"I'll be the judge of that."

Quimby shook his head. "I've already got a fiver from someone who wants it worse. With the promise of ten more."

Samuel tapped the coin on the table. "I'll give you twenty pounds sterling, if I think it's worth that."

Quimby considered the offer. "Twenty quid?"

Samuel nodded.

" 'Ere's a man at the Green Dragon askin' about Baron Wetherly. Where he can be found, and all."

"What did the man look like?" Samuel asked.

"Meant to look like a docker, but he ain't. The clothes were all right, but he had a lily-white face. No dirt on his hands, neither. He was a gentleman, in the least." Quimby leaned back in his chair. "Oh. An' he had a scar above his lip, too."

Maris covered her mouth with her hand, stifling a gasp. Gray! It had to be Gray Quimby was talking about.

"Was he still at the Green Dragon when you left?"

"Aye. But we agreed to meet at Southside Dock. He was to give me the other ten pounds there. Prob'ly there waitin', I'd say."

Samuel leaned in. "What did you tell him, exactly?"

Quimby grinned. "Nothin'. Thought the Baron would appreciate a bit of loyalty."

"He will." Samuel left the table and returned with a small leather sack. He counted out twenty silver coins.

Quimby scraped them into the bottom of his long shirt and tied it in a knot. Then he tucked the shirt into his breeches. "Can't be too careful."

"Southside Dock?"

"Aye. And he was carryin' a knife and a pistol."

"How do you know?"

Quimby laughed. " 'Cause there isn't a body who goes to the Green Dragon without 'em."

Quimby left the captain's quarters, the coins jingling as

he walked. Samuel went to a chest in the corner of the room, where he withdrew two pistols.

Maris scrambled to the gunwale. She had to get to Southside Dock before Samuel did.

Quimby whistled out of tune, the notes echoing off the grimy cobblestones.

The silver in his pants felt pleasantly cold and heavy against his skin. Twenty quid! And another fiver in his pocket.

Surely, he had died and gone to heaven. The things he could do with twenty-five quid!

He scratched his head. But for thirty-five . . .

For thirty-five, he could leave London. Get away from the ceaseless damp, the rats, and rot of the docks. Visit his mum in Derbyshire.

It was risky. But it was worth the gamble.

If he could get to the Southside Dock before Pardee, he could give the stranger the information he wanted, collect another ten pounds, and be gone before anyone was the wiser.

He doubled his pace, the weight of the coins in his shirt slapping against his belly as he ran.

"Who the hell are you?"

Hands snagged Maris about the waist before her feet could even touch the dock. In her hurry, she'd forgotten about the guard at the bottom of the gangplank. He'd grabbed her as she'd slid down the mooring line.

"Captain asked me to check the ropes." She kept her voice low and her eyes averted, hoping that in the dark, he wouldn't be able to tell she was a woman. "Paid me half a crown."

"In the dark? Yer lying, ye filthy little beggar."

"I ain't."

"Show me the coin, then."

"Let go of me."

The sailor released her. She put her hands in her pockets and withdrew a fist. "Here."

The sailor bent to look at what was in her hand. She braced her fist with her other hand and drove it up into the sailor's nose. It connected with a satisfying crunch, and he howled with pain.

She pushed past him and flew toward the street, but he followed close behind, grabbing for her shirt. He came away with her hat, instead.

The thick braid she'd tucked up beneath the hat unfurled, slapping against her back as she ran. Behind her, she could hear the sailor cursing.

She darted between carts and wagons, scrambled over thick coils of mooring line, and finally lost her pursuer when he slipped in a pile of horse excrement, his head hitting the street like a ripe melon.

When she finally stopped long enough to catch her breath, she realized that she'd run in the opposite direction of Southside Dock. With a sick feeling in her stomach, she reversed direction, praying she could make it there before one of the men she loved was killed.

Ships swayed on silvered water. Mooring lines groaned against the current of the Thames, sending melancholy sounds through the damp night air.

Behind a cluster of barrels, a cat screeched.

Ethan kept to the shadows of the ramshackle building that was once a customs house. He waited for Quimby against the side of the building for a long while, listening to the distant laughter of prostitutes trolling for business.

Had Quimby stopped to spend his five-pound note with one of them? Perhaps he shouldn't have paid the man anything until he had the information he needed.

By the time the moon had settled low over the mist-covered river, he'd begun to doubt that Quimby would show. Perhaps he'd gone back to the Green Dragon to drink away his fortune. Or perhaps he'd decided that ten more pounds wasn't worth his time—or the risk to his scrawny neck.

It seemed unlikely, from all Ethan knew of the man. What was more likely was that he'd passed out somewhere close by.

Ethan crossed the narrow street that ran between the river and the buildings, heading toward the water. Southside Dock was surely one of the vilest places he'd ever been. A far cry from the piers where passenger ships disembarked, this place served mostly fishing boats and cargo ships carrying perishable goods.

All about him, the stench of fish guts and rotting fruit and vegetables permeated the night air. Rats abounded, scratching and squealing to each other amongst the culinary treasures they found. Dogs with matted fur eyed him with suspicion from behind piles of rubbish.

He entered a maze punctuated by towers of empty shipping crates and barrels slick with fish slime, the hair raising on the back of his neck. He moved slowly through the maze until something on the ground between two barrels caught his eye. When he crouched down to investigate, a cat darted over his feet, hissing and spitting before disappearing into the night.

Ethan leaned against one of the barrels, his heart hammering against his ribs. When it calmed, he leaned down again, only to realize the thing he'd spied on the ground was—

A hand.

He shouldered one of the barrels aside to find Quimby sprawled behind it, his legs and arms splayed out at awkward angles.

Drunk.

Ethan made a noise of disgust, and slapped Quimby's cheeks. He shook his shoulders, but Quimby didn't move. Ethan withdrew his hands, his fingers slick with blood.

Ethan pushed the barrels farther aside to allow moonlight to filter onto the body. The anemic light revealed poor Quimby's fate. A dark river of blood ran a route as crooked as the Thames across the boards. And much to Ethan's horror, beside him lay his tongue.

Quimby's eyes stared up at him with a flat, lifeless gaze.

As Ethan reached down to close Quimby's eyelids, one of the crates behind him splintered, crashing to the ground.

"What the—"

Before he could react, something struck him hard from behind.

He landed facedown beside Quimby's body, a crushing weight on his back. Wetness seeped through his coat, soaking his shirt and neck.

"He's shooting at you," a voice whispered over his shoulder. "Stay down."

The peacock?

The weight lifted from Ethan's back. He rolled over to find himself staring not into the peacock's eyes, but into the Raven's. Water dripped from her hair onto his face. Her clothing, too, was soaked.

Another loud *crack* sent a crate tumbling down beside them.

Ethan pulled the pistol from his boot.

Maris grabbed his wrist, and shook her head. "What if there are more than one? I have no weapon." She rolled up into a crouch. "Follow me."

Keeping their heads low, they made their way through

the maze of empty crates and barrels. Footsteps echoed behind them, moving quickly, growing close.

A mutter. A curse as the shooter met a dead end in the labyrinth. Crates crashed and tumbled about them as Maris pulled Ethan deeper and deeper into the stacks until they reached the water's edge. Wooden planks shored up the banks of the Thames, creating a sheer drop into the river.

Footsteps echoed in the maze, but it was impossible to tell how many men pursued them.

Maris dropped to her belly and slid to the edge, swinging her legs over the bulwark. "Follow me," she whispered. She lowered herself over the side until all that were visible were her head and shoulders.

He hesitated.

"Trust me," she whispered.

Trust her.

Ethan fingered the handle of his pistol—a weapon that would be useless if he immersed it in the water.

Maris hung on the bulwark, waiting. "Hurry!"

He fell to his belly and lowered himself down. Maris released her grip and slid silently into the water, and Ethan followed. They clung to a piling post, listening.

Footsteps again drew close, then retreated. Crates and barrels were pushed about. Ethan and Maris remained still many minutes after the footsteps receded.

"We cannot scale this wall," Ethan whispered. "It is too slippery."

She nodded. Then she swam, gliding through the moonlit water with the ease of a water nymph, her strokes sure and even against the current of the Thames. Ethan followed her, his limbs growing numb by degrees in the frigid water. They hugged the shoreline, searching for a place to climb out. So focused was Ethan on that task, that he almost missed the noises above him.

He looked up to see a flash of gunpowder before he

heard the pistol's report. Beside him, the water bubbled. He could hardly feel his arms and legs, and wondered if he'd been hit.

"Hurry!" Maris urged.

He swam faster, matching her strokes as they moved farther away from shore. Another shot hit the water close to his right side. He separated from Maris, cutting the size of the shooter's target in half. He made for the opposite bank, his arms churning through the waves.

A final shot reverberated from the dock, missing its mark again. Or so he thought.

When he turned to look for her, Maris was gone.

"Raven!" He called for her over and over, with no reply. The moon was nearly gone now, making it difficult to see across the water.

He swam to where he'd last seen her and dove beneath the surface, hoping to make contact with her by thrashing his arms and legs under the water. His strength waned.

Finally, she broke the surface twenty yards away, gasping for air.

"Are you hit?" he called.

"No." Her voice was weak. "My foot is tangled in something."

He reached her side in a moment. Plunging under the water, he worked to uncoil a thick, slimy section of fishing net that had tangled about her ankle. After several attempts, he was able to free her by removing her boot.

But her struggles had clearly exhausted her.

"Let me help you to shore."

He rolled her onto her back and crossed an arm over her chest, supporting her body on his hip as he swam. Fighting the current, he pulled her farther and farther out into the river, lungs burning with the effort.

They had to make it to the opposite side. If they turned back, they'd be swimming toward certain death. Whoever had been shooting at them would hardly have given up the chase.

Halfway across, a cramp in his left side nearly took him down, and Maris with him. Only the thought of watching her slip beneath the water and disappear renewed his resolve. Treading until the pain eased, he managed to keep both of their heads above water until he could swim again.

He made for a set of stairs on the bank, ignoring the stares of the watermen as he hauled Maris out of the river and onto the stone platform. She shivered violently in his arms. He wrapped his body around her and held her close, rocking her, giving her what little heat he had left. But she faded into unconsciousness.

"Stay with me. *Stay with me,*" he whispered, holding her close to his chest.

One of the watermen took pity on them and pulled a blanket from a seat in his barge. "Here, mate."

Ethan wrapped it around Maris's shoulders, chafing her arms and back until she roused. She attempted to speak, but her teeth chattered too violently.

"Shh." He pressed his lips lightly to her forehead. "I'm taking you home."

All was quiet and dark at the house on Bloomsbury Square.

Gray spirited her past the carriage house and in through the rear entrance. He carried her down the stairs to the kitchen, depositing her on a tall stool beside a huge black stove. She shivered when the heat from his body left her.

"The servants are asleep," he said. "They're housed on the third floor, so we shouldn't have to worry about them. They're accustomed to my coming and going at odd hours."

She nodded. It was best if no one saw her there.

"I'll light the stove," he said.

Within moments, a fire flared in the iron behemoth, sending heat out in waves to warm the kitchen. Maris stretched her hands out over it. A drop of water fell from her sleeve and hissed on the stove's surface.

Through a haze, she watched him stoke the flames in the stove. A drop of water rolled from his hair down his neck, and into the collar of his shirt, which clung to his shoulders and back. When he turned, she could see the splash of auburn hair covering his chest through the wet linen.

Her mind flitted back to the night in Kent when he'd stood in nothing more than his breeches over her bed, scaring the duchess's maid half to death. And later, when she'd run her hands over his bare chest. She remembered every inch of it. The hard, knotted muscles and the warm skin. The coarse triangle of hair that became a silky splash across his belly . . .

"This should dry us out nicely." He slammed the stove door closed. "The rest of the house is cold, of course, but it won't be long before the kitchen is bearable."

Maris concentrated on warming herself as Gray placed two teacups on a small silver tray. He measured a few spoonfuls of tea leaves into a teapot and filled a kettle for the stove. She wondered where he'd learned to do such a thing.

"We should get you into dry clothes," he said. "Wait here. I'll be back in a moment."

He returned shortly with several towels and a dark blue dressing robe in hand. "The robe is mine. It might be a bit large, but it will be warm."

He'd changed into dry breeches and a plain white linen shirt, buttoned wrong in his haste.

"Come here," she said.

He stood before her and she pointed to his shirt. "You've missed one."

"So I have." He handed her the towels and the robe, and unfastened the buttons down to his navel.

When he began to button them again, she said, "No. Don't."

He gave her a curious look, then indicated the robe. "I would have brought you a fresh pair of breeches, but I've seen the way mine fit you, and they don't do you near the justice as those." He motioned to her own soaking-wet clothes, which clung to her like an image to a mirror.

She resisted the urge to cover herself. "I tailored some of the stable hand's clothes, for nights such as this. Can you imagine running and swimming in a gown?"

He looked amused. "I can't."

Her eyes met his, and she started at the naked desire she saw there. She bit the inside of her cheek.

"Why don't you change in here, where it is warm, and I'll go set a fire in the library."

When he'd gone, she stripped off the thick wool stockings she'd worn beneath her now-missing boots. The breeches came next, and she hung them on the back of a chair beside the stove to dry. She worked at the tiny buttons of her own shirt, with no success. Her insides churned. Her fingers were numb and shaking.

She was still trying to work them open when Gray returned.

"Let me help you," he said, his voice low and rough, a cat's tongue on her senses. He came to her slowly, perhaps giving her time to protest. Time to escape. But that notion never crossed her mind.

She thought about what might have happened if she hadn't gotten to Gray at the docks before Samuel had. If he had died there, she never could have lived with herself.

He pushed her hands away from the buttons, slowly unfastening them. "Seems I'm always having to undress you, Miss Winter. Perhaps I might fill the position of your lady's maid."

Button by button, inch by inch, he revealed her. A chill

ran over her skin. She'd worn nothing beneath the breeches, or the shirt. When it was gone, nothing would lay between her and Gray.

Nothing, of course, but her lies and deception.

She ignored that small voice—the one that would have her feel guilty for taking pleasure in Gray's touch. The one that reminded her he was the enemy.

No, not her enemy. Samuel's.

But wasn't that the same?

His hand slid beneath the shirt to cup her breast, burning hot against her frigid skin.

The devil's touch.

Her nipples, already taut from the cold, grew even tighter against his palm. Her breath caught.

"By God, Maris, you are beautiful."

He drew the plait of her hair, which hung down her back like a length of wet rope, over her shoulder. His fingers loosened the ribbon that held it in place and worked the braid loose until her hair hung in damp waves over her breasts.

He fell to his knees, burying his face against her belly. She tangled her fingers into his hair, gasping in surrender. She pushed his shirt from his shoulders and it dropped to the floor, forming a pool of linen around him.

Her hands found the muscles of his shoulders and arms as he gripped her waist. He looked up at her, heat smoldering in his eyes, turning her insides to liquid. His hands grazed her thighs, her knees, her calves. He traced her toes and ankles with his fingertips, and massaged every inch of her legs, climbing in blissful, agonizing ascent to the damp curls between her thighs.

His touch burned, but she wanted more. She wanted that heat inside her.

"Please," she whispered.

Chapter 17

"Please."

The word unleashed every shred of desire for her that had built within him. Every unanswered craving and forbidden dream.

He struggled to his feet, gathering her against him and crushing her mouth to his. She answered his kiss with one equally as tumultuous and punishing, as if she, too, were fighting—and giving in.

Memories of Madeline lurked at the edge of his mind, but they were soon chased away by the reality of Maris Winter. There was no one before her. No one like this. He'd never, ever desired a woman this way.

He would not take her here, though. Not in the kitchen.

He wanted her in a familiar place, a place amongst his things, so he could look upon her and feel at last as if he had her. As if she were his.

She would not elude him tonight.

He swept her into his arms and carried her not to his bedroom, but to the library, where he kept his most precious possessions. He stretched her out upon the rug before the fireplace, his breath catching in his throat.

She was there for him, now, every inch of her. The light of the flames danced across her pale skin, bathing her in light and shadow. He made love first to the light, and then the shadow, caressing the hollows of her body, tasting her, devouring her. She moaned and shuddered her release, and he felt a surge of victory.

The Raven was his.

Limbs entangled, tongues entangled, skin heated by longing and the fire, they pleasured each other. Her fingers slid over him, stroking, sliding in gentle rhythm, and he panted against her shoulder, his desire building to a fevered pitch.

"Now," she demanded. *"Now."*

"Say my name. I want to hear it on your lips."

"Gray," she whispered.

"No . . ."

"Ethan. Now."

He obliged her, moving into her slowly until she took all of him. Until he melted into her heat.

Their hips joined and retreated, the rhythm exquisite. Relentless. Until finally she shuddered, and cried out his name. He drove into her one last time, binding himself to her, body and soul, as he found his release.

They lay there, entangled and exhausted, her body finally warm. He tipped her chin with his finger. She looked into his eyes, and smiled.

His heart lurched. "Are you . . . Did I hurt you?"

She shook her head. "Quite the contrary. You are the best lover I've ever had."

He opened his mouth, but she covered his lips with her fingers. "Please don't feel compelled to say the same of me. I know I am not . . . I cannot hope to compete with the others."

But there was nothing to compete with. No one. He'd never felt the way he had with her, had never come close. Being with Maris was like the thrill of deciphering an impossible code. Like the comfort of his favorite chair and the pleasure of a good book. All those things together, times ten.

It was the closest thing to perfection he'd ever felt.

He could not tell her that, though. There were no words.

He touched his lips to hers, trying to say it all with a kiss.

She smiled, and stretched out on the rug with a contented sigh. He traced the line of her jaw with his fingertip. "Stay here."

He pulled his breeches on, and returned with the robe he'd fetched for her, as well as a decanter of brandy and a single glass on a tray.

"I'm afraid tea is impossible," he said. "The water has long boiled away, and the fire in the stove has gone out. But would you care for a brandy instead?"

She nodded, and he poured half a glass, sitting down beside her before he handed it to her.

"Won't you have one, too?" she asked.

"I rarely drink spirits."

"You don't care for them?"

He shook his head. "I don't care for what they do to a person. They make one careless."

Maris reached up and brushed a lock of hair from his eyes. He stretched out beside her before the fire, and she slid closer to him, curling an arm around his waist. He looked into her eyes, and his heart stopped. When had he grown so attached to her, this capable, serious, utterly disarming woman? And how could he possibly deserve her, after what he'd done to her father?

She kissed his neck. "My clothes must certainly be dry by now."

She attempted to rise, but he held on to her.

"Wait."

He wanted to tell her he trusted her, and ask her to help him with the weapons investigation. But if he did, there would be no turning back.

She rolled over to face him, her hip touching his. "What is it?"

"I want to ask—" He took a deep breath. "I want to thank you for tonight. For finding me at the docks. How did you know I'd be there?"

She lowered her eyes. "I was working on a lead. I saw you at the Green Dragon."

He sat up. "You were at the Green Dragon? Dammit, Maris. That place is dangerous. You could have been killed."

Her pinched expression returned. "I am perfectly capable of taking care of myself."

His frown softened. "I know you can. That's why I . . ."

"What?"

He rubbed the back of his neck. "Come upstairs with me." He took her hand and pulled her to her feet with him.

"I must get home—"

"Please, Maris. Spend the night with me." He pulled her into his arms, running kisses along her jaw.

She leaned against him, her head resting on his chest. After a moment, she said, "Just for a little while."

Maris had planned to go straight to Baliforte after she'd left Gray's.

But she couldn't fix this mess at Baliforte. She couldn't end this. And she wanted to, desperately. She couldn't deceive Gray any longer. Her conscience wouldn't allow it.

Somehow she had to convince Samuel to go home, back to Philadelphia.

It wasn't yet dawn, and the dock where his ship was moored was all but deserted. An exhausted prostitute lay sleeping on a hay bale against the side of the building where Maris hid, and a waterman snored in his tender nearby. Once again a single guard stood watch at the gangplank of Samuel's ship, but there was no movement up on the decks.

Before she had a chance to figure out a way aboard, she spotted Newcomb approaching the gangplank. He and the guard spoke briefly, and then the guard let him pass.

Quickly, Maris formulated a plan.

She shook the prostitute awake. The woman gave her a surly look. "I ain't takin' customers."

"I need you to talk to someone."

The doxy shook her head.

Maris pressed a coin into her palm. "Just for a few minutes."

She explained what she wanted the woman to do.

The prostitute stuffed some hay beneath her skirts, and Maris helped her arrange it so it looked as if the woman was with child.

"All you have to do is distract him for two minutes. If you manage it, I'll pay you double when I return."

"How do I know ye'll be back?"

"I'll leave these." Maris removed the pair of boots she'd borrowed from Gray. "You can sell them if I don't come back."

The prostitute examined the boots, and hid them behind the hay bale.

She adjusted her "baby," and stumbled across the dock toward the ship's gangplank, moaning and cursing. "Help me. Help me, please. Oooohh, Lord. Help me."

She staggered up to the guard and grabbed his shoulder, doubling over. "The baby's comin'."

The guard was clearly out of sorts. "What—"

"Oh, help me. Help me to the tender. I got to get home."

The guard slung the prostitute's arm over his shoulder and guided her to the tender, where he woke the sleeping waterman.

As the two men argued and the prostitute moaned, Maris slipped past them and up the gangplank, moving as silently as a cloud across the sun in her bare feet, heading directly to the skylight.

"I've cleared the way for you to leave early next week," Newcomb said, stretching his legs out beneath the table.

"How are the guns packed?" Samuel asked.

"With crates of farming tools. The bill of lading says they're bound for Jamaica. My men will go in and change the bills, and move the cargo over to the other warehouse the night before you load, after your shipment has already been inspected."

"Good. When the transaction is complete, your payment will be waiting for you at the Green Dragon."

"I don't think so." Newcomb leaned back in his seat, and sucked his teeth. "I want it now."

Samuel shook his head. "It isn't how I do business."

"It is now, *Baron Wetherly*."

Samuel tensed. "Baron Wetherly is the head of this operation. I am only his assistant."

"I don't think so." Newcomb smiled, showing a set of sharp, gray teeth. "You see, when I got this from the Frenchies," he pulled an envelope from his waistcoat and threw it on the table, "I met an old man who is familiar with you. Says you and Wetherly are one and the same."

"He must be crazy."

Newcomb laughed. "At first I thought so, too. But the pretty little piece with him seemed awfully determined to shut him up. So I did some research. Found out that a Baron Wetherly passed his title on to a bastard nephew in colonies."

"How did you—"

"I make it my business to know things."

Samuel studied the man for a moment, impatient for the day when his dealings with Newcomb would be finished. He had just one more load of weapons to ship, and he'd never have to look at the man again. From now on, all arms deals would be handled by a Frenchman named Beaumarchais. The details were included in the envelope Newcomb had just given him.

"Fine," Samuel said. "You want your payment now, you'll have it."

Newcomb grinned. "Good. But that isn't quite enough."

"What else?"

"Hollister."

"Hollister? Hasn't he been found yet?" Samuel asked.

"You know he hasn't. And I think you know where he is."

"I don't."

"You worked with him for two years."

"Yes, but he disappeared six months ago. I haven't any idea where he's gone."

"Well, you'd better find him, because he has something I need. And if it gets into the wrong hands, you, Baron, will go down as hard as I will."

"What does he have?"

"A ledger. He stole it from me just before he tried to strangle the duchess. The whoreson wanted me to buy it back from him."

"How do you know he still has it?"

"Because if anyone else had found it before now, I would not be sitting here. And neither would you."

He was almost afraid to ask. "What's in it?"

Newcomb shrugged. "Let's just say it's a personal diary of all the favors I've done for friends. Baron Wetherly included."

Samuel rubbed his temples. He couldn't wait to leave England.

"Sir."

The word roused Ethan from a sound sleep. He covered his head with a pillow.

"Sir, forgive me for disturbing you, but there's a Lord Popper to see you."

Ethan opened one eye just a slit. His valet, Peabody, stood beside the bed, hands folded behind his back.

Ethan bolted upright, expecting to see Maris asleep beside him. But she was gone, the only evidence of her existence the tangle of sheets at the foot of the bed.

Peabody cleared his throat. "Sir?"

"Tell him I will be down shortly," Ethan snapped.

"Yes, sir. Very good, sir."

Peabody retreated from the bedchamber.

Ethan rolled from the bed, unsure whether to be relieved that Maris hadn't been seen there, or annoyed that she'd left without saying goodbye. He hadn't even had a chance to speak to her about assisting him with the weapons investigation.

He'd forgotten what it was like, to be the one remaining in the bed alone after a night of lovemaking. Usually it was he who sneaked off in the wee hours of the morning.

He rolled from the bed and plunged his face into the icy water in the washstand by the window, attempting to wash away the fog of exhaustion. He never would have guessed Maris could be such a passionate and energetic lover.

Peabody returned to help him dress, informing him that a pair of his best boots had gone missing.

Maris.

The thought annoyed him. The image of her stealing his boots and skulking out in the middle of the night, as if she couldn't bear to spend another moment in his bed. Why had she done it?

A thought niggled the back of his brain. *Because you question her abilities. You treat her like a child.*

He managed to pull himself together by the time he greeted Lord Popper in the library, where, he noted, all traces of his and Maris's evening there had been carried off by the help.

"Lord Popper. Thank you for coming."

The barrister, a tall, thin man sharply turned out in a forest-green embroidered waistcoat and breeches and a wine-colored jacket, stood when Ethan entered, flashing him an eager smile.

Lord Popper tended toward male companionship, and Ethan often felt like a hare at a fox's luncheon in his presence. But the man was an excellent barrister, quite accomplished and capable, and if Ethan had been one to lean toward such proclivities, he could have done far worse than Lord Popper.

"Good to see you again, Mr. Gray," Popper said. "How is your aunt?"

The question was a courtesy rather than a genuine curiosity.

After Aunt Charity's husband had passed away, Lord Popper had served as administrator of the duchy. He and the duchess had mounted a war of words that spanned nearly two decades, skewering each other ruthlessly in public until the responsibilities of the duchy were finally transferred back to the family a few months ago.

Popper was surely relieved to be done with her.

"The duchess is the same as ever," Ethan said.

"More's the pity. One would have hoped she'd soften with age."

Ethan stifled a grin. "Would you care to have a seat?"

The two men settled down across from one another in a set of comfortable chairs.

"I am sure you are wondering why I wished to see you," Ethan said.

"Are you looking for someone to handle your affairs?"

"Not at the moment. But there is something I had hoped you might help me with. Something rather, ah, sensitive."

Lord Popper leaned forward in his chair. "Go on."

"I must be certain this conversation never leaves this room."

Lord Popper looked injured. "Discretion is my hallmark, I assure you."

Ethan tented his fingers beneath his chin. "I have a friend. A lady friend who finds herself in a bit of trouble."

"Oh, I'm *sorry*." Lord Popper gave him a sympathetic frown.

"No, no. 'Tis not *my* trouble. I only wish to help her find the man who . . ." He patted his middle.

"I understand. But what does this have to do with me?" Lord Popper's eyes grew wide. "Surely you know *I* wouldn't have—"

"Of course not! But I believe you know the man who did."

"I do? Who?"

"One Baron Wetherly."

"Baron Wetherly?"

"Yes."

"He is a client of mine."

"I've heard. Which is why I've asked you here. I was hoping perhaps you could tell me where to find him."

Lord Popper leaned back in his chair. "As I said before, Mr. Gray, discretion is my hallmark."

"Of course. I understand." Ethan shook his head. "Unfortunately, I've exhausted every other resource I had in searching for the man. I've hit nothing but dead ends."

"I might be able to get a message to him," Lord Popper suggested.

"That would be one way to handle it. However, my lady friend is afraid he might not take the news of his impending fatherhood very well, unless it comes directly from her."

"But I have no idea where he is. In fact, I've never even met the man. I only handle his legal affairs."

"If I knew where to begin looking, I might be able to find him myself."

"I don't know. I . . ."

Ethan looked directly into Lord Popper's eyes. "I beg of you, sir, on my lady friend's behalf. She does not wish for her child be born a bastard."

Lord Popper's face grew red, and Ethan knew he'd hit his mark. Lord Popper himself had been raised a bastard, his father acknowledging him only on his deathbed for lack of another heir.

The barrister shook his head. "I will help you. What do you wish me to do?"

"May I see your files on Wetherly? I can accompany you to your office right now."

"I'm afraid I have another appointment, and it cannot be postponed. But I can bring them to you tomorrow night."

Ethan ignored the suggestive tone. "Tomorrow night? Can't we do it after your appointment today?"

"Sorry, but the appointment is in Southwark. I will be gone until tomorrow evening."

"Very well. I shall be at the Mayhews'. Can you meet me there?"

Lord Popper's face fell. "The Mayhews'?" He sighed. "I will be there."

It was close to noon by the time Samuel returned to his ship.

He shed his heavy wool coat and hung it on a hook beside the door in his cabin, rolling up his sleeves as he crossed to where his papers lay spread out on a small desk. The desk was nailed to the wall to prevent it from sliding about in nasty weather at sea.

Samuel seemed far too large for the cabin's compact efficiency, and Maris wondered how he managed to live in such a small space for months at a time. But despite the room's size, it still took him a while to notice her sitting on the tiny bunk in the corner.

"What are you doing here?" His voice held none of the tolerant amusement with which he usually spoke to her.

Her heart constricted. He looked exhausted. Spent.

She longed to take him in her arms. Smooth the curls from his forehead.

She removed the black felt tricorn she'd worn to the docks to cover her hair, and twisted it in her hands. "I want to speak to you."

He shrugged. "So speak."

"Samuel, you must stop this madness immediately," she said, trying, failing to keep the desperation she felt from seeping into her words.

Samuel gave her a tired smile. "To what madness do you refer?"

"All of it. The weapons. The auctions." She took a deep breath. "Shooting at Gray."

He gave her a questioning look.

"At the docks last night."

"It was Gray who spoke to Quimby?"

She nodded.

"And it was you at the docks with him?"

"Yes."

He shook his head. "I could have killed you."

"You could have killed Gray."

"He would have deserved it. He is getting too close. I cannot ignore that anymore."

"You can't kill him. He risked his life for—"

"He did what any other man in his position would have done." Samuel's face clouded. "He tried to rescue a comrade. It doesn't make him a saint."

She made a noise of disgust. "He's going to catch you, Samuel. It's only a matter of time."

"I don't care if I am caught."

"You'll be hung if you are!"

He shrugged. "There are worse fates than to die for something I believe in."

"You pigheaded fool."

"Why? Because I am willing to give my life for a cause?" He grabbed her by the shoulders. "And what about you, Maris? You are a hypocrite. You go against the Crown, against everything you believe in to 'save' me. A man who has no need, no desire, to be saved. Leave me be, Maris."

She touched his cheek. She wanted to heal the pain in his eyes, though she knew she could not. She doubted anyone could. His course had been set a long time ago.

"You are right," she said. "I have gone against everything I believe in, because I love you. But I won't cover up for you anymore, Samuel. I cannot."

He released her from his grasp. "Congratulations. You are finally becoming a woman of your convictions."

"I always have been. I believe in England. But I believed in you, more."

She went to him and put a hand on his shoulder. He flinched, but did not shrug it away.

"I know about the guns, Samuel. I know where they are, and how you plan to ship them. I am going to inform Lord North. It is my duty as an agent for the Anti-British Activity Committee."

He smiled and shook his head. "You won't do it."

"As you said, I am becoming a woman of my convictions." She let her hand fall from his shoulder. "Forget about the weapons. Leave for Philadelphia tomorrow, or you *will* pay the price."

He turned to face her. "Now you are asking me to go against everything *I* believe in."

They stood looking at each other for a long time, locked in a silent battle of wills.

"Please be careful," she said.

She walked out, not knowing if he'd heed her advice, or if she'd ever see him alive again.

Chapter 18

"How are Father and Mother faring at Lockwell Hall?" Ethan asked.

Freddie pulled a face. "Bored to death. You know how Father always adored hawking there. But now that the mews are closed and Randolph is building the mine, they've nothing to do but sit around and stare at one another. Aunt Charity's honed her tongue to a finely sharpened instrument of torture."

"I can only imagine." Ethan was grateful he wasn't the one confined to Lockwell Hall, waiting for Hollister to come out of hiding.

"It's funny, though. I really do think she and Father are mending their fences. They're like two vultures circling the same carcass, ready to do battle. They seem to enjoy it." Freddie scanned the faces the Mayhews' soiree. "Where is Maris, these days?"

Ethan shrugged. "I couldn't say."

The truth was, he'd sent her a note apologizing for his heavy-handedness, but had received no reply.

His sister's eyes narrowed. "What did you do? What did you say to her?"

"Why do you assume I did something to her?"

"Because you did, didn't you?"

He thought about the night before, when he'd scolded Maris for going to the Green Dragon. He realized it was only one of many times he'd called her abilities as an agent into question, or insulted her by treating her like a child.

"Honestly, Ethan," Freddie scolded. "If you muddle this one up, I shall never forgive you. You two are perfect for one another. You both have so many of the same . . . interests." She gave him a pointed look.

He raised his eyebrows. "What *interests* are you talking about?"

Freddie put her hands on her hips. "You'll never find another like her. If you don't marry her, I'm afraid you will end up a bitter old man, and I shall never invite you to supper."

The hapless Lord Staunton appeared at Freddie's side, a look of adoration plain on his face. He handed her a cup of syllabub. "Here you are, Lady Frederica."

To Ethan he said, "I am grateful your sister agreed to let me steal her away from the duchess for the evening."

"Yes, Freddie's company is always so enjoyable," Ethan replied dryly.

Freddie accepted the glass of sweetened wine from Staunton and smiled up at him, fluttering her eyelashes in an effort obviously designed to kill him with elation. Staunton turned purple.

Ethan wondered if Freddie had heard anything from her Captain Blackwood, or if she'd finally accepted the fact that he was simply not meant for her.

She could do far worse than Staunton. It was clear the man would turn himself inside out to make her happy, and she deserved a suitor like that. But Ethan wondered if

Staunton truly had the stomach for it. It would take persistence, and a thick skin, for sure. Ethan imagined that loving Freddie would be a bit like walking into a swarm of bees.

Ethan gave his sister a clandestine smile of approval, and moved away to leave her alone with her new beau.

As he waited for Lord Popper to arrive, he thought about what Freddie had said about his marrying Maris Winter. He poked at the idea like a sore tooth. He didn't want to think about it, but he couldn't help it.

There was no doubt Maris was an excellent partner, as well as an attentive lover. But a wife?

He laughed the thought away. He was not the marrying type. Nor, he suspected, was she. He enjoyed his freedom, and suspected that she did, too.

A stunning woman across the room caught his eye, and smiled coyly at him from behind her fan. As she leaned over to speak to a friend seated beside her, she gave him an excellent view of her bosom, which threatened to spill from her bodice at the slightest provocation.

The show failed to arouse a shred of interest in him. His thoughts drifted instead to Maris and the severe necklines she favored. The ones that had at first annoyed him, then driven him crazy with the desire to discover what was beneath them.

He recalled her prudish expressions and chastising looks, and how her feet were constantly bare beneath her gowns. Her perfectly lovely feet.

Could there possibly be a more contrary woman in England?

A voice roused him from his daydreams.

"Pardon, Mr. Gray. Your presence is requested in the foyer."

Ethan followed the Mayhews' footman to the front door. Lord Popper stood just inside it, draped in a floor-length black cape, which Ethan thought a bit excessive for the weather.

"May I take your cape, sir?" the servant asked. Lord Popper pulled the corners of the garment together, his eyes bugging with nervous energy.

"Never mind," Ethan told the footman. "Lord Popper won't be staying."

The servant bowed, and shuffled out of the narrow foyer.

"Do you have it?" Ethan asked.

Lord Popper's gaze darted about, making certain there was no one about to witness his appalling breach of discretion. He opened the cape, producing a sheaf of folded papers.

"This is all I've got. The current Baron Wetherly has held his title, and the previous Baron Wetherly's financial accounts, for only sixteen months."

"He's the son of the last baron?"

"No. A distant relative, I believe. From Philadelphia, no less."

Ethan perused the papers at a leisurely pace, not wishing to reveal his excitement to Lord Popper. "Do you handle all of the baronecy's finances?"

"No. Although, the maintenance of Battenborough Hall is paid from one of his private accounts that I manage, and he draws drafts for some rather large purchases on it as well."

"What sort of purchases?"

Lord Popper was silent.

Ethan looked up at him, and raised his eyebrows.

The barrister gave a resigned sighed. "Guns. Large numbers of them."

Ethan fought to keep his face impassive. "Why does he purchase so many weapons?"

"He sends them to Africa, I believe. Apparently he is in partnership with a gun merchant there, who pays him his cut from an account maintained in France."

"Is that legal?"

Lord Popper looked injured. "I wouldn't be a party to it if it weren't. He's perfectly within his rights."

Ethan nodded. "In any case, Wetherly's finances don't interest my lady friend. She is not after his money. She would be happy just to know where she might find him. To tell him about the child, of course."

"That could prove tricky," Lord Popper said, eyeing the papers in Ethan's hand as if he were mistreating a baby. "From handling his accounts, it would seem Wetherly spends quite a bit of time in London, but I haven't a clue where he stays. I've tried to locate him several times, with no success. Though his estate is but a few miles outside of town, he never makes use of it."

"Hmm." Ethan flipped through the papers. There, on the last page, was the man's signature.

Ethan's mouth went dry. His nemesis finally had a name.

Samuel J. Pardee.

He indicated one of the cancelled bank drafts paid to the gunsmith. "May I keep one of these?"

Lord Popper's eyes bugged. "Keep it? Whatever for?"

"Perhaps my friend can trace him through someone at the bank, or the gun quarter in Birmingham. It would help if she had proof she actually knew the man."

Lord Popper shook his head. "This is all terribly, *terribly* improper."

"I understand. But please, Lord Popper, think of the child."

After a long pause, the barrister said, "You must return it to me as soon as possible. If it were made known that I'd done something like this, my reputation would suffer sorely."

"Of course, of course. I will handle it with the utmost care and discretion, I promise you."

Lord Popper seemed slightly mollified. He tucked the rest of the papers beneath his cape. Ethan bid him farewell at the door, before returning to the party in the salon.

His mind raced. He was getting close. So close he could taste the victory. But instead of celebrating, he thought of Maris, and how pleasant it would be to share this triumph with her.

Across the room, the woman with the ample bosom flirted, her rouged lips puckered in a sensual pout. And that's when he knew, with all certainty, that Freddie was right.

If he didn't marry Maris Winter, he would end up a bitter old man.

Baliforte rested in the mellow sunlight, a grand dame sunning herself on a warm spring day. And much like a grande dame, she'd begun to sag in the middle, her beauty now resting less in her appearance than in her character.

Maris's father had loved this place, and Maris wished it wasn't falling to wrack and ruin. If only Olivia, her mother, wasn't so stubborn. It would make all of their lives so much easier, Maris thought, as she swept the leaves from the crumbling terrace that overlooked the shrinking formal garden in the rear.

These days, all of them had to lend a hand to maintain the estate, and she was no exception. But she did not mind this, sweeping in the sunlight. It gave her a chance to enjoy the warm spring air while she thought about things.

Her present dilemma had kept her awake the whole of last night.

How could she betray Samuel? How could she inform Lord North of the weapons shipment, knowing she might put Samuel's life in jeopardy? If Samuel ignored her warning and failed to remove himself from the course of action, he *would* be caught. And if caught, he would hang.

That was something that would be on her conscience—and in her heart—forever.

She'd spent most of the night composing a letter to Lord North, outlining where he might find the weapons, and how they were going to be shipped. She'd kept Samuel's name out of everything, of course. There was still hope he'd come to his senses and get out of this mess with his life intact.

Then she'd written a long letter to Ethan, trying to explain herself without actually telling him anything. In the end, she'd torn it up.

She hadn't sent the letter to Lord North yet, either. Perhaps she should rethink things. Maybe she could find the weapons and somehow dispose of them herself . . .

No.

She'd spent the past two years protecting Samuel, putting her own life on the line to save his. She'd warned him. If he chose to ignore her now, it was his own damned fault, she thought, stabbing the broom at a stubborn leaf, chasing it from the terrace.

Maris leaned on the broom and looked out over the sloping yards of Baliforte. She was tired. So tired. And not just from the lack of sleep the night before.

She was tired of trying to hold her family together, and her home, and even herself. She was tired of being strong.

She was tired of being the Raven.

To have someone to hold her, protect her—like Ethan had, just for a night. Most women took such things for granted, but she'd never had it. With an oft-absent father, a mother who cared for no one save herself, and a grandfather who'd been gradually fading away for a dozen years, Maris's life at Baliforte had been painfully lonely. Only Ajala had made it all bearable.

And that hadn't lasted long enough.

Her eyes filled with tears as she finished up the sweeping.

She was just about to fetch the watering can when the tattoo of horses' hooves echoed on the front drive.

Who could that be? They weren't expecting company. They never were.

Maris dropped the broom and stuffed her apron beneath one of the bushes beside the terrace, smoothing the wrinkles from her faded apricot gown. She rounded the house on a crooked little path, arriving at the main door in time to see Ethan dismount from a stunning white mare.

She began to run to him, but the wary look in his eye stopped her. She suddenly regretted the way she'd left him the other night, sneaking off in the dark without so much as a goodbye.

"Ethan, what a surprise. What brings you to Baliforte?"

He came to her, and stood close, just an arm's length away. She hoped for a moment he would kiss her, but he didn't.

"I wanted to apologize. In the flesh, this time. No letter."

"Apologize?"

"For the way I spoke to you. I treated you as if you were a child, when I know you are capable of handling yourself. I never should have taken issue with your visiting the Green Dragon.

Her throat tightened with emotion. "Thank you."

His expression grew even more serious. "I also came because I need to speak with you about something important. Is there somewhere we might go? Somewhere private. This is not a conversation to be had on the drive."

"Of course. How rude of me." She buried her suddenly shaking hands in her skirts. "I'm afraid our stable master is . . . ill today. But if you take your horse to the stables, one of the boys there will care for it. I will wait for you inside."

She ran up the wide steps and through the door, pressing a fist into her stomach to keep it from somersaulting. Had he somehow found out about Samuel? What did he know? It was obvious he hadn't simply come for a visit.

Then it struck her.

Perhaps he wished to discuss what had happened between them. She knew it was a mistake. Behavior unbecoming of two people who had to work so closely together.

They'd simply been caught up in the moment. But she didn't regret it. She never would.

She knew she would never have the Wolf 's heart, but at least she would have that night.

Suddenly remembering that she still wore her working gown, she dashed up the stairs to change before Gray returned to the house.

Though he knocked several times, no one answered the door. Where was the housekeeper? Where were the other servants?

It occurred to Ethan that he'd seen no footmen, no maids, while he and his aunt had been there the last time. Just the Indian woman. Was it possible she was the only house servant they had?

He opened the door and called out. When no one replied, he entered the house, and began to think it very possible, indeed. The place was tomb-quiet.

Gavin Winter had been a wealthy man. Between his service to the Crown, his work with the East India Company, and his well-placed investments, he should have been able to afford a houseful of servants. Surely, he had left a small fortune for his family.

"Maris?" His query echoed off the walls of the foyer.

"Mr. Gray. You've come back."

Olivia Winter appeared from nowhere, drifting toward him as silent as fog over water. Her dark-gray gown reminded him of Maris's predilection for somber colors. He supposed living in such melancholy surroundings had affected her tastes.

"Good afternoon, Mrs. Winter. I am sorry to have let myself in, but there seemed to be no one else about."

"Mother has given some of the house staff a free afternoon." Maris descended the staircase at the back of the hall.

"Very decent of you, Mrs. Winter."

Olivia shrugged her thin shoulders. "Excuse me. I am off to the conservatory."

"Of course, Mother."

Maris waited until Olivia had gone before she turned to Ethan. "If you'd like, we can take a walk. There won't be anyone about outside. It will afford us more privacy."

"Very well."

Maris rang for the housekeeper, and requested a luncheon be packed for Ethan and her to take with them.

At first the air between them was tense. Ethan imagined Maris regretted that she'd let her guard down with him. But after a few minutes they began to relax a bit in each other's company, chatting at length about the paintings hanging in the hall until the housekeeper returned with their provisions.

Maris handed him the basket and led him to the door. "Shall we?"

Outside, they followed a narrow path around the side of the house to a lovely stone terrace. A broom stood against the marble railing. Something white lay crumpled beneath one of the bushes.

"What is this?" he said, picking it up.

She threw it aside and tugged him toward the lawn. "Never mind. One of the maids must have left her apron behind."

They trod a wide grass lane, through a labyrinth of boxwood shrubs in dire need of pruning, until they reached a grove of blooming rhododendron trees. There, amongst the dark green foliage and pink blossoms, a path spiraled down to a little pond edged with water violets. Bluebells and the white blooms of wood sorrel blanketed the opposite bank, creating a spectacle of color on the water. The beauty of the place was overwhelming, the air thick with the scents of the different flora. Spicy, musky, sweet.

"My favorite place," Maris said, gathering her skirts beneath her and sitting on the grass. "I come here every day, even when it rains."

Ethan found it difficult to connect her with this place, which seemed so contrary to her serious nature.

His thoughts must have shown on his face, for she laughed. "Come now. You don't think me so cold and rigid that I cannot appreciate something beautiful?"

He sat down beside her. "I'm sorry I ever said such things about you."

She kicked off her shoes. "You weren't so terribly off the mark. I *am* rather cold at times, I admit it."

"You are practical, and resourceful, and responsible."

She took up a fallen rhododendron petal and twirled it in her fingers. "How awfully dull I must be."

"You're hardly that." He plucked the petal from her hand, taking it in his. "Why did you leave me the way you did?"

Her face clouded. "We shouldn't have done what we did, I know. But I do not regret it."

He took her chin in his hand and turned her to face him. "I don't regret it, either." He sighed. "Perhaps it wasn't the wisest thing to do. But I care for you, Maris. A great deal. And I want to ask a favor of you."

"A favor?"

"Yes. I need your help with something. An investigation."

He could see the wariness in her eyes. "What investigation?"

"General Gage found a cache of weapons in Concord last April, which had been hidden there by the colonial rebels. Some of the guns he found had come from a shipment that originated in London. An illegal shipment. Since then there have been at least two more. Hundreds of weapons. I've been working for months to find out who is responsible, but I haven't been able to break the case. Will you help me?"

Maris's heart skipped a beat. Ethan was asking for her help. He was confiding in her about the weapons investigation. The very thing she'd been hoping for all along.

But this was far from the victory she'd imagined when this all began. Instead, she was trapped between Ethan and Samuel now, having to choose which of the two she must betray.

"I've been using this mission to prove my worth. To prove to my men—and my father—that the Wolf still has fangs. I wanted to do this on my own."

"Then you should."

He shook his head. "I know you must think it odd, my asking for your help. Especially after the way I've treated you. I've shown you no respect."

"Ethan—"

"I trust you, Maris. You are the most proficient agent I've ever known."

She knew how difficult it must have been for him to ask for help. She knew how it tormented him to think that he'd lost the respect of his men. It was the highest praise he could give her.

"I don't know what to say. I . . . thank you. But I cannot—"

"Please, Maris." He pushed up onto his knees and turned to face her, taking one of her hands. "Don't let the things I've done and said in the past keep you from agreeing to work with me. I need you."

Her throat closed with emotion. She never imagined she could feel so deeply for a man. For *this* man. She'd set out to trap the Wolf, and he'd trapped her, instead.

He touched her cheek. The scent of the rhododendron he'd crushed between them lingered on his fingertips. She pressed the palm of his hand to her lips, closing her eyes, breathing deep.

She couldn't bear to look at him. "Ethan, I cannot work with you on this."

He cupped her face in both hands and drew her closer, his eyes searching. "Why?"

She tried to look away but he wouldn't allow it. He kissed her, slow and deep.

She could taste the apology on his lips. His regret for misjudging her. It hurt so badly, she wanted to cry. She'd betrayed him, time and again. Put him in danger. He'd risked his life to try and save her father, and she repaid him with a Judas kiss.

When he drew away, she said, "You don't understand."

"I do understand," he murmured. "I hurt you. I insulted you when I implied that you weren't good enough to stand beside me. But I was wrong. I want— Nay, I *need* you by my side."

She couldn't breathe.

Ethan lay back on the grass, bringing her with him. "I need you, and I love you, Maris."

His words hung on the air like the sweet scent of the flowers. She wanted to tell him she loved him, too. That she'd never loved anyone so deeply in all her life. But her feelings were so open, so raw, she found could not bear to say it.

His smile faded. "Perhaps I was mistaken. I thought you might return my regard for you. Freddie seemed to think—"

He stopped himself. "Never mind. I'm sorry if I offended you."

She saw the pain flicker behind his eyes before he turned away.

"Offend me?" She touched his hand. "I could not feel more honored. But I am not worthy of you, Ethan."

"Don't." He pressed a finger to her lips. "Don't say that. We fit together so completely. So perfectly."

Confess. *Confess*, her mind whispered, but her mouth refused to form the words. If she told him now what she had done, he would hate her forever.

She busied herself spreading the picnic cloth out between them, and then the food—a feast of honeyed nuts, dried fruit, bread, and preserves. The activity eased the strain. As they ate, they listened to the music of the birds and the trickling of water in the springs that fed the pond. More than once she caught him watching her, and her stomach fluttered at the hunger she saw in his eyes.

When they finished, Ethan cupped his hands to collect water from one of the springs nearby, offering it to her to drink.

She held his hands in hers, and brought them to her lips. Drops of cool water trickled down her wrists and escaped into the sleeves of her gown. When his hands were empty, she licked the water from his fingertips.

He groaned, and buried his hands into the hair at her temples, capturing her in a wild kiss. His lips were cool and sweet with the water from the stream. She tugged his lower lip between her teeth, coaxing a noise from deep in his throat. And then, his hands were everywhere, touching, teasing, heating her skin.

She knew she should stop him, but, the devil help her, she didn't want to. Just one last time, she wanted him. Even if she could not tell him how she felt, she could show him.

Afterward, she would give him the letter that had been

meant for Lord North. It was his investigation, after all. And he could use the information to prove to Lord North, and his father, and his men, that he hadn't lost his edge.

Then, she would resign her post with the committee.

Samuel had been right when he'd said she was a hypocrite. If she wasn't, she would have led Ethan straight to Samuel. Perhaps she would leave England altogether, Baliforte and her mother and Samuel be damned. She could begin a new life, with no one to worry about but herself.

She looked into Ethan's eyes. An image of him, bathed in firelight, came into her mind. Her heart shattered. She would never know another man like him, should she live to be a hundred.

"I need you, Maris," he said. And she knew that he wasn't talking about the investigation.

She kissed him, taking everything she could from the kiss, hoping it would be enough before it all had to end. He removed the pins from her hair and unbound it, sifting it through his fingers until it fanned about them, catching up rhododendron petals.

He buried his face in her hair. "No one has meant anything, until you. I don't know what I would do without you."

"Oh, Ethan." His name caught in her throat.

He rolled onto his back, bringing her with him. She straddled his hips, pressing against his arousal. His hands roamed her body, touching her breasts, encircling her waist, cupping her hips and bottom. Her skirts rode up to her waist, leaving her legs bare, and he stroked them with his palms.

He raised her up, moving his hand between them, circling the soft bud of flesh there until she cried out. She tore at the buttons of his breeches until she'd freed him, drawing him into her until it seemed as if they were a single person.

They moved together and apart, stirring heat like a gathering storm. Ethan held her hips, driving into her until the thunderheads erupted, releasing the rain. Her climax ripped through her like lightning, setting every nerve on fire.

She shuddered and cried his name, clutching his hips with her thighs. Never had a man filled her so completely, in every way. Never had she wanted to know such intimacy, or allow this possession by another person.

Ethan groaned beneath her, the sound rolling over her like thunder. She collapsed on his chest, panting, and he gathered her close, stroking her back and winding his fingers into her hair.

"I love you, Maris," he murmured.

She wanted to say it. Her heart ached to say it, but she could not.

He kissed the top of her head gently, as if he forgave her for not repeating his words. He did it for her.

"I love you," he said again.

CHAPTER 19

Ethan awoke to shouting coming from the direction of the house.

He lay curled around Maris's body, the two of them lying atop the picnic blanket. The sun had settled amidst the trees, and he estimated it was close to tea time.

He shook Maris awake, helping her to straighten her gown before donning his own shirt and jacket.

They ran up the path to the terrace, where Riya stood with Lord North's courier. The man seemed vastly relieved to see them.

"Thank you, Riya. You may go," Maris said. The housekeeper stared with narrowed eyes at Maris's hair, which, Ethan realized, was loose and full of rhododendron petals. She hurried away, the bangles on her wrists and ankles jingling softly.

Maris turned to the courier. "What is it?"

The young man turned over the correspondence he'd been dispatched to deliver. She quickly broke the seal and scanned the message.

The courier said, "Mr. Gray, I did not realize you would be here, as well. I left a letter for you with your valet. Lord North was quite determined to contact you, as well as Miss Winter."

Ethan thanked the young man, and dismissed him.

"What does it say?" he asked Maris, pointing to the letter.

"It's from your father. Hollister has finally shown his face. He has the duchess locked in her quarters. A shot has been fired. Your father doesn't know if she's alive or not." She handed him the missive.

Maris shouted for Riya, who bustled out in moments, as if she'd never gone far from the door.

"Tell Mother and Grandfather there is an emergency. I will return as soon as I can."

Maris drew up her skirts and flew to the stables, with Ethan only steps behind. They saddled their horses in silence, and in minutes they were on the road, headed for Lockwell Hall, Maris once again cursing her decision to sell their best mount.

"I cannot believe this has come to pass on my watch." Lord Maldwyn sat on the edge of a bench in the third-floor hallway of Lockwell Hall, his face buried in his hands. Lady Maldwyn hovered over him, touching his shoulder, stroking his hair.

For the first time, Ethan noticed the white that once streaked his father's temples had now proliferated to cover the better part of his head, and his shoulders, which had always seemed strong enough to hold the world, had fallen just a bit.

"What happened?" Ethan asked quietly.

Maldwyn raised his head to look at his son. "It was my fault. I left her alone. Unguarded. She'd been arguing with me all morning, picking at old wounds. Making my blood boil. I went for some air, and when I returned—" He pointed to Charity's room. "When I returned, Hollister was in there."

Ethan rattled the door knob. It turned, but the door wouldn't open. "He's barricaded them in."

"There's already been one shot fired. She may be dead, for all we know."

"What does he want?"

"I'm not certain. He's been ranting about some box. He's convinced Charity's got it."

"Where is Randolph?"

"He's taken some men to search the house, from top to bottom."

Ethan looked at Maris. "Did my aunt mention anything about this box to you?"

"I'm afraid not."

Ethan rubbed the back of his neck.

Maldwyn's head sank lower in his hands. "I am too old to be trusted with her protection. I failed."

Ethan laid a hand on his shoulder. "You made a mistake, Father. No one is perfect."

The two men exchanged a glance. Ethan could have sworn he'd seen forgiveness in his father's eyes, but he didn't dare to hope. In any case, there was no time now to explore it further. They had to get to the duchess.

Ethan tapped on the door to his aunt's chambers. "Hollister?"

A bump and a curse behind the door, and then he answered. His voice sounded shrill, even through the muffling thickness of the wood. "Who's there?"

"Ethan Gray. I wish to speak to my aunt."

A laugh. "I am afraid she's unavailable at the moment."

"I want to speak with her. Now. You'll not get a damned thing from us until I know she's safe."

"No. *You* will not get a damned thing from *me* until I get my box. She told me—she promised me—I could have it. My life isn't worth a fart in the wind without it."

"How can you be sure the duchess knows where it is?"

"Because I had it here, in this room, the last time I saw her. Unfortunately, I had to make a hasty retreat, and I forgot it on the way out. She *told* me to come for it, sent me a note, and now she refuses to tell me where it is. Bloody *bitch*."

Hollister's ranting made no sense. Aunt Charity asked him to come for the box and then wouldn't tell him where it was?

"Good god." All color drained from his father's face.

"What?" Ethan said. "What is it?"

"She said she was going to kill him. I told her she wouldn't be rid of me until Hollister was dead, and she said she would just have to kill him."

Ethan looked over his shoulder at Maris. Her eyes held the concern he felt.

"She's a bloody fool," his father said.

"Maldwyn! Do not speak of your sister that way," Felicity scolded.

"Hollister tried to strangle her once. She knows what he's capable of," said Ethan. "She's playing with fire."

"I will kill her," Hollister yelled. "*I will*. Do you hear me, Charity? I will cut your throat!"

Beyond the door, there was silence once again. Minutes ticked away on a standing clock at the end of the hall. Still no sound from within.

"Perhaps she is doing the best thing," said Maris. "If she gives Hollister what he wants, he'll most likely kill her anyway."

"If she isn't already dead." Maldwyn spoke it aloud. The thought they'd all had, but no one could voice.

"What if I try to go in through the window?" Ethan said.

Maldwyn shook his head. "It's three stories off the ground. How will you get to it without Hollister seeing you?"

"We could wait until tonight, when it's dark."

"It might be too late by then."

Ethan paced in front of the door, scattering the fringes of the carpet there. "If we cannot get in, we've got to find the box. It's bound to be here, somewhere. Why else would Hollister have been so determined to get into Lockwell Hall?"

"We've already done that, twice," Felicity said. "Every servant was enlisted, and we turned the place on its ear. Even Randolph helped."

"What about the stables, or other outlying buildings? What was the cottage we passed on our way here?" Maris asked.

Ethan shook his head. "The falconer's cottage. It's been closed since my cousin . . . Since he was killed."

"Canby?"

"Yes. Besides, how would the box get there? As far as I know, my aunt has never set foot there her entire life."

Something the duchess had said came back to Maris in a rush. "Are you certain?"

"Certain of what?"

"That she's never set foot there."

Ethan shook his head. "She couldn't stand anything having to do with falconry. After my cousin died and the falconer's daughter left the estate, she ordered the cottage closed for good. Why?"

"When we were at the wedding, she passed a remark. I didn't think much of it at the time, but now . . ."

"What did she say?"

"She said her son found a home without her, elsewhere.

That there were a lot of secrets hidden there. Secrets that will never be discovered."

"He found a home without her?" Ethan ran the words through his mind.

"It's worth a try."

"This place will soon be torn down to make way for Randolph's coal mine," Ethan said as they negotiated a stone pathway strewn with leaves and debris. The door to the falconer's cottage gave way easily beneath the weight of his shoulder.

Inside, it looked as if the residents had gone out for a walk and never returned.

A cup and plate sat beside a washing basin on the cupboard. A falconer's bag hung on a peg beside the door. Half a dozen leather-cutting tools were lined up on a low workbench, between the miniature kitchen and a small sitting room. A thick coat of dust cloaked everything, muting the colors to dreamlike quality.

"Canby all but lived here when he was a child," Ethan said. "He and the falconer's daughter spent all of their time together."

"Selena?"

Ethan nodded.

The story of Canby's "return from the dead" the year before had been on everyone's lips, and some version of the tale had been printed in every newssheet in England. The Duke of Canby had reappeared just in time to save his love, Lockwell Hall's falconer Selena Hewitt, from hanging for his murder.

His subsequent romance with the woman the papers described as "a regal, raven-haired beauty" was the stuff of fairy tales, and his death a few months later, tragic.

"What happened to her?" Maris asked.

Ethan's voice turned wistful. "After Canby died, she disappeared. I like to imagine she found a happy life, somewhere."

Maris's throat grew tight. Soon, she would lose the man she loved, too. Her heart went out to Selena Hewitt, wherever she was.

"Shall we check the kitchen first?" he asked.

An hour later, after turning the house on its ear, they still hadn't found the box. Ethan sank to the floor, and Maris followed. They sat cross-legged in the middle of the mess they'd made.

"I really thought it would be here," Ethan said.

"I'm sorry." Maris touched his sleeve. "Perhaps I didn't remember your aunt's words correctly."

"Tell me again what she said, as well as you can remember it."

Maris closed her eyes, thinking back to the grand gallery in Kent, where she and the duchess had spoken about Canby. "She said her son found a home without her, elsewhere. There are secrets hidden there. Secrets that will never be discovered now."

"A home without her?"

"Yes, I believe that is what she said."

Ethan scrambled to his feet and grabbed her by the hand, dragging her out the door. They went in the opposite direction of Lockwell Hall, into the woods.

Trees and brush had begun to reclaim the narrow path, making passage difficult. Maris and Ethan pushed their way through to a large, open area ringed with logs.

"The weathering area for the birds," Ethan said, in explanation. "The mews are this way."

The long, narrow building had seen better days. Moss spotted the roof, and a clematis vine climbed one side, heavy with large, white flowers.

"Be careful," Ethan said, taking her hand and guiding her over a loose board on the step.

The sounds of the forest followed them into the mews, and when they pushed open the door, muffled scuffling and scratching told them they were not alone. But in the four small enclosures that once held magnificent birds of prey, the perches stood empty.

Maris glanced about, trying to imagine the former duke and the tall, dark-haired falconer at work with her birds, their heads bent together over a newly hatched hawk, or an injured falcon.

"I suppose Canby would have considered this home, even more so than the falconer's cottage. He practically lived here."

She nodded.

"Where shall we start?" he asked.

She pointed to a small tack room. "In there."

They left the door open for the light and fresh air it afforded. Dust motes and mottled down feathers swirled about them as they searched. They worked until sweat soaked their clothes, lifting loose boards, digging in the sand pits beneath the perches. Exhausted and dirty, they ended their quest in the last of the enclosures. They had found no box, just a lot of dust and animal droppings.

"Damn." Ethan wiped his hands on his breeches. "Let's go back to the house. Perhaps by some miracle one of the servants has found it."

"And if they haven't?"

Ethan looked grim. "Then I'm afraid there isn't much hope for my aunt."

Maris followed him out of the mews, snagging the leather door handle to pull the door shut. Before it closed, through the crack between the frame and the door she spied a falconer's glove, hung on a nail. They hadn't seen it with the door open. She went back into the mews and closed the door, removing the glove from the nail.

Aside from a coating of dust, the glove looked almost new. She thought it mustn't have been used much, if at all. A set of initials was burned into it—*JM*. John Markley, the Duke of Canby. Maris traced the initials with her fingertip.

She unhooked the glove from the nail and reached inside. In the bottom, by the fingers, lay something stiff and smooth.

Reaching deep, she fished out a small wooden box no longer than her hand, and maybe twice as thick. There was no lock, but nevertheless she was unable to open it.

She dashed from the mews, running to catch up with Ethan on the path.

"It's locked," Lord Maldwyn said, examining the box from every possible angle. "But how? Where is the key? The lock?"

"We should break into it," Ethan said, as his father passed it over to him.

"We haven't got much time," Maris said. "The sooner we get the box to Hollister, the sooner we can get Her Grace out of that room. Besides, if he sees that it has been tampered with, he might kill the duchess after all."

Ethan examined the box again. Maris knew what he was thinking. It might contain something that, under normal circumstances, he would kill for.

He was probably right.

"It's true," Ethan said. "We would endanger Aunt Charity's life if we open it. I will take it to Hollister immediately."

"No, you won't. I will." Lord Maldwyn stood. "It was I who put her in harm's way, and I will get her out. If I must give my life to do it, so be it."

"Husband . . ." Lady Maldwyn touched his shoulder. Her eyes filled with tears.

Maris's quelled an attack of nerves. She could not allow that box to get into the hands of either of these men, if it contained what she suspected. She cleared her throat. "Might I make a suggestion?"

Ethan nodded.

"Let me go in."

Lord Maldwyn immediately dismissed the idea. "Absolutely not. I'll not put another woman in danger."

But Ethan was quiet.

Maris looked him in the eye, her expression carefully neutral. She suspected that beneath all of the maneuverings, Lord Maldwyn was testing Ethan yet again. She waited for him to refuse her.

"Let me go in," she repeated.

"How?" Ethan ignored his father's look of disapproval.

"Hollister has never seen me. He wouldn't know me from the maid."

"True," Ethan said, waiting. But Maris said no more, and soon her meaning struck him.

"Use the 'maid' to deliver the box," he said.

She nodded.

Lord Maldwyn raised his head. "You'll only succeed in putting yourself in the hands of a madman, young lady." Lady Maldwyn gave him a stern look. She seemed to understand that this was between Ethan and Maris, alone.

Maris stood, silent and still, leaving everything in the hands of the man who had been her gallant, her enemy, her partner and her lover.

"Hollister *is* a madman. Do you really want to do this?" Ethan asked her quietly.

"I do."

He kissed her lightly on the forehead. "Then I suppose we should get you ready."

* * *

Maris tucked a stray lock of hair up under the gray mob-cap. She smoothed the apron on the maid's gown she wore with nervous hands, but when she knocked on the door to the duchess's suite, they hardly shook at all.

"What do you want?" Hollister's voice filtered through the heavy door.

"I 'ave the box, sir."

She heard things being moved about, and then Hollister's voice again, closer to the door.

"Where did you get it?"

"From Mr. Gray."

"Describe it to me."

"'Tis small and green, with a pretty gold scrolling across the top—"

"Slide it beneath the door."

"I cannot sir. I'm not to deliver it until I see Her Grace for myself." Her voice quavered, and not completely from playacting.

Swearing from within. And then, "Gray!"

"I am here." Ethan spoke over her shoulder, his voice at once comforting and disconcerting. The faint smell of rhododendron petals lingered on his jacket. She longed to lean back against him. Absorb his strength, his protection. But she was afraid to touch him, for fear she would break into a million tiny pieces.

"Send the box under the door," Hollister repeated.

"I'm afraid not," Ethan said. "You would then have no incentive to spare my aunt's life. That is, in fact, if she is still alive."

"She's alive," Hollister said, "and it has taken every ounce of my will to leave her that way."

"I want a witness to that fact."

"I'm afraid not," Hollister mimicked.

"Then it would seem we've reached an impasse. For you will not receive the box until I know my aunt is alive."

Hollister was quiet for a few minutes. The clock behind them ticked off the moments, growing louder with each.

"Go out on the lawn," Hollister finally shouted. "Beneath the window where I can see you, Gray. You and your father, the butler, the footmen. Everyone. When I see the rest of you, I will open the door to the maid. If there be any attempt to deceive me, any attempt at all, I will gut the both of them."

"Give me ten minutes to gather everyone together."

Ethan gave Maris an encouraging look, and squeezed her hand. Then he and the others disappeared down the servants' stairs.

Maris took a deep breath and closed her eyes. She rubbed her hands on her skirts, feeling naked without the knife and tiny, pearl-handled pistol she carried everywhere. She and Ethan had debated whether or not she should carry it, but in the end decided she shouldn't, in case Hollister searched her when she entered the room.

She opened her eyes and glanced at the clock in the hall. Ten minutes had passed. She knocked again on the door.

After much thumping and dragging, the door latch clicked. The barrel of a hunting rifle eased through the crack in the doorjamb, aimed directly at her face.

"Please sir," Maris whined. "Please don't shoot me."

A hand reached out beneath the rifle and grabbed her arm. Hollister dragged her into the room, the weapon still pointed at her head.

Her first look at him was shocking. She'd heard that Hollister had been something of a rake, a handsome bounder, but there was no evidence of that anymore.

He was gaunt and pale, the skin of his face drawn tight and shiny, like the skin of a smoked pig. Yellow sores covered his neck and hands—the signs of a syphilitic in his final stages. A red stain spread over his left arm.

"Do you have the box?" He shoved the gun barrel against her nose.

"N-no, sir. Mr. Gray has it. He says he won't give it over until I bring word that the duchess is well."

"Piss."

He pushed Maris up against the door. Her heart banged against her ribs. She willed herself to stand still as a pock-marked hand groped her bosom, her waist, her skirts, touching her intimately, presumably in a search for weapons.

When he concluded his assault, he shoved her toward the bedchamber. "Go on, then. See for yourself."

Hollister locked the door as Maris inched into the suite of rooms. The duchess was indeed alive, gagged and bound to a chair shaped like a giant golden swan, her little white dog whimpering on her lap.

Her face was so bruised and swollen that Maris would not have recognized her save for the emerald brooch she always wore. Blood caked her hands and smeared the front of her jade-green silk gown. The right sleeve had been almost completely torn away.

"Oh, Yer Grace. Are ye hurt?" Maris fell to her knees beside the chair. Charity's eyes grew large, and she blinked furiously.

Maris gave an almost imperceptible nod.

"As you can see, the old bitch is alive," Hollister said, poking the dog with the butt of the rifle until it yipped with pain.

Tears streamed from the duchess's swollen eyes.

Hollister shifted the gun beneath his other arm and wiped the sweat from his palms. "I want my box."

"I am to tell Mr. Gray, through the window. He said he'd put it under the door when I do."

Hollister went to the window overlooking the rear lawn. He unhooked the latch, and pushed it open. Then he grabbed Maris by the collar and dragged her to it, pushing her head outside. Maris saw Ethan and his parents, along with a dozen household servants, milling about on the lawn. She signaled to Ethan.

"I want my box," Hollister shouted over her shoulder. Apparently, he was using her as a shield should anyone decide to take a shot at him.

On the lawn, Ethan waved the box in his hand and headed for the house.

Several long minutes later, he slid the box beneath the door.

"Get it," Hollister demanded. "And if you touch that doorknob, I'll put a lead ball between your tits."

Maris retrieved the box and scurried back to Hollister. Her hand shook as she handed it to him.

"Over there." He waved the rifle in the direction of the duchess. Maris ran over to the chair, huddling beneath the wing of the gold swan. She gave the duchess's hand a gentle squeeze, wishing she could undo the ropes around her wrists. She looked up into her eyes. They were dull. Resigned. The eyes of a woman who knew, without a doubt, she was dead.

Maris looked away. She would not think about what would happen if she failed.

She focused on Hollister. What was his weakness? He was tall, but not muscular. All that had been wasted away by his illness. She imagined that seven months of hiding had taken a toll on him, as well. Still, she didn't dare assume he'd lost his strength. Desperate souls fought with desperate strength.

On top of his desperation, he was clearly mad. The condition was divulged in his wild, red-rimmed eyes, and in the facial tic that caused an unrelenting twitch above his lip. She knew from experience, however, that insane did not mean foolish.

He was also, she surmised, quite a dandy. He'd taken

the time to comb his thinning blond hair and pull it back into a neat ponytail at the nape of his neck. Despite the torn and dirty lace sleeves, his fingernails were clipped, and his face clean-shaven. Not the grooming habits one would expect from a desperate criminal.

Hollister played with the box, turning it this way and that before sliding a small dowel from the back of it. The lid sprung open, revealing a row of thin cigars. Maris blinked. He'd held the duchess hostage over a box of cigars? Truly, he wasn't that insane.

Was he?

He took up one of the cigars, and held it beneath his nose. An expression of ecstasy washed over his face, and he closed his eyes for a moment.

He replaced the cigar before removing another piece of the box. The bottom dropped open. A small book fell out onto the bed. Hollister giggled like a child. He leafed through the book, which was about the size of a deck of faro cards.

Maris glanced at the duchess, but the older woman's eyes were closed now. Her forehead rested against the long, curving golden neck of the swan, whose head was tucked beneath a wing. Maris prayed she was still alive. She knew had to act soon.

She sat up straight. "Sir?"

Hollister ignored her.

"Sir?" she said again, this time a bit louder.

Hollister tore his attention away from the book, clearly annoyed with her.

"May I leave now, sir?"

The corners of his mouth curled into something she supposed was meant to be a smile. A chill ran up her back.

"You wish to leave?" His eyes crinkled in amusement.

"Aye. Yer finished with me, aren't ye?"

"Not by half, my dear. Not by half."

He tucked the book into his waistcoat and grabbed the rifle, swinging his long legs over the side of the bed. "Stand up."

She rose, gripping the wing of the swan as if to keep herself steady.

"Come here."

She shook her head silently.

He strode over to her and grabbed her by the back of the neck, tossing her to the floor like a dirty shirt. He brought his knee up as she fell, catching her on the cheekbone, sending a shower of stars behind her eyes. She battled a wave of nausea as she lay at Hollister's feet.

Every instinct told her to fight. To bring him down. But it wasn't the right time yet.

She got up onto her knees, wiping a trickle of blood from her lip with the back of her hand. "You've a hole in your coat."

He grabbed her braid and yanked her head back so she was looking up at him. "What did you say?"

"You've a hole," she whimpered. "A hole in yer coat."

He looked at her with a mixture of curiosity and incredulity. "Why would you say that?"

She whimpered. "I dunno. Please don't kill me, sir. I 'ave two babies . . ."

"Shut up."

He stepped back, and examined his coat, poking a finger through the bullet hole. He made a noise of disgust. "That bitch shot me. Lucky for me, it only skinned my arm. But it ruined the jacket." Yanking her to her feet, he said, "Can you fix it?"

She sobbed.

He shook her until her teeth rattled. "I asked if you could fix it."

She cried harder. "Aye. I am handy with a needle, but I haven't got one with me."

"The maid used to keep her things in there." He pointed to a vanity table with three drawers running down one side.

She looked at him in surprise.

Hollister laughed. "At one time, the duchess and I were close . . . *friends*."

Maris searched the vanity, locating a small sewing box in the bottom drawer.

Hollister slipped one arm out of his jacket, and then switched the rifle to the other hand to shed it completely. As he held the jacket out to her, she noticed that he'd lost quite a bit more blood than she'd originally thought. His entire sleeve was soaked from elbow to shoulder.

"Fix it," he said.

She held it away from her, as if it might attack her. "I—I need more light."

He looked toward the windows, but it had already begun to grow dark. Maris wondered if Ethan and Lord and Lady Maldwyn had taken up their posts in the hall again.

"Use the fire," Hollister said.

"May I put another log on?"

He waved a hand in permission.

This was the moment.

She laid Hollister's jacket over the back of a nearby chair and moved the fireplace screen aside, tossing another log on the flames. Poker in hand, she moved the logs about, leaving the hooked metal end of it against a burning log for as long as she dared.

Hollister moved toward her, the sewing box in hand.

She took a deep breath. Then she swung around, landing the glowing poker hook square on Hollister's injured arm. The sewing kit flew from his hand, the contents scattering on the carpet. Then she moved the poker up until the hook of it rested against Hollister's temple. With a sickening sizzle, it wiped the shocked expression from his face and turned it into one of pure agony.

He screamed and swung the rifle about, jamming it into Maris's side. She bucked it away with her hip just before it went off, sending a shot exploding into the carved mantel behind her.

To her right, so far away, she heard the sound of pounding. But she ignored it, focusing with single-minded purpose on the man before her.

Hollister grabbed the hot shaft of the poker, howling as it melted the flesh of his hand. He jerked on it, pulling her up against him.

They danced, locked in combat, across the green and blue carpet of the duchess's bedchamber. The poker was lost. She had no weapon, now, save herself.

He grabbed her neck with his huge hands, squeezing the delicate bones of her throat. Maris suddenly went limp, catching Hollister off balance and pulling him onto the floor with her. Desperation took control, and she drew strength from untapped depths.

She rolled atop him and kneeled on his throat. His face mottled red, then blue; the spot where the poker had burned him turning into an ugly black *J*.

He scratched at her legs, and managed to push her off of him, rolling over onto her, his face just inches from her own. He sat on her chest, the weight of him forcing the air from her lungs, and then he took her by the throat again, staring into her eyes with frightening calm. She knew then that he believed he'd won.

She flailed her arms, groping for something, anything that might save her.

She found it.

Swinging her hand upward, she stabbed the point of the tiny sewing scissors into his neck. Hollister clawed at it, releasing her long enough so she could struggle out from beneath him.

She scrambled to her feet. Before he even had a chance to

move, she drove her knee up under his chin. Hollister's neck snapped back with a *crack*, and he crumpled to the floor.

Behind them the pounding grew fierce, and she realized at last that someone was attempting to break into the room.

The duchess opened one eye. Her lips moved.

Maris went to her, and took her hand. "What is it?"

"The book," the older woman rasped. "Take it. Please. Get rid of it."

Maris nodded her promise, as if it hadn't been her intention to take it all along. She felt a momentary stab of guilt.

Then she quickly searched Hollister's waistcoat and withdrew the book, tucking it into the pocket of her apron just as Ethan burst through the door.

CHAPTER 20

"Maris!"

Ethan started for her and Hollister, but she waved him on to the duchess. "Over there."

He ran to the swan chair where Charity slumped, white as King Henry's ghost. The blood spattered on the front of her gown had dried to a dark crimson.

The dog peeked out from beneath the bed, yipping at him.

"Aunt Charity, can you hear me?" He untied her wrists and ankles, and laid her gently upon the carpet.

Lord Maldwyn arrived moments later. "I've sent for the physician. Is she . . . ?"

"She's breathing," Ethan said. "But she's badly bruised. It looks as if he tried to strangle her again, among other things." He tilted her head to the side, revealing a lattice of ugly purple marks across her neck. Her lower lip had swelled to twice its size.

Lord Maldwyn kneeled beside his sister, his hands clenched into fists in his lap as if he were afraid to touch her.

The duchess opened her eyes. She and Maris shared a long look before her eyes moved to her brother. Maris imagined she saw a look of appreciation and forgiveness pass between the two.

Ethan went over to Hollister's body, and nudged it with his toe. "What happened to his face?"

"I burned it with the poker."

"His neck?"

"Scissors."

"His arm?"

"That is where your aunt shot him, I believe."

"Where is the box?"

She pointed to the bed. The box lay open, the cigars scattered around it. Ethan went over and picked them up.

"This is it?"

She nodded.

"Cigars?"

She nodded again. "I'm afraid he'd gone round the bend. He looked completely mad, Ethan. His eyes . . ." She shuddered.

He came to her and folded her in an embrace. She closed her eyes. Pressing her cheek against his chest, she breathed deep, taking the scent of him into her. She would remember it always, no matter what happened.

As he held her, the little book stuck in her ribs—a reminder of all that lay between them. All that would keep them apart.

"I must go." She pulled away from his embrace, still trembling violently from all that had happened.

"Why? Where?"

"Home. I have things I must see to."

"Don't be ridiculous. We'll send for the physician. Make sure you are well—

"Ethan, please. I must get away from this place. I can't bear to be here."

His expression softened. "Then I will ride with you. It will be dark before you reach Baliforte."

"I don't need your protection—"

He took her by the shoulders and forced her to meet his gaze. "Maris," he said quietly, "I am not offering to escort an operative. I am offering to escort the woman I love."

Her belly clutched at his words. She lowered her head. "Thank you, Ethan. But I must refuse. You should take care of your aunt, and surely Lord North will want to know what occurred here."

"I suppose." He brushed a lock of hair from her eyes. Reluctance clear in his voice, he said, "Very well. I will see you in a day or two, then." The tender kiss he placed on her lips almost made her cry.

She changed her clothes quickly while Ethan saw to the removal of Hollister's body. A little while later, a groomsman brought her mount around. Ethan helped her onto her horse, his hand lingering at her waist.

Although she would never admit it to him, it would have been nice to have Ethan beside her on the ride home. Her nerves had been badly shaken by her confrontation with Hollister. It was never easy to kill a man, even in self-defense.

But there would be no comfort for her today. She would be alone, as always. The thought made her sad, although she knew it was for the best.

She needed to see exactly what the little book contained, and she wouldn't be able to do that with Ethan lingering close by.

"I'm off for one afternoon, and miss all the excitement."

Freddie had returned to Lockwell Hall from a day of calling upon friends in the country with Staunton, when she heard about what had happened with Sir Ambrose Hollister.

She stared glumly at her aunt, who lay stretched out upon a chaise in the drawing room, covered in a thick woolen blanket. Freddie's father and mother sat nearby, looking far older than their years.

"Be happy you were elsewhere, young lady," her father snapped. "Hollister's attack hardly qualifies as an evening at the theater. He could have killed your aunt."

"Perhaps *I* might have been the one to rescue her, were I here," she said.

"Of course you might have, my dear." He hadn't laughed outright, but amusement danced in her father's eyes.

Freddie simmered. The shadow of her father's patronizing manner, in which she'd lived her whole life, had not grown easier to stomach over time. As the youngest child, as well as the only girl, she'd been cemented in his mind as a fragile creature, capable of nothing more risky than wearing silk when the skies threatened rain.

"We are fortunate Maris was able to dupe Hollister so skillfully. Otherwise, things may not have come out so well," her mother commented.

"Indeed." The duchess stared into the fire.

"You have no idea why he would hold you hostage for a box of cigars?" Maldwyn asked.

Charity gave Maldwyn a puzzled look. "Cigars?"

"Yes. That is what the box contained. Didn't you know?"

Charity shook her head. "I had no idea."

"I wonder how Maris was able to overpower Hollister," Freddie said. "It seems a bit odd, don't you think, for a woman to be able to do that?"

Maldwyn cleared his throat. "Enough of this talk, now. I imagine my sister is full up with it. Let us allow her to rest peacefully and put this business behind her."

"Thank you, dear brother." For once, there wasn't a single note of sarcasm in the duchess's words. "Thank you for everything."

"It is not me you should be thanking," Maldwyn said quietly. "I never should have left you alone, knowing that Hollister might have been out there."

" 'Twas I who pushed you away." The duchess sighed. "I do not know why, except that I cannot abide relying on anyone."

"I suppose I could have been a more pleasant watchman, under the circumstances," Maldwyn said.

The duchess smiled at him. "I must admit, I rather enjoyed having a dueling partner. It took me back to our youth."

Felicity patted Maldwyn's hand. "We should go upstairs, now. You are going to need your rest." To Charity and Freddie she said, "We have decided to head off to Gillamoor for holiday a week from today, if no one objects."

"Of course not. I wish you a grand adventure," Charity said.

"I wish you would join us, Freddie," said Felicity.

Though she'd accompanied her parents a few times on their trips to her father's holding in Northern Yorkshire, Freddie more often stayed in London to amuse herself with friends, or the cadre of cousins they had nearby.

"I don't believe I will, this time. I'm working on a new endeavor at the moment."

Felicity smiled. "Well, we wouldn't wish to tear you away from that."

Freddie knew that her mother lived in hope that, one day, her "endeavor" would turn out to be a well-connected young man.

Maldwyn rose, and helped his wife to her feet. "Good eve, ladies."

Freddie watched her father go, thinking how rather old he'd been looking, and wondering when he was going to stop pushing himself so hard.

Before their footsteps had faded, Ethan entered the room. "I'm off to London."

"So soon?" Freddie smiled. "Does your haste have anything to do with a certain lady?"

Ethan sighed. "I thought you'd given up on this silly venture to marry me off."

She shrugged. "Oh, not to worry. I am on to something else, entirely."

"Good." He came to her and kissed her forehead. "I was beginning to worry that you'd become stuck in a rut."

"May I accompany you to London? If you don't mind."

"Fine. But I plan to leave shortly, so you'd best hurry."

Weariness had gripped Maris by the time she arrived home.

Her thoughts and emotions had battered her the whole way, and now she wanted nothing but to strip off her gown and climb into bed, and not open her eyes for three days.

That was what she wanted, but she would not get it. She felt at her hip for Hollister's little book, secreted in a linen pouch beneath her skirts. A rush of guilt overwhelmed her when she thought of how she'd lied to Ethan.

She sneaked through the great hall and up the stairs, directly to her rooms, praying no one had seen her arrive. She couldn't manage her mother right then, and even the thought of trying to pull her grandfather into the present exhausted her.

She untied the pouch from her waist and removed the book. For a while, she simply stared at it, wishing she didn't have to confirm what it contained. Once she found out, her betrayal would be complete. This was the information the Duchess of Canby—her friend—had nearly been killed for.

What did it matter now? There had been nothing but lies, from the very beginning.

She opened the book. Inside, the pages were filled with names. Lists and lists of names, written in a small, cramped hand. Beside the names were monetary amounts, dates going back at least two decades, and words like *Rum, Sugar, Cotton, Tobacco, Tea,* and *Wool.*

As she'd suspected—feared—it was Newcomb's book. The list of all the people whom he'd helped to illegally import and export goods throughout the years, most recently to and from the colonies. It was the ledger he'd told Samuel about on the ship the other night.

She had no idea why Hollister had stolen it. Perhaps he'd planned to extort money from Newcomb for the return of the ledger. Or maybe he'd planned to blackmail those listed in it.

She flipped through the pages, searching for names she recognized.

Kellam Markley, the Sixteenth Duke of Canby—Charity's husband—was listed quite often, as was the name of his shipping company, Two Moons. That would certainly explain why the duchess had defended the book with her life. If word of her husband's illegal activities came to light, the scandal would forever mar her family's reputation.

Monsieur Belange was on the list, as well. Maris's heart sank. She knew Belange and Toureau had given the customs agent at least one envelope, but she couldn't believe they actually knew what they were doing.

She didn't believe they would ever do something so foolish as to become involved in the war. They'd been recruited, she was certain, by friends and relatives in France to act as ignorant dispatches. Unfortunately, Belange would pay the price for his naiveté.

Samuel's name was there, too, of course. Twice, in recent entries. And beside his name were the dates of the previous weapons shipments, and the word *Guns*.

A feeling of dread crept over her. This ledger—it was the one place she hadn't been able to remove evidence of his association with the colonial rebels. Or was it? How many more places had his name been listed beside the word *Guns*? Places she'd missed when attempting to erase his sedition?

It was time she faced the ugly truth.

Samuel was entangled in this war—on the opposite side from her—whether she removed all proof of it or not.

The time for games was over.

"Hollister is dead." Ethan sat across from Lord North in the prime minister's comfortable study. The surface of the wide, walnut desk between them was uncluttered, no curiosities to sit about collecting dust.

Lord North tented his fingers beneath his chin. "Were you able to learn anything before he died? What was he looking for at Lockwell Hall?"

"Cigars, apparently."

"Cigars?"

"I don't know." Ethan shook his head in disgust. "The man was syphilitic, I'm afraid. Quite insane. Who can say how his mind worked at the end? He was either insane, or whatever he'd come to retrieve at Lockwell Hall was already gone. Perhaps my aunt had removed it."

"Did you ask her?"

"I did. She maintains that she knows nothing about his motives. I did not press her, because she was in a weakened state. She'd been through quite an ordeal. But I shall speak with her again, of course."

"Very good. In the meantime, have you come up with anything at all on the weapons smuggling?"

"I have a name. Samuel Pardee, Baron Wetherly."

"Baron Wetherly?" Lord North frowned. "I vaguely remember the name. An elderly gentleman, I believe. Removed from society for quite some time."

"Apparently when he died, the title was passed to a long-lost nephew. A colonial. Which would certainly explain the man's misguided loyalties."

"Where is he?"

"I'm looking for him. He's rather slippery. I've spoken with Lord Popper, who serves as barrister for the baronecy. Seems the young Wetherly has drawn several large bank drafts, paid to a certain Birmingham gunsmith."

"Congratulations, Gray. It would seem you've finally discovered your mysterious fourth man. Have you found out where the latest haul is, yet?"

"No, not yet. The episode with Hollister has slowed things down. When I leave here, I am going straight to the docks."

Lord North leaned back in his chair and rubbed his chin. "Tell me, how did you find working with the Raven?"

He had been expecting this question. But even so, when Lord North spoke Maris's name, Ethan's heart tripped.

He chose his words carefully.

"Frankly, sir, I am humbled. I was wrong, on every account. Not only is the Raven an excellent agent, both intelligent and instinctive, but she is one of the bravest I've worked with, as well. I cannot imagine anything coming in the way of her service to the Crown."

Lord North smiled. "I am happy to hear you say that, Gray. Does this mean you've brought her into the weapons investigation?"

"Not yet, but I will."

There was no need to tell Lord North that Maris had been less than enthusiastic about his invitation to her to join the probe. He *would* convince her.

"I would not be adverse to having her work with me on tactical considerations, either. I trust her completely," Ethan said.

"Very good. Bring her with you the next time you come, and we shall fill her in on all of our operations. Have you any idea what duties you'd wish her to handle?"

Ethan shrugged. "Contacts in France, perhaps. And maybe Prussia. Her language skills are excellent."

"Ah! Speaking of Prussia . . ." Lord North removed a key from his pocket and opened a drawer in his desk. He slid a small square of paper across to Ethan. "This came from Leer."

Ethan scanned the missive, sent by one of their agents there. "Litchfield is the informant for the Prussians? I met him in Kent."

"He's gathering information on mining techniques."

In the back of his mind, Ethan saw Maris and Litchfield, their heads bent together, laughing and joking at the wedding party in Kent. He pushed the image away.

"Who do we have watching him?" Ethan asked.

"Badger. He expects to have him in custody by early next week. Litchfield will be in Prussia until then, ostensibly to buy horses."

Ethan rose. "Let me know when he's been arrested."

"I will. And you'll bring the Raven in soon?"

"Of course."

As Ethan's carriage pulled away from the prime minister's house, he ignored the concern that gnawed insistently at his conscience.

Old habits died hard, didn't they? It would take some effort on his part not to slip back into the suspicious mindset he'd developed after Madeline's betrayal. She'd sold the Crown's secrets—secrets Ethan had shared with her—to the highest bidder. A man she professed later to love. In turn, good men had died.

They hadn't died because of Madeline's greed and lust. They'd died because *he* had trusted the wrong woman.

But Maris would never sell secrets to Litchfield. He was certain of it. Absolutely certain. And by the time he reached home, the words had become a mantra in his head.

Absolutely certain. Absolutely certain. Absolutely certain.

He shed his jacket and headed straight for the library, craving a good, stiff brandy and a new book.

When he arrived there the door was closed. He was surprised, when he opened it, to find Freddie seated in the chair behind his desk.

Almost as surprised as she was to see him.

"Ethan! I . . ." She took a deep breath. "I hope you don't mind, but I wished to write a letter, and I've run out of ink. I thought I might find some in your desk."

"But of course." He went to it, producing a small glass jar of ink. "Why didn't you ask the housekeeper?"

"I rang, but she never came." Freddie went to the door. "Thank you."

"Freddie, wait."

She turned back, an odd expression on her face. "Yes? What is it?"

"I wondered—" He stopped. "Never mind."

She stepped back into the room and closed the door. "Is something bothering you, Ethan?"

"No." He sat at his desk.

Freddie stared at him, much the way a dog will do while waiting for his supper. Ethan knew that like a persistent dog, Freddie would stand there all night until he answered her.

He sighed. "I wondered if I might ask you a question. About Miss Winter."

Freddie smiled, lethal dimples forming at the corners of her mouth. "Go on."

She sat on the edge of the chair across from him.

In spite of her flighty appearance, his sister was a shrewd observer of human nature. She watched people. Studied them. She knew them inside and out, and could often predict what they would do before they did it.

"I wondered if you thought that Litchfield and Miss Winter have any kind of history together."

She raised her eyebrows. "A history? You mean, were they lovers?"

He bit back the urge to scold her for her rough language. After all, it was exactly what he'd meant.

"I don't believe they were," she answered.

"Is he interested in Miss Winter in that way, do you think?"

Freddie's eyes sparkled. "No, he's interested in someone else entirely." She rose. "Is that all you wished to ask me?"

"Yes. Go write your letters."

She flounced out of the room, leaving him not with the comfort he'd hoped for, but with an uneasy sense that she knew something he didn't.

Newcomb wiped the blade of his knife on the dead man's shirt, and tucked the weapon back into the sheath at his waist.

This one hadn't been as easy as Quimby.

Quimby, who'd been skimming from his take for years. The twenty-five quid he'd found in the man's pockets after he'd slit his throat hadn't come near to covering what he was owed. Quimby was a worthless piece of dung, if ever there was one.

But this one . . .

Newcomb kicked the corpse with his boot. This one he'd had hopes for. This one could have risen high in Newcomb's little empire, if only he hadn't gotten greedy. If only he'd played by Newcomb's rules.

He'd broken the biggest one: Never ask for more.

More power. More glory. More money.

Newcomb had paid the man well to search for Hollister, who—by some miracle of miracles—he'd found. But then he refused to tell Newcomb Hollister's whereabouts unless Newcomb paid double.

So Newcomb had paid. And then he listened. And then he killed the man, and took the money back. That, and everything else he had in his pockets.

So now he, Newcomb, had the power, and the glory, and the money.

And he knew that Hollister had been killed at Lockwell Hall, in the presence of the Duchess of Canby's brother, and nephew.

And a woman with white-blond hair.

Newcomb smiled. He thought he might know who she was, and who she'd been working for.

Samuel Pardee.

It would seem the good Baron Wetherly had taken Newcomb's words to heart, and had retrieved the ledger Hollister had stolen from him.

Now all Newcomb had to do was get it back from Pardee.

Ethan arrived at Baliforte just before dark, riding directly to the stables. As he dismounted, Maris appeared from the little tack room at the back of the stable.

"Ethan?"

He drank in the sight of her like a man who'd gone for days without water. "What are you doing in the stables?"

She lit a lantern and hung it on a nail on the beam above them. "The stable master is ill, so I came out to check on the horses."

He cared for his own horse, watching her as she worked beside him, admiring the way she handled the mount with a firm but gentle hand. Some of her hair had escaped its braid, and rested on her shoulder like a fine web of silver. She'd rolled up the sleeves of her gown, and he could see the muscles working in her arms as she brushed the mare's flanks.

By God, she was beautiful. The most beautiful woman he'd ever known. He couldn't believe he'd ever thought her plain. She turned him upside down, while seeming to have absolutely no idea the power she held over him.

How could he have compared her to Madeline? The two were more different than air and earth. Madeline was like the peacock—exciting, mysterious, bewitching—and in the end, nothing but vapor. But Maris . . .

Maris was solid. Strong. She was the earth beneath his feet. The army at his back. He knew he could count on her, always.

When they'd finished with the horses, he took her hand, leading her to a bale of straw and motioning for her to sit. "Have you thought about what I asked you? Will you help me with the weapons investigation?"

"I—" She withdrew her hand from his. "I don't know."

He kneeled before her. "I've managed to track down three of the four men involved. Two are locked away in Newgate, and one—Hollister—is now dead. The other, the last one, has eluded me. But with your help, I know we can find him."

"Do you know who he is?" she asked quietly.

"Yes. I know his name, anyway. Samuel Pardee, Baron Wetherly." The name tasted bitter on his tongue. "I haven't been able to find him. I believe there is another cache of weapons at the docks bound for the colonies, even as we speak. But when I try to locate this Wetherly, to connect him with the weapons, all records of his involvement have been destroyed."

"Ethan . . ."

"There is another person working with him, I think. A woman. We'll find her, too."

"Ethan—"

He took her by the shoulders and kissed her, his passion for her melding with his passion for their work. "We'll do this together, I know we will. But time is running out."

When she didn't return his kiss, he released her. Her face was pale and pinched. "Are you unwell?"

"I—"

A voice calling from the house interrupted her.

"My mother." She seemed almost relieved. "Wait here."

Ethan watched as she disappeared through the door and into the almost-dark of the night.

"Damn me." Ethan kicked a bale of straw. Maris had run from the stables as if the devil chased her. Did she believe, as did North and his father and his other operatives, that he wasn't capable of handling this mission?

No. He knew in his heart she believed in him. He wouldn't love her if he thought she didn't.

There was something else holding her back. But what?

Another possibility sprang to mind. Was it because he'd told her he loved her? She wasn't exactly the kind to wear her emotions on her sleeve, and perhaps it made her uncomfortable to discuss such matters openly. Or worse, maybe she did not feel the same way about him.

Was that why she refused to work with him?

He lit another lantern and trod the stable's floorboards, until the space seemed too small to think in. Arturo, Gavin Winter's old horse, whinnied in his stall. Ethan went to the gate, and Arturo nuzzled his hand. He scratched the horse's nose, feeling a surge of guilt over Winter's fate once again.

As he caressed the horse, he noticed that the rear wall of the stallion's stall didn't quite match up with the other stalls. The other stalls seemed to be several feet deeper.

Curious, Ethan took the lantern off its nail and went

around the back of the stall, to the small tack room that abutted it. This was the room he'd seen Maris come out of when he'd arrived. The one that was usually locked. But tonight, the lock lay on a bench beside the door.

He pushed the door open with his foot. He'd expected to find that the room opened up to the right, behind Arturo's stall, but the wall there was solid. A familiar scent lingered among the smells of hay and leather and manure. He couldn't quite place it, but it seemed to be coming from behind that wall.

An assortment of riding accoutrements hung there, crops and whips, reins and stirrups. Ethan put his hand to the wall, and could feel a light breeze coming through the cracks in the boards.

His interest piqued, he knocked on the boards, receiving a hollow thunk in answer.

Working from left to right, he removed each item from the wall, searching. Looking for what, he didn't know. But his gut told him there was something there. He pressed against each board until finally, on the second to last before the door, he heard a small click. The wall swung inward, just a fraction.

He pushed it open, and found himself in a small antechamber off the tack room, directly behind Arturo's stall. It was no more than six feet long, and when he stepped inside, he could span the width of the place with his arms. The floor was hard-packed dirt. Iron hooks studded the beams of the ceiling, bare and rusting.

The smell that had lured him there grew stronger when he entered, but he still could not place it.

Several sets of shelves were built onto the walls, but by the thick layer of dust that covered them, he surmised they hadn't been used in some time. He guessed that the space had once been part of the tack room, but at some point had been partitioned off, made into some sort of secret chamber.

Besides the shelves and hooks, the only other article present in the space was a large trunk, which sat against one wall. Ethan went to it, hanging the lantern on one of the hooks above his head. The musty odor was stronger here.

He opened the lid of the trunk.

The smell that escaped it hit him like a fist to the gut. With an unsteady hand, he reached in and withdrew a handful of clothing. A man's shirt and a pair of breeches.

The clothing Maris had worn the night she'd rescued him at the docks. The night they'd first made love. The garments smelled exactly like the trunk. Exactly like—

Tobacco.

Chapter 21

Maris said from the doorway. "My father used to keep his tools in it. Ciphers. Invisible inks. Journals."

She came to him and took the garments from his hand, dropping them back into the trunk and closing the lid before he could see what else it might contain.

"It's a tobacco trunk. I hide my clothes here because I don't want my mother or Riya to find them. As with my father, they don't know what I do for the Crown, and I want to keep it that way."

"What *do* you do for the Crown?" His voice sounded harsh, even to him, and very far away.

"What do you mean?"

"Do you give yourself in service to our fair country? Or do you whore yourself out to the highest bidder?"

Even in the murky light, he could see the color drain from her face.

"Ethan, what has gotten into you?"

The ground seemed to shift beneath his feet. He felt as if he might vomit. He'd been duped by a woman—again.

Last time, his gaffe had cost the lives of two of his operatives. This time, it could cost the lives of hundreds of British soldiers.

Maris Winter cared nothing for England. Nothing for him. She was a whore, just like Madeline. But the question was: Did she whore for money or for love?

He yanked open the trunk and grabbed the clothing, holding the shirt and trousers in his fist. "Did you wear these the night in Lord Shelbourne's study, when you made off with the very evidence I sought?"

Her eyes widened. She opened her mouth, but no sound issued forth.

"Did you wear them the night of Lady Jersey's masque, beneath the peacock's feathers? You must have, under the costume you stole."

She took a step back.

"You wore them at the docks. But they were wet then, weren't they? I couldn't smell the tobacco on them." He moved closer, towering over her. "And you wore them the night in the warehouse, when you held a gun to my head. When you threatened my life."

Her voice was hoarse. "Ethan, I can explain—"

"Ah, but there is no need. I am not blind, Maris. I've seen the threadbare carpets in your home. I know you haven't any servants. How much were you paid to betray your country?"

"Paid? You think I did this for money?" Her breathing came fast, heavy. "As you said yourself, our financial troubles are more than evident."

"Which would make it all the more plausible, no?"

"No! If I did this for money, where is it?"

He moved closer—the Wolf stalking the Raven. Darkness pulsed behind his eyes. He reached out, stopping just before he touched her cheek. His hand fell to his side. "If it wasn't for money, then it must have been for love," he sneered.

"No!" She moved toward him, but stopped when she looked in his eyes.

"Are you in league with Litchfield, as well? Selling the secrets of my cousin's mine to Prussia?"

"Litchfield?" Her voice was incredulous. "Ethan, you're mad. Please listen to me."

"Why? So you can attempt to lie your way out of this treachery?" He threw the clothing at her feet. "I've been such a fool."

"No, it is I who am the fool. I did what I thought I must. I didn't think I had a choice. But I was wrong."

He pressed his fingertips to his eyes, desperately trying to stop the throbbing behind them. "Tell me, Maris. Did you betray England?"

She said nothing, and for the first time, her emotions were plain on her face.

She would not deny it, then.

He felt sick. Physically ill. He shook his head, and said quietly, "Just tell me why."

"Ethan, I care for you. And I love my country. I would give my life for it, and for you. I've proved that, again and again." She touched his shoulder. "I did what I had to do, but it is over, now."

"It is over now?"

"Yes. You will have to trust me on that."

"Trust you?" His laugh was wild. "I ought to kill you."

Her eyes flashed. "Then do it, if you must."

It was all a horrible dream. It had to be. He turned away. He couldn't bear to look at her anymore, or he just might do it. He might kill her.

She put her hand on his shoulder. "You risked your own life to try and save my father's. I am forever indebted to you. Please know that I never wanted to hurt you."

Her words brought his ceaseless guilt back to the surface. But for once, he refused to acknowledge it. What was happening now was not about *his* long-ago mistake. It was about *her* betrayal.

"Whatever the consequences to me, personally, I cannot compare them to the danger you've wrought on England's men. The sons and father and brothers who will be killed by the weapons you helped to send to the rebels."

"I didn't help to send them!"

"You did. You interfered with my ability to stop it."

A sob escaped her. "I am so sorry, Ethan. I wish I could change things—"

He spun, and took her by the shoulders, shaking her. "Then do it. Tell me where to find the man who is making those shipments."

She fell to her knees and dug through the trunk.

"Here!" She pushed a letter to his chest, folded and sealed, the head of a raven embedded in the wax.

It was addressed to Lord North.

"Read it," she said.

He cracked the seal and unfolded the missive, holding it up to the lantern to read.

His mouth went dry. "The next shipment is at the docks?"

"It is due to be shipped next week. All the information you need to stop it is there."

"And you planned to send this to Lord North?"

She nodded. "Yesterday, in fact. Before you asked me to help you."

"Why wouldn't you give it directly to me?"

"Because you didn't know I knew about the case. I was certain Lord North would pass the information on to you, so you could use it."

He read the letter again, wondering if the information was real, or if it were another of her tricks.

"It says nothing about Wetherly."

She lowered her head, but not in time to hide the pain

in her eyes. "I know I have no right to ask, but I beg of you, if you care for me at all . . . please, keep him out of it."

A flash of something—jealousy, perhaps—flared within him. Why was she protecting him? "Wetherly is a traitor. Tell me where he is, Maris."

She shook her head.

"I will be forced to arrest you if you do not." A desperate, sick feeling overwhelmed him at the thought of her, a rope about her neck, hanging from the gallows at Tyburn.

He dropped to his knees before her, grabbing her hands. "*Tell me,* Maris. I do not want to arrest you."

She closed her eyes. Tear spilled over her cheeks. "Arrest me if you must. I'm sorry."

Ethan's chest squeezed painfully. So her betrayal wasn't for money, after all.

He rose from his knees, his heart a lead thing, cold and hard and dull. "Do you love him?"

"I told him I won't help him any longer. But I cannot lead you to him."

Ethan crushed the letter in his hand and threw it on the ground. He grabbed her by the arms, forcing her to look at him. "Where is he, Maris? Where?"

She would not answer. He pulled her closer, kissing her, wanting to force the answer from her lips. "Where?"

She was stiff. Unyeilding. He wanted to shake her. To hurt her the way she'd hurt him.

But God help him, he still loved her.

He released her and stalked to the door, leaving her standing like a fallen angel in the circle of the lantern's light.

"I am duty-bound to tell Lord North," he said. "It won't go well for Wetherly. Or for you."

She didn't lower her eyes. Didn't flinch. "Do what you must."

* * *

"I pegged you for a man of action, and you didn't fail me."

Pardee started at Newcomb's voice. He threw the rolled-up map he'd been carrying onto the table in his cabin. "How did you get in here?"

"I convinced the guard to allow me aboard."

"How? With your knife?"

Newcomb laughed. "Nay, with my considerable charm."

Pardee shed his jacket and rolled up his sleeves. "What do you want?"

Newcomb's favorite words.

"I want the book, of course. The journal Hollister stole from me."

Pardee shrugged. "I've put some men on it, but so far they haven't had much luck."

Newcomb narrowed his eyes. "What do you mean?"

"I mean, my men haven't been able to locate Hollister."

"But Hollister's dead. He was killed at the Duke of Canby's home, Lockwell Hall. He'd taken the Duchess of Canby hostage."

"Well, then. There you go. Dead men cannot talk. And they certainly cannot produce journals for perusal by the authorities."

Newcomb didn't appreciate Pardee's cavalier attitude. "But you must have the journal."

Pardee shook his head. "I told you, none of my men could find Hollister."

"Perhaps none of your *men* could find him, but your woman certainly did."

Pardee went pale. "My woman?"

"Aye. The blond I met at Baliforte, Maris Winter. She was at Lockwell Hall when Hollister was killed. From all reports, she was in the very room."

Pardee's shoulders relaxed just slightly, a move not lost

on Newcomb, who was accustomed to detecting even the tiniest motes of fear and relief. "I don't know who you are talking about."

"Of course you do. The piece who protected your good name the night I supped with the Frenchies. The night that daft old man told me who you really are."

Pardee shrugged.

Newcomb withdrew his knife.

Pardee merely pushed it away. "If you kill me, you'll not get your pay." He shoved past Newcomb and spread the map out on his table, studying it.

Newcomb stabbed the point of his knife into the map. "Who is she?"

"No one."

"Horseshit."

Pardee sighed, and looked up from his map. "She is just a woman I once knew. She has no bearing on any of this. If she was at Lockwell Hall when Hollister was killed, then it was only a coincidence."

He removed Newcomb's knife and handed it back to him, handle first. "Mr. Newcomb, I am glad that Hollister has met his demise. But it had nothing to do with me. Now, I would appreciate it if you left me in peace."

Newcomb took his knife. "I want my money. Now."

"I'm afraid that is impossible. The bills of lading must still be changed on the shipments, and the weapons moved to the other warehouse."

"You know where they are. Do it yourself."

Pardee raised his eyebrows. "Fine." He went to a trunk in the corner and unlocked it. He took out a small leather sack and removed half the contents. Then he tossed the bag to Newcomb.

"That is all you'll receive from me. Take it, and get out."

Newcomb gripped the bag. His hands itched to get around Pardee's neck. To slice it with his knife.

But he knew he'd probably never make it off the boat alive. And even if he did, he'd spend the rest of his life a hunted animal.

Pardee was an important man amongst many dissatisfied merchants. Merchants who wanted this squabble with the colonies resolved, one way or another.

Pardee's death would be noticed. Avenged.

And that was one game Thomas Newcomb did not play. He tucked both his knife and the bag in his waistband, and walked away.

He may not have been able to get to Pardee, but he could get to a certain female acquaintance of his.

One he had no doubt could tell him exactly where his journal had gone.

CHAPTER 22

"Miss Maris. You are up early." Riya was elbow-deep in a mass of dough for the household's daily ration of bread.

"I have too many things to do today." Maris gathered up all of the household accounts and receipts she kept in a small desk just outside the pantry and spread them out on the wide, scarred table in the kitchen.

She intended to spend the morning writing out instructions for the care of Baliforte, although she had absolutely no idea who would carry them out in her absence.

It would be a shock to her mother and grandfather when she was arrested. Perhaps she'd be wise to ride to London and turn herself in to Lord North, before they had a chance to come for her. Perhaps things would go easier that way.

Not for herself, of course. She had no illusions about the way things would go for her. She touched her throat.

No, she had no illusions at all.

She pushed thoughts of arrests and hangings from her mind. There was too much to do, and very little time to do it.

After she balanced the household accounts, she folded all the money she'd been able to scrape together into a piece of parchment and tied it with some twine. She debated who she might entrust with such a precious bundle—God knew it was all they had—and concluded that Riya was the only person capable of handling financial matters in her absence.

She summoned the housekeeper to the table.

Riya came to her, wiping her hands on the white starched apron that always looked so foreign over her colorful saris. "Yes, Miss Maris?"

"I need you to do something for me." She indicated the receipts and the household journals stacked beside the small packet of money. "There is enough money in that bundle to pay our accounts until winter has passed. But in the spring, you will have to find a way to make more. Sell whatever you can. Perhaps you will be able to convince my mother to sell Baliforte. Convince her it will be the only way."

Riya's eyes widened. "Why are you telling this to me, Miss Maris? Is this because of Samuel?"

Maris was silent.

Riya's expression turned to one of anger. "That boy is a fool, just like his mother was."

Now it was Maris's turn to be angry. "Ajala was your sister. Your own flesh and blood. As is Samuel."

"Fools, the both of them," Riya repeated, and marched out of the kitchen, the usually musical sound of her bangles ringing harsh in Maris's ears.

"Shall I bring your breakfast now, Lady Frederica?"

"Hmm?" Freddie turned away from the window. "Oh, no thank you, Louise. I am not very hungry this morning."

"That's fine, miss. If you want for anything, please ring."

"Of course."

The maid retreated, closing the doors behind her. Freddie slid further into the crewelwork pillows on the comfortable window seat in her room. When her parents were away, Freddie rarely dined in the formal dining room, but took her meals in the small sitting room in her suite. It seemed senseless to set such a large table for one.

She stared out at the burgeoning London day, her spirits sagging. She supposed she could host a small dinner party, make a distraction for herself. But who would she invite? She spread the handkerchief she held out on her lap.

She could invite Captain Blackwood.

She wondered where he was. She hadn't seen him since the night at the wedding, with the flautist and the fat priest. But she'd thought of him almost constantly.

What was his purpose, finding her there like that? Telling her those things—things that he knew would only serve to confound her? What did he want?

She'd finally been able to go a day without him occupying her every thought, and then, there he was again. She smoothed the wrinkles from the handkerchief. She'd slept with it beneath her pillow since he'd given it to her, like the silly child he once told her she was.

As she worried the lace on the edges, she noticed something she hadn't seen before. Tiny holes formed a pattern in the corner, where something once was embroidered.

She held the handkerchief up to the window. The holes formed letters! Initials, she supposed. She squinted, trying to make them out.

SJP

Who in the world was SJP?

She twisted the handkerchief into a knot and threw it on

the floor, amazed that even Blackwood would have the audacity to give her someone else's handkerchief.

The narrow shaft of sunlight fighting through drawn curtains pierced Ethan's consciousness. He rolled over, trying to escape it, with little success.

He'd forgotten how miserable it felt to awaken the morning after drowning one's sorrows at the bottom of a glass. The evening before he'd been on a single mission—to wipe the Raven from his mind with drink.

Falling in with a group of old acquaintances, Ethan found himself matching the debauched group whiskey for whiskey, ale for ale, until he could neither think or feel. Exactly his aim.

He didn't want to think of her betrayal. Nor of the fact that he should have been on Lord North's doorstep rather than in the back room of his club, getting dissipated.

However, all of the thoughts he'd avoided the night before today once again flooded his brain in a most violent fashion. His head pounded with them.

The need to relieve himself finally drove him from the bed, and as he passed in front of a mirror on his way to the chamber pot, the man who stared back at him was a stranger.

He was not Ethan Gray, a sharp-witted tactician and spymaster for the Anti-British Activity Committee. He was not Ethan Gray, loyal subject of the Crown.

But who had he become?

He'd become a man who was willing to give up everything, including his deepest convictions, for the woman he loved.

In the cold, cutting light of morning, he could finally admit the truth. He would never turn Maris over to Lord North—but he could not say the same for her lover.

According to Maris's letter, the cache of weapons was stored in a warehouse at St. Saviours' Dock near London Bridge, packed with farm equipment and slated to be carried aboard an unnamed ship the day after next.

The bill of lading would list a destination of Jamaica. But tonight, the crates would be transferred over to the cargo bay beside it.

Ethan would be there to witness it. And, he hoped, so would Wetherly.

CHAPTER 23

Organizing the household didn't take nearly the amount of time Maris thought it would.

There were precious few details to handle, she realized, when money was scarce. She'd organized, collected, outlined, and arranged for every possible situation her family might face. But without the funds to pay gardeners, caretakers, stable masters, and the like, Baliforte would slowly crumble into ruins. She only hoped Riya could convince Olivia to sell the place before it deteriorated into worthlessness.

Maris collected the last of the papers and stacked them neatly on the desk beside the pantry, next to the packet of money she'd left for Riya.

She'd decided she wouldn't wait for Lord North's men to come for her. She would ride to London and face him, and ask him for compassion. She would confess, so that there needn't be a trial, and request that her hanging be private. Whatever difficulties she and her mother had between them, she wouldn't wish for Olivia to suffer through a public execution if she could possibly avoid it.

With all details straight, there was nothing more to do now but say goodbye.

Maris found her mother and grandfather in the conservatory, Olivia seated at the harp. Her long, slender fingers plucked a whimsical melody that reminded Maris of rain. Olivia's face was serene, with none of the tortured look about her that she wore at other times.

Her grandfather sat on the window seat, his eyes closed, a smile playing upon his lips. Perhaps he was asleep, dreaming of her grandmother. Or of better days, when the curtains weren't frayed, and when he could still watch his son through the window, riding Arturo across a meadow filled with bright yellow cowslip.

Maris was reluctant to disturb their peace. She realized it would be far kinder to let each of them go on this way as long as possible. Her mother would only become angry at Maris's leaving, and her grandfather would not understand, anyway.

She watched them for a while before closing the door. Then she dressed in a black gown, and took the small bag she'd packed to the stables where she kissed Arturo's regal nose before helping her driver to ready the coach.

As they took the final bend on the drive, she hung out of the window for one last look at her home. Baliforte was awash in golden sunlight, and she could have sworn she saw the ghost of her father waving to her from the steps.

"I'll join you soon, Father," she whispered.

Newcomb spurred his horse around the final curve to Baliforte, nearly hurtling headlong into an oncoming coach.

His mount reared, lunging to the left to avoid a team of horses that pulled a creaky blue carriage behind them.

The driver cursed him, and Newcomb nearly shot the man on the spot. He would have, if he hadn't caught a glimpse of the passenger inside. Or rather, a glimpse of the back of her head as she looked out the opposite window, toward Baliforte.

Maris Winter.

Sometimes, he marveled, Lady Fate could be a bloody cooperative bitch.

He debated whether or not to attack the coach right there, on the road, but he decided to wait. If he did, he would certainly have to kill the driver. And if the woman didn't have the journal with her, he'd be buggered.

No. Better to wait until a more opportune moment.

Lady Fate would not disappoint. He was sure of it.

Maris ordered the driver to stop before Ethan's house on Bloomsbury Square, her heart in her throat.

She wanted to see him again, just once more. She wondered if he'd even be there, or if he was at the warehouse, looking for the guns. Looking for Baron Wetherly.

She hoped to God Samuel had taken her advice and sailed for America two days ago. She'd warned him. Heaven knew, she had warned him.

The letter she'd written to Ethan laid in her lap. It was a grand entreaty, filled with pleas for forgiveness, and pledging her love. All the things she hadn't been able to tell him face to face.

He would hate her forever, but at least she would hang knowing she'd done her best to explain herself.

A cart driver behind them yelled to her man that he was blocking the street. Maris waved to him from the window.

She took one last moment to gather herself, and alighted from the carriage.

"Go through the alley," she told her driver, "and park in the back, beside the carriage house. I won't be long."

He nodded and drove off, the old blue coach groaning in protest.

Maris went through the tall, open iron gates that separated Ethan's home from the street. It was but a short walk to the front door, but it seemed like a mile. She clutched the letter in her fist, and straightened her back.

"Psst."

The sound caught her off guard, and she stumbled as she turned, finding herself in the grip of Thomas Newcomb. His breath reeked of liquor, his smile menacing.

"Mr. Newcomb!"

"Miss Winter. What a coincidence."

"Indeed." But it was no coincidence, she knew. She wondered what Newcomb was doing there, and what he knew.

"Do you have business with Mr. Gray?" she said.

"No. As a matter of fact, my business is with you."

She pulled away from his grasp, giving him an icy stare. "Really? And what might that be?"

"I believe you have something that belongs to me."

She said nothing.

"A book. A journal that Ambrose Hollister had, ah, *borrowed* from me some time ago."

"I am sorry, Mr. Newcomb. I am not familiar with Mr. Hollister, nor any book he might have had."

"Oh, I think you are." Newcomb gripped her arm. Pain shot from her shoulder to her wrist. "Samuel Pardee told me you had it."

Samuel! He couldn't have . . . He never would have told a maggot like Newcomb any such thing.

"You are mistaken, Mr. Newcomb. Now please, release me."

Newcomb backed her up against one of the great brick pillars that held the gates, effectively blocking the view of them from the street. She prayed someone in the house would look out of a window, and see them.

He pushed his face into hers. His fetid breath blew warm on her cheek. "I know you were there at Lockwell Hall when Hollister died. I know Samuel Pardee sent you there to get the journal. And the fact that you refuse to own up to being there makes me doubt I am mistaken."

Maris controlled her breathing. She musn't panic. Every instinct she had told her that Newcomb was a malicious man. Evil. And if she didn't handle things exactly right, she would end up dead on Gray's small, neat lawn on Bloomsbury Square.

"Unhand me, Mr. Newcomb. If you want your book, I shall have to get into Mr. Gray's house."

Newcomb relaxed his grip. "The duchess's nephew has the book?"

She smiled. "Perhaps."

He held her arm and marched her up the path toward the front door.

"Not this way," she said. "We need to go round back."

"Why?"

She raised her eyebrows. "You will have to trust me, Mr. Newcomb."

Maris led Newcomb around toward the side door of Ethan's home, away from the street, and anyone who might witness what she was about to do.

When they were out of sight of prying eyes, she stopped suddenly, bending at the waist. When Newcomb's middle struck her bottom, she reached behind her and grabbed him by the jacket, pulling him onto her back and using leverage and the element of surprise to throw him over her shoulder.

In less than a second, a shocked Newcomb stared up at her from the ground. She trapped his neck beneath her foot, pressing on his Adam's apple with the spooled heel of her proper shoe. Her mind reveled briefly in the thought that she'd finally found a decent use for that instrument of torture.

She wished she hadn't left her weapons at Baliforte, but she hadn't dreamed she would need them to simply turn herself in to Lord North.

Newcomb clawed at her leg, nearly managing to throw her off, until she drove her other heel into the soft mound of flesh between his legs.

Newcomb screamed like a woman, writhing ineffectively beneath her feet like a worm on a pin.

She found a dagger at his waist, and released it from the scabbard. She should kill him right there. What he knew about Samuel alone should have driven her to do it. But she wouldn't.

Thomas Newcomb would prove too valuable a prisoner to the Anti-British Activity Committee. What he knew—what was in his book—would prove crucial to the security of England, and send a great many men to ruin.

The fact that Samuel could be one of them pained her greatly. But as he'd said himself, it was time for her to prove her commitment to her cause.

And her cause was England.

Slowly, she replaced her heel with the knife at Newcomb's neck. He ceased his writhing, staring up at her with naked disbelief in his eyes. With one hand, she pressed the point of the blade to the hollow above his collarbone. "Move, and you shall have a hole in your throat that will make drinking ale a futile exercise."

With her other hand, she reached up and untied the scarf she wore about her neck. Forcing Newcomb to roll over, she tied his hands behind his back. Sticking the knife between his shoulderblades, she said, "Get up slowly. And if you try to attack me in any way, I will kill you. Do not test me."

Newcomb crawled to his knees. Apparently the blow to his ballocks had caused more damage than she imagined, for he whimpered with pain as he rose. She poked the tip of the knife into his back. "Walk."

She forced Newcomb on past the side door and around to the rear of the house, where her carriage and driver waited. He stared at her with wide eyes.

"Help me," she said. "Hurry. This man tried to rob me."

Her driver found some rope in the boot of the carriage, typically used for securing trunks and the like, and trussed Newcomb like a prize pig.

"Put him in the carriage, and take him to Bow Street, to the magistrate. Tell him your lady said this man should not be released until he hears from Lord North."

Ethan's knees ached.

He'd been sitting behind a stack of barrels for hours, waiting for someone to come and move the weapons.

He'd located them easily enough. They were exactly where Maris had told North in her letter, and it gave Ethan some satisfaction to know that she'd been honest about that, if nothing else.

She'd apparently warned Wetherly off, though, for Ethan had been sitting in this god-awful place for thirty-six hours, without anyone coming near the guns. Surely the man was long gone.

He stood, stretching a cramp from his leg. If nothing else, he could confiscate the weapons, and there would be one less shipment to reach colonial shores.

The slamming of one of the warehouse doors sent him down to the floor again. He struck his knee hard against the side of a barrel, and swallowed a yelp of pain.

An absence of voices told him that whoever had entered was probably alone, a fact that was confirmed when the sound of only one set of footsteps drew near.

Ethan held his breath, waiting.

The newly arrived guest moved assuredly through rows of cargo, as if he knew exactly where he was going. From Ethan's vantage point he could see the tops of the two large wooden cartons that held weapons hidden beneath hoes, plow blades, and other farming instruments.

The footsteps grew closer, passing Ethan on the opposite side of the barrels behind which he hid, and stopping before the crates that contained the guns. Ethan could see the back of the man, who was dressed in a black coat and breeches, his dark hair tied with a black ribbon. The man withdrew a piece of paper—a bill of lading—from his pocket and, untacking the one on the crate, replaced it with the one he held.

Ethan rose slowly, a pistol in each hand trained on the man's back. At the sound of the hammers cocking, the man spun to face him.

"Blackwood?" Ethan said.

"Gray." Freddie's beau hardly seemed surprised to see him.

"What are you doing here?"

Blackwood's face registered surprise. "I would have thought Maris had told you, considering that you are here, waiting for me."

His reply stymied Ethan for only a moment. He raised the pistol and pointed it directly at the man's chest. This was the man Maris had risked her life for?

She hadn't been protecting Wetherly, after all. It had been Blackwood all along. He should have known.

Blackwood had captured the fancy of every woman in London, Ethan's own sister included. Why should Maris be immune to the man's charms?

Blackwood seemed nonplussed. "She actually had the nerve to do it. She told me she would, but I didn't believe her."

"What?"

"I didn't believe she would tell anyone about this." He swept a hand toward the crates.

"Maris warned you, and you still came 'round?"

He gave a rueful smile. "She's threatened to tell you before, but she's never done it."

"Me?"

"Of course. You've been chasing me for months, haven't you?"

"I've been chasing Baron Wetherly."

Blackwood smiled.

"*You* are Baron Wetherly?"

"So it would seem."

Ethan stepped out from behind the barrels, keeping both pistols leveled at Blackwood's chest. "You think yourself clever, using an English title to purchase these guns?"

Blackwood's smile disappeared. "Not clever. Just determined."

"Determined to spit in the face of your countrymen?"

"England is not my country, Wolf. I'm an American."

Ethan didn't flinch at the mention of his code name. He supposed there was much that Blackwood knew about him. And some of it he'd undoubtedly learned from Freddie. He'd used her just as Ethan had used all those other women.

The thought made him as furious as Blackwood's words. "The colonies belong to England. The crown provides you protection and support in return for loyalty. Your actions are a crime against England. You are not worthy of the title of Baron, nor the title of Englishman."

Blackwood spat. "Believe me, I don't want either one."

"Turn around." Ethan shoved the barrels of the pistols in

Blackwood's back, tempted to pull the triggers. Instead, he pushed him toward the door. "You are far worse than a traitor, Blackwood. You're a coward. The kind who would have a woman hang for protecting you."

"I never asked Maris to protect me, and I certainly don't want to see her hang. She acted of her own accord."

Anger surged through Ethan's veins. This man had abused Maris's trust. Taken advantage of her love for him.

He shoved Blackwood up against a wall and pressed one of the guns to his cheek. "I should shoot you right here."

"Don't! Please!"

Maris. She appeared from nowhere, like an apparition.

She wore the same gown she'd had on the day they'd made love at Baliforte, in the rhododendron grotto. The scent of the blossoms still clung to the dress, and it filled the air between them.

"This is between the Wolf and me," Blackwood said, through clenched teeth. "Get out of here."

"I will not." Maris came closer. "If you are foolish enough to wish to die, then I am foolish enough to try to save you from it, Samuel Winter."

"Winter?" Ethan repeated.

"My name isn't Winter," Blackwood said, his voice filled with rancor. "It never was. It is Samuel Josiah Pardee Blackwood."

Maris came forward and took Ethan's wrist, moving the gun from Blackwood's cheek. "It *should* be Winter. He is my brother."

"Your brother?" Ethan's eyes moved between her and Samuel, as if looking for some resemblance. He wouldn't find it. They were as different as night and day.

"His mother was Ajala Pardee, our housekeeper. Riya's

sister. My father fell in love with her when he was working in India, and brought her back with him to England. When she became pregnant with his child, my father moved her out of Baliforte."

"Maris, don't." Samuel's eyes blazed.

But she wanted Ethan to know. He had to know why she'd betrayed him. What she thought was more important than loving him.

"Samuel and I saw each other often as children. But when my father was killed, Ajala took Samuel to the colonies to start a new life." Her voice broke. She swiped a tear from her cheek with the back of her hand.

Ethan's expression softened. He lowered the pistol to his side.

"Ajala married a man there named Blackwood. She died shortly after that."

"Stop it, Maris. He doesn't need to know this. It doesn't matter." She could hear the pain in Samuel's voice. But he needed to confront this as much as she did.

Maris continued. "Samuel came to Baliforte a little more than a year ago, looking for Riya and me. We were the only family he had left by then. My uncle, who'd always been moved by Samuel's plight, had just died, leaving Samuel everything he had. His title and all of his money—"

"I never wanted it," Samuel interrupted. "You know that."

Maris nodded. She said to Ethan, "As you can imagine, my mother was less than overjoyed to meet Samuel. My father's will states that Mother is to get nothing until she acknowledges Samuel as his rightful heir. Of course, she never will."

"That explains the state of Baliforte," Ethan said. "But what about the guns? What is your part in this, Maris?"

"By the time Samuel came home, I was already spying

for the committee. I was following up information that suggested King Louis had promised support to the colonials, when I discovered Samuel was involved. And when I realized that you'd begun to search for him, I knew he was in trouble. I did not want to see him killed."

"Maris does not understand, Wolf, that I am fighting for a cause," her brother said. "And that I am fully prepared to die for it."

"But *I* am not prepared!" Maris cried. "You are all that I have, Samuel. Don't you understand?" Her heart ached to look at him. To her, he was still a boy, fighting to be recognized. Fighting to be important.

Maris turned to Ethan. "If I can hope to mean anything to you, anything at all, let him go. He is my last link to my father, Ethan. I love him."

An image flashed in Ethan's mind. Maris's father—*Blackwood's* father—lying in a pool of his own blood, his fingers and toes severed, his legs broken.

He pressed his palms to his forehead, trying to rub the memory away. "I cannot . . ."

"Please." Her voice was rough with anguish. "He will leave England immediately—"

"I won't," Blackwood interrupted.

Maris shot him a deadly look before turning back to Ethan. "He *will* leave England, and never return. If he does, you may shoot him on sight. Please, just let him go."

Ethan shook his head. "I'm sorry, Maris. I am duty-bound to arrest him. You know that."

Maris withdrew a small book from the sash at her waist and held it out to him. "We shall make a trade, then. Within these pages are the names of every man in England who has made a deal with the devil. Everyone who has paid Thomas Newcomb to arrange illegal shipments, avoid taxes on imports, or send aid and support to the rebel forces in the colonies. Weapons, supplies, even monetary support and gifts directly from King Louis. All those names, with the exception of one."

"Baron Wetherly," Ethan said.

She nodded. "Let my brother go, and this book is yours."

"Where did you get it?" he asked.

She was silent.

"Is that what Hollister was after? Is that what he was looking for at Lockwell Hall?"

"Yes."

Ethan's stomach turned. "How can you call yourself an agent for the Crown? It is your duty to turn over all evidence of traitorous activity."

She raised her chin. "I love England. But I am bound first to my family. To those I love. I am not ashamed of it. If you arrest my brother, you will have to arrest me, as well." She stepped between him and Blackwood, and covered Ethan's hand with hers, drawing the muzzle of one of his pistols to her breast. "If you shoot him, you must put the bullet through me, first."

Ethan's pulse rushed in his ears. He looked into Maris's eyes, and knew that she meant what she said. She would die before letting him take her brother.

His anger mixed with admiration for the woman before him. She did what he would have done—she risked her skin for the sake of her family, such as it was. He would do the same for his parents. For Freddie. So how could he fault her for it?

And had he not so grossly mishandled that mission so long ago, Maris and Blackwood's father might still be alive. They might have been a true family.

But all of these things put together mattered only half as much as one other: He was in love with Maris Winter. And if he did anything but set Blackwood free, it would surely destroy her.

Ethan uncocked the pistols.

He looked over Maris's shoulder at Blackwood. "Your sister has given you a great gift, Captain Blackwood. I hope you accept it. I ask for your word as a man that you will desist with all orders and shipments of weapons to the colonies. That you will relinquish the title of Baron Wetherly. And that you will leave England as soon as you have gathered your crew, and never, ever return."

Maris turned and grabbed Blackwood's hands. "Please, Samuel."

Ethan could feel Maris's anguish, and he wanted to reach out to her. To hold her. But the three were suspended there by Blackwood's indecision.

Finally, the other man nodded. "I will accept your terms."

Ethan extended his hand, and Blackwood took it. The two men stood for a moment, locked in a private battle disguised as an accord.

Ethan released Blackwood's hand. "Be gone by morning, or our agreement will not hold."

Maris folded Blackwood into an embrace. She cried freely now, and Blackwood returned the embrace, his own eyes filled with tears.

Ethan turned away.

When Maris came to him and touched his shoulder, Blackwood was gone.

"Thank you," she said quietly.

He said nothing. He couldn't speak. He simply took her into his arms and kissed her.

Samuel pulled tight the leather straps that held his trunk to the floor of his quarters.

Preparations were nearly complete for their journey back to America. Back home. He felt a hum of anticipation building in his bones, and in his soul.

He missed Philadelphia.

But he knew that his city would have a rough road before her. Even now, British soldiers threatened occupation of the whole region surrounding the city. Tensions grew daily there, and it wouldn't be long before Philadelphia was deep into the war, if it hadn't already occurred.

Samuel did not know if he would make it through the war with his life—or even if he and his crew would ever make it back to colonial soil with their skins intact. But he would die knowing he'd perhaps done one small thing in the name of freedom.

His heart grew heavy when he thought of Maris, but she'd chosen her own path, same as he. This war was not between them, but between the places they each called home. He wished her nothing but good.

In fact, he'd left instructions for Lord Popper to transfer the remainder of his inheritance from his uncle, as well as what had been withheld in his father's will, into an account in Maris's name. He had his own fortune in America, and didn't need Gavin Winter's money.

He knew Olivia Winter would never accept him into Baliforte, or name him as Winter's rightful heir—and he did not blame her for it. In fact, he didn't care, really. He wanted nothing from her, and nothing more from England, either.

No. That wasn't completely true. There was one thing he wanted. But he could never have it.

Or rather, he could never have *her*.

Lady Frederica Gray.

What had begun as a game, a way to torment the Wolf, had ended in true affection. He would miss Lady Freddie's stubborn optimism and thirst for adventure, her witty banter, and wild red curls. She'd become a good friend, and it was difficult to imagine that he would never see her again.

He threw the last of his clothes into the trunk and slammed the lid closed.

By noon tomorrow, Freddie, Maris, Wolf, and England would be but a shadow at his back.

CHAPTER 24

Maris awoke wrapped in Ethan's arms, certain that everything that had happened the last few days was a dream. But the wedding ring on her finger—and the warmth of him pressed against her—assured her it was not.

They'd been married four nights ago by a sleepy priest in a midnight ceremony, witnessed only by the rector and his wife. They'd been bound to one another with a vow to always be truthful, which they began straight off, confessing their sins to one another and forgiving them, too.

The fact that she'd given him Thomas Newcomb proved to him that her loyalties really did lie squarely with England—even if she did use Newcomb's book under false pretenses to free her brother.

They'd made a truce, as well, about Samuel. Ethan was uncomfortable with his decision to let her brother go. She knew that. But she also knew that Samuel was a man of his word. He'd proved it.

His ship, the *Christina*, was gone from the docks the next day.

Maris was heartbroken, not knowing if she'd ever see him again. But at least her last moment with him wasn't a farewell at the gallows.

Her new husband had given her the greatest wedding gift she could ever have received—her brother's life. She rolled over in the bed to face him, and kissed his forehead. Ethan opened his eyes, smiling at her, spinning a strand of her hair around his finger. "You are glorious."

Maris felt her face grow warm. It was all so new, these feelings of pleasure at a man's admiration. She was glad they'd taken a few days for themselves, before announcing their marriage to anyone. But it was finally time to let the world know.

"What time are we to meet with Lord North today?" she asked.

"Not until later," he murmured against her neck. "Much, much later."

"What shall we do until then?" she asked, although she had a feeling she knew what his answer would be.

As Ethan had predicted, much, much later they informed a shocked and rather pleased prime minister that they'd become husband and wife, and assured him it did not mean that either one was going to give up working for the committee.

After they'd left Downing Street, they decided that Freddie should be the next to share their news. When they arrived at Ethan's parents' house, however, the place was in a state of nervous confusion.

Louise, Freddie's lady's maid, hurried to greet them, her face pinched with worry. "Mr. Gray! I'm so glad you're here. We've sent a post to Lord and Lady Maldwyn, but I'm afraid it will be days before they receive it."

"What is it? Has something happened?" Ethan guided the women into the drawing room.

Louise bobbed nervously about. "Lady Frederica left a few days ago, Mr. Gray. She said she was visiting with friends, but she didn't take a trunk. No fancy gowns, no shoes, no gloves. Imagine! Just one small bag, and she was off."

Ethan fingers tightened on Maris's arm. "Where did she say she was going? Who was she to visit with?"

"She didn't say, sir. But she did leave something for you."

Louise hurried off, and reappeared a few minutes later with a letter, addressed to Ethan in Freddie's delicate hand.

He quickly unfolded it, and Maris read over his shoulder:

My dearest brother,

I am off, at last, on a grand adventure!

Captain Blackwood stopped by for a visit—his last, he said, as he was leaving England for quite a long time. Perhaps forever.

I realized, as I bid him farewell, that I am not meant to be a bluestocking, nor am I particularly skilled in my "endeavors." It is a shabby matchmaker, brother, who cannot even recognize a match for herself until it is nearly too late!

But I will not let him go this time. I love him, Ethan, and I feel certain he loves me.

I know he would not take me with him if I asked, so I will not ask. My adventure will begin as my own secret, to be revealed to Captain Blackwood only when we are finally at sea! I feel sure it will be a welcome surprise.

Please do not be angry with me, dear brother. My heart yearns for adventure, and for Josiah Blackwood as well.

Be a comfort to Mother and Father, and tell them I will write as soon as we arrive in America.

With greatest regard, I remain
Your loving sister,
Freddie
P.S. Do hurry up and marry Miss Winter.

"Great God." Ethan had gone white.

EPILOGUE

"You cannot go with me," Ethan said.

"I can, and I will."

"You get seasick, Maris."

She looked at him with surprise.

"Did you think I didn't notice? You made a valiant effort to hide it, but I know you suffered on our short trip to France. And it may take us days, perhaps weeks, to catch up with your brother's ship. They've had nearly a week's start."

"It doesn't matter, Ethan. I am going with you. We'll find Freddie together."

Ethan gazed down into his new wife's face as their coach rocked its way through the crowded London streets. By the stubborn set of Maris's jaw, he knew that he would not dissuade her.

Much to his surprise, he found he did not mind. His wife, his partner—his equal—would be right where she belonged.

Beside him, always.

Don't miss the
"fabulous historical romance"* of

Donna Birdsell

The Painted Rose 0-425-19804-9

The reclusive Lady Sarah hides from the world behind her veils. But the sad eyes of her handsome young tutor, Lucien, seem to burn right through them, willing her to face her fears. Yet how can a man so used to beauty ever desire a woman whose face he hasn't seen?

Falcon's Mistress 0-425-20634-3

The Duke of Canby is a spy, working as a falconer in France, privy to the secrets of the nobility. But when he learns that his only love, Selena, is imprisoned for his own, faked murder, Canby must return to England to save her. His sudden reemergence into society will come at a price to his freedom—and the ultimate cost to him may be Selena herself.

**Best Reviews*

Visit the author on her website:
donnabirdsell.com

Available wherever books are sold or at
penguin.com

Penguin Group (USA) Online

What will you be reading tomorrow?

Tom Clancy, Patricia Cornwell, W.E.B. Griffin, Nora Roberts, William Gibson, Robin Cook, Brian Jacques, Catherine Coulter, Stephen King, Dean Koontz, Ken Follett, Clive Cussler, Eric Jerome Dickey, John Sandford, Terry McMillan, Sue Monk Kidd, Amy Tan, John Berendt…

You'll find them all at
penguin.com

Read excerpts and newsletters, find tour schedules and reading group guides, and enter contests.

Subscribe to Penguin Group (USA) newsletters and get an exclusive inside look at exciting new titles and the authors you love long before everyone else does.

PENGUIN GROUP (USA)
us.penguingroup.com